AMBERGRIS

AMBERGRIS

Antonia Price

The Book Guild Ltd
Sussex, England

This book is a work of fiction. The characters in this story are imaginary. No resemblance is intended between these characters and any real persons, either living or dead.

The Book Guild Ltd,
25 High Street,
Lewes, Sussex

First published 1997
© Antonia Price, 1997

Set in Baskerville
Typesetting by
SetSystems Ltd, Saffron Walden, Essex

Printed in Great Britain by
Bookcraft (Bath) Ltd, Avon

A catalogue record for this book is
available from the British Library

ISBN 1 85776 296 7

In memory of my mother

1

Belize, Central America, 1993

Albertine had never been in the tropics before. There were
travel brochures in Mr Lee's office showing pictures of
Jamaica and the Bahamas, but none of Belize; it was not on
the tourist map and she had no idea what to expect, but it
was in the Caribbean Sea so she assumed there would be
wide, white, coconut-clad beaches and single-storeyed hotels
with swimming pools surrounded by thatched cottages with
their own verandahs; that nightlife would revolve round
dark-skinned girls in grass skirts who would be garlanded
and dancing to the rhythmic drumming of equally dark-
skinned and grinning musicians. *Enjoy a typical evening of
tropical romance in an island paradise* said the advertisement
for Jamaica. She thought it would be like that.

It was November when Max had said, 'I don't think I can
stand another bloody winter in this country; I think we
should go away, find the sun, have a change.'

'I didn't think you liked the sun,' Albertine had said, her
mind already travelling from India to Peru, from Mexico to
Thailand, from the Seychelles to the Bahamas.

'Somewhere not too hot, but at least away from this
infernal drizzle.'

It was a damp raw day, the leaves were almost off the trees
and lay in sodden piles where the wind had driven them
across the lawns.

It was so unlike Max to suggest going away. He was the
sort of Englishman who considered all foreigners to be a

1

different species. His relaxations were shooting in the winter and playing tennis in the summer. Occasionally, mostly to please her, he would be prepared to go away in the spring. For him to suggest that they leave England in the middle of the shooting season was like suggesting to a robin that it should try South Africa for the winter. Though now she thought about it, she realised he had not been shooting as often this year. Perhaps he was feeling his age, although for a man of 65 he was still very fit.

'Where would you like to go?' she asked, allowing herself a tiny frisson of excitement at the possibility of change.

'Well, certainly somewhere where they speak English.'

This excluded most of the countries on her imagined list. Max had drawn an atlas from one of the shelves in the book-lined room in which they were sitting. It was over 50 years old and most of the countries were coloured pink.

'South Africa would have been all right if they weren't all bent on killing themselves . . . So would Kenya if we hadn't given it back . . . Australia's too brazen . . . New Zealand – nothing but sheep farmers . . . India's too smelly.'

The possibilities became fewer and fewer.

'California – ghastly.'

His finger hovered over Central America.

'Here's something,' he said. 'British Honduras. They'll speak English there.'

Albertine remembered her stamp collection. British Honduras had always had very large and colourful stamps, triangular ones too, which she had loved. She had never had the faintest idea where it was or the interest to find out.

'Do you know anything about it, anyone who's been there?' she asked.

'No, but I'll go to the travel agent's tomorrow and find out.'

He had sounded as if he meant it and she had seen a little crack in the dark monotony of her life.

'It's called Belize now,' he said, triumphant on his return the next day. 'They became independent ten years ago. It's a very peaceful country apparently, with very little tourist trade; that's why we've never heard of it. We still have some forces there, English is the main language and at this time of year it never gets hotter than seventy-eight degrees. I've booked us onto a flight at the beginning of December. We'll miss bloody Christmas too.'

'Amanda and the children are coming for Christmas,' Albertine complained, already seeing the collection of things she had brought for their stockings wasted.

'They'll have to make other arrangements.'

There was never very much consultation in this marriage.

Mr Lee, the travel agent, had managed to find them a house to rent on Ambergris Caye, which was one of the many islands off the mainland and only about a quarter of a mile from the coral reef which ran the whole length of the tiny country. They were going to spend Christmas there and then do a tour of the whole country, staying in lodges in the rainforest, canoeing down rivers, riding through the jungle and visiting Mayan ruins. Mr Lee had never been asked to arrange a trip like this before and he put his whole heart into it. 'I've been in touch with a colleague in the States who says ...' he would tell Max, and yet another possible itinerary would be added to the already overloaded list of things they could do. They were to fly to Houston, where they would spend a night, and then to Belize City; from there they would take another plane to the Caye.

After a dismal and sleepless night in the airport hotel in Houston, Albertine found flying over Mexico a disappointment; she was glad that they had decided not to stay there though it had been on the original list of countries she would like to visit. It seemed a deserted scrubland with nothing to break the barren monotony but long white roads which had only a very occasional group of houses nestling beside them. When they crossed the border into Belize the desolation became even greater. The scrub turned to marsh; it was a watery wilderness with no road and no sign of habitation. The reddish-brown earth was cut by a wide and winding river which looped back upon its course and by

3

dark pools of umber which did not reflect the brightness of the sun but which lay in threatening stagnancy. It was a sinister and brooding landscape, it was like the moon with vegetation, it was like nowhere.

They were coming down to land and still she had seen no sign of life; it was only when the wheels descended and the aeroplane completed a circle that she saw the cluster of houses that was Belize City tipping into the sea. As they landed, the skies opened and they had their first experience of a tropical rainstorm.

The rain stopped as suddenly as it had begun. They had been through immigration, drunk their first rum punch in Jet's bar and were waiting for the announcement of the flight to Ambergris Caye. The departure lounge, with one exit onto the tarmac, was abuzz with the confident and strident tones of the many Americans gathered there, some brown or red returning home, some as white as Max and Albertine themselves; some dressed as if for a smart cocktail party, some in shorts with backpacks, but all of them assured and certain of their welcome, unlike Max and Albertine, who sat in silence, suddenly very aware of what they had left behind and of the strangeness of the world they had so impulsively, and now possibly unwisely, decided to enter. It was not only their silence that set them apart. Max, dressed as usual in a blue and white striped shirt, Brigade of Guards tie, blue blazer and, as a concession to the heat, immaculately pressed white trousers, and Albertine in a crumpled dark blue linen suit, proclaimed their Englishness as loudly as if they had shouted it from the rooftops.

They were halfway through their second rum punch, feeling increasingly uncomfortable, when a small neat man came up to them and very politely said, 'If you are ready I can take you to your flight now.'

They looked at each other in amazement at this courtesy, so far removed from the usual impersonal screens flashing the sign *boarding now*. They rose, expecting others to follow, but alone they were escorted across the tarmac, where a plane which appeared no bigger than a large motor bike

4

awaited them, the interior piled high with their luggage, and the pilot standing beside the propeller smiling, more like a chauffeur than an aviator. Albertine climbed nervously into the back seat; Max, with an expression of boredom which only she could have recognised as suppressed excitement, sat beside the pilot, who, after putting on earphones, pressed a button. The tiny aeroplane shuddered into life, bumped slowly down the runway and miraculously lifted them into the air and over the emerald pin-striped sea.

Once her fear had subsided enough to look out of the window, Albertine saw that this wide expanse of rippling cloth was dotted with dark patches, islands and islets, uninhabited, low and mysterious, the earth coming up to breathe, like whales. Ten minutes later they could see in the distance and near the horizon a larger and more intricately patterned patch.

'Ambergris,' said the pilot, pointing.

The plane jerked unsteadily as he lowered the wheels to begin the descent. It wobbled crazily over apparently abandoned building sites, pools of orange water, expanses of grey sand, until finally, veering its way down the short and potholed strip of tarmac, it drew to a halt beside a blue and white wooden hut. *Island Air*, read the sign hanging above the verandah. Children were playing round it; two stringy horses, who barely raised their heads from their vain attempt to graze on the sparse leaves of grass struggling through the sand, were tied to the verandah rail. They were in San Pedro.

Houses stood all round the strip; over a knee-high fence children in dark blue tunics and white shirts played in the school yard, paying as little attention to their arrival as had the horses. A squat, flat-faced man with gold teeth and a large gold crucifix hanging on a chain round his short fat neck stepped from the verandah.

'I am Orlando. You Mr and Mrs Stevens? I take you to the water taxi, OK.'

He carried their luggage to his car, a large six-seater van almost totally eaten away by rust.

5

'What would we have done without the admirable Mr Lee,' Max whispered to Albertine, who barely heard him, so entranced was she by the strangeness of their arrival, by the charm of Orlando and by the extraordinary sight of the sand street down which they were travelling at no more than five miles an hour. Three hundred yards later they drew up on the beach. The water taxi as promised was waiting, their luggage was transferred yet again and they were on the last leg of the journey which had taken nearly two days.

The house Mr Lee had found for them was two miles north of San Pedro. The northern part of the island was separated from the southern by a river, which they had been warned that they would have to wade across in order to shop. They could see it now; it was wider and deeper than Albertine had imagined and she wondered how they would manage to bring back their supplies, which she could see in her mind's eye; the 12 or more bags from Safeways piled into the back of her car. San Pedro was a busy, active, densely built little town which stretched as far as the river, but beyond it the island seemed nearly deserted. This was not the Caribbean beach of Albertine's imagination. The palm trees touched the shore, their roots, like bunches of shoelaces, clinging hopefully to the wooden sea wall; the two or three houses they could see stood in sandy clearings surrounded on either side by dense bush. Opposite each house long docks pointed into the sea and beside each dock a boat was moored.

'We'll have to hire a boat,' Max shouted above the roar of the engine.

'Tres Cocos,' the boatman said, pointing to a cluster of houses, and as he spoke the rain came down. For the second time in a day they arrived at a new destination soaked to their skins. Beaten by the wind, they struggled out of the boat, along the dock, over the sandy frontage to their house, a small, corrugated-roofed bungalow with a wide screened verandah on which hung two hammocks; their home for two or three months.

'Well, we're here,' Max said, joining Albertine on the verandah. 'What do you think of it?'

'Heaven must be like this,' she answered, looking out across the still sea towards the line of surf breaking over the reef, and added tentatively, 'Is it what you were expecting?'

'I must admit I hadn't expected anything quite as primitive.' Max looked with barely concealed distaste at the plain slatted wooden chairs on the balcony.

Albertine felt a familiar flutter of panic. So still she was to be the cajoler, the supporter. As if trying to persuade a boy that he was enjoying himself at a party he had not wanted to go to, she said, 'It's going to be fine; come on, let's unpack, we'll feel better then. Did you notice that someone's put some flowers on the table and a bottle of wine in the fridge? There's some cold chicken and lettuce too. Why don't you relax while I sort everything out and then we'll eat. Where did you put the duty-frees? Have a drink even if it is a bit early. You deserve it after that journey.'

Max had a rule that he never drank before six o'clock.

'Yes, you're right,' he said. 'I think I'll have a whisky.' He sat back in the sofa and watched Albertine arrange their life round him: books on the shelves, clothes in the wardrobe, medicines in the bathroom, tapes and tape recorder on a table and beside them a large photograph of Amanda and the children. He had all the appearance of a contented man but, as so often, appearance belied the reality.

Max was a man who could rarely admit his mistakes, even to himself. Watching Albertine attempting to turn the inhospitable room into something resembling a home was reminding him painfully that in this instance he could blame no one but himself. If they had been in England now there would be logs burning in the fireplace, the curtains would be drawn, he would be feeling pleasantly relaxed after a hot bath following a day's hard exercise, not drained as he was now, both mentally and physically. He would know that Albertine was busy in the kitchen preparing dinner, but as he would not be looking at her he would not be feeling, as

7

he was now, that perhaps he should be helping. He never told her so, but she was a good cook and he looked forward to his meals. Cold chicken and lettuce was not what he felt like now. He would like pheasant cooked as she often did with apples and cider or even plain roasted, with lots of bacon, paper thin potatoes, cranberry sauce and perhaps some creamed spinach.

He knew that it had been his idea to come here though why he was no longer sure. Unlike some men, he had not experienced a mid-life crisis. His routine had remained the same for most of his adult life and he had never had the slightest desire to alter it. Nor had Albertine's sometimes obvious unhappiness disturbed him enough to consider how their lives should change. If she was bored – and he did suspect that boredom was her problem – it was up to her to do something about it. Other women he knew had involved themselves in charity work when their children had grown up. Some of the more eccentric of his friends' wives even did Open University degrees though he was baffled why they should bother.

When he decided that they should go away he had been thinking about himself not her. For the last two shooting seasons he had had to wear glasses for long distances. His eye was therefore not as good and in the rain he had to keep taking them off to wipe and so missed a lot of birds. Having the reputation for being one of the best shots in the county, he resented the fact that younger men were overtaking him in the individual tallies. He had begun to notice too that the hearing in his right ear was being affected. He had a horror of going deaf and though recently he had started wearing ear muffs when shooting, he was afraid he might have left it too late. If he had to cut down on his shooting, it had suddenly seemed a good idea to go away for the winter. Now, he realised that he should perhaps have involved Albertine more in the choice of house – she was better at things like that. She would probably have enquired more about what was available and not simply left it to Mr Lee. He could not conceive what they would both do for the months they had planned to stay.

Albertine, though relieved that she had succeeded in warding off a tantrum which would have meant hours of sulky silence, felt sickened that after all nothing was to change. It had been his idea to come here, he had made all the arrangements without discussing them with her and she knew he would not have asked any questions about the house itself, which he was making only too obvious he hated; it simply would not have occurred to him to do so. He would have assumed it would have all the comfort of his own home only in a different place. She had been excited by the idea that in a new place she would find a new Max, that without the constraints of long-ingrained habits and cultural conditioning, he would somehow, like a butterfly from a chrysalis, emerge a new man and from the new man there would develop a new relationship; they would have a marriage where in some way that she could not at the moment imagine, she would be recognised, not for what she was, Max's willing wife, but for who she was. Surely, somewhere there was a who. Somehow the fact that he had not even taken off his tie killed this hope before it had barely had time to breathe.

Neither of them slept well under the flimsy sheet which was more a protection against insects than the cold. They were used to a six-foot bed and the standard four foot six meant that whenever they turned over they woke each other up. The hard foam mattress on plain board was uncomfortable and this, combined with jet lag, made it impossible for either of them to sleep much after four o'clock. Neither of them admitted that they were awake; to do so would have meant that they would have to speak, inevitably revealing their thoughts, which were gloomier than even normal 4 a.m. thoughts.

The next morning, while they were eating breakfast and wondering how they could get into San Pedro to shop, they heard someone shouting outside.

'Hi, you guys!'

'Do you think they mean us?' Albertine asked nervously.

'I wouldn't think so,' Max answered.

They heard a faint knocking on the screen door.

'Can we come in?'

Standing on the steps leading to their balcony were two Americans, looking straight out of the cast of *Thirty-Something*.

'Hi!' they said together.

'Bill,' the man said, holding out his hand to Max.

'Max Stevens,' Max answered, 'and my wife Albertine.'

'Hi, Albertine,' Bill said.

'How do you do,' Albertine responded as she shook his hand.

'Ellen,' said the tall blonde young woman, stepping forward. 'I'm sorry we weren't able to greet you last night. I hope Orlando met you all right. Did you find everything?' Ellen looked round the room. 'Your man in England said you would probably want something to eat in the house when you arrived. I hope it was all OK.'

'Everything was wonderful,' Albertine said. 'Thank you so much.'

'You're welcome.'

'We did not want to complicate your arrangements from England any further but you will need a boat of some sort here. We've got to go ourselves for some shopping so we could show you round and fix you up with a dinghy.'

'That's very kind of you. We'd like that, wouldn't we, Albertine? We were just discussing how we were going to get there,' Max answered.

'We'll call for you in about half an hour . . . if that's OK?'

'Aren't they nice,' Albertine said to Max when they had gone. 'I suppose they must be our landlords.'

'I wonder why Americans always look so healthy. Do you think Ellen lives entirely on muesli and yoghurt? Frightening isn't it?'

Albertine was intimidated by most people. The feeling of inadequacy covered most areas of her life, not least her

10

appearance. She preferred not to look at herself in the glass. When she did so, she saw 5 foot 11 inches of fat. 'You're tall, you can carry it,' people said to her, but Albertine did not feel this. If she had to be fat she would have rather been fat and dumpy, small and round like Mrs Tiggywinkle, comforting and comfortable and most of all not taking up so much space. She always kept her shoulders bowed, which added to the humps of flesh already there at the back of her neck and at the top of her collar bones. She felt more comfortable sitting than standing; she felt most comfortable sitting on the floor with her legs curled almost out of sight. She always kept her legs hidden if she could, covered mostly by trousers, now and then by a long skirt, and if she had to wear a short one, by dark tights to conceal the dimpled cellulite and the small but multiplying patches of brown and white skin which she was horrified to discover were symptoms of incipient old age. Her lumpy knees, which she had always hated, were now not only fat but padded and cushioned by pockets of fluid which rolled when she straightened her leg. They hurt too, which she tried to ignore, afraid of arthritis, which had crippled so many of her female relations. Her arms below the elbow she did not find too unpleasant, though the skin, once hard and firm, was beginning to soften into tiny creases not unlike the surface of calm water ruffled by a gentle wind. Above the elbows they were thick and heavy, with two or three inches of loose and flabby flesh hanging in bluish lumps, slightly speckled with red, which wobbled when she moved them. Her mother used to say that women over the age of 45 should never show the tops of their arms. She now knew why and never did if she could avoid it. Since this was one of the few pieces of advice she had received from her mother it had remained in her mind, as had other more surprising warnings: never to marry a man with a small nose and on no account to sit next to a hospital nurse on railway stations or in the theatre, or to get into a taxi without first checking if there were handles on the doors. 'White slavers,' she had added enigmatically.

'What on earth can I wear?'

'I thought you did a lot of shopping before we came.' Max was always bored by this perpetual cry which arose whenever they had to go anywhere, not realising it came from the humiliation Albertine experienced every time she went to buy clothes.

She had no idea how to dress as a fat woman, and struggling in tiny booths in front of what must be distorting mirrors left her almost weeping with disgust. Anything she tried on was always too tight and looked terrible and after only one or two attempts she would buy something if only not to have to go through the same process again somewhere else. Her cupboard was full of unworn clothes bought in this manner. The clothes she wore were invariably navy blue or black; she hoped in this way to minimise her bulk, to somehow remain always in the shadows. She admired fatter people than herself who managed to carry their flesh with flamboyant pride like galleons in full sail or giant tropical flowers, waxy and brightly coloured. She should have worn scarlet or emerald green but she felt small inside and could not recognise herself as herself in the reflected overblown rhododendron; she saw a violet, definitely shrinking.

'I can't wear any of the shorts I bought, I'd look absolutely ridiculous. Didn't you notice Ellen? She looked wonderful, so thin, so brown . . .'

'Well, wear some trousers then.' Max was too irritated to point out that since Ellen was probably 25 years younger than she was it was only natural that she should be slimmer.

'I'll boil.' The sun was already high in the sky and it was hot.

'It doesn't seem the sort of place that it matters much what you wear or what you look like. Do come on, for God's sake. They'll be here in a minute.'

It was easy for him, Albertine thought bitterly as she struggled into a pair of knee-length shorts which she had bought despite the fact that they did not quite meet round her waist; ever hopeful, she was expecting to lose some weight and then they would fit. In spite of his age Max was still slim and wore his 'abroad' clothes – khaki shorts and blue linen shirt – with the same ease as he had on their honeymoon 30-odd years before. He had no need of the long navy tee shirt she was wearing to cover the gap; in fact, she noticed, he had even less of a stomach than Bill.

There were three main streets in San Pedro, Front, Middle and Back. Front Street faced the sea, Back Street the lagoon. Most of the shops were in Middle Street. The tourist shops sold carved wooden fish or birds and tee shirts, there were dive shops selling fins and goggles and diving suits. There were vegetable kiosks selling papaya and mango and rather dead-looking greens amongst root vegetables which Albertine could not identify. There were liquor stores and general stores selling everything from fish hooks to tinned tuna and casserole dishes to mattresses and rubber sandals. There was Rocks, the supermarket. It was to Rocks that Ellen took Albertine while Max went with Bill to arrange the hire of a boat.

Used as she was to the abundance and variety of food in the English supermarket, Albertine was uncertain what to buy. There was no butter and no bread, there was no milk and the only cheese came in orange slices. There was a deep-freeze which contained nothing but a few packages of chicken wings. There were tins of beans – refried beans, green beans, baked beans – and some sweetcorn, there was rice and flour in plastic bags, there were no eggs. She bought some chicken wings and some tinned tomatoes, she bought rice and some salt, she eventually discovered pepper, loose, in a very small plastic bag. She could see that her culinary skills would be stretched to the limit.

They had arranged to meet in Fido's, a covered courtyard overlooking the sea. It was very crowded. Albertine and Ellen found a table, ordered two rum punches and waited for the men to return.

They had to wait for some time. Albertine, still very conscious of her fat white legs sticking out from the end of her shorts, was having difficulty speaking to Ellen, who was exuding warmth and friendliness in such a bounteous stream that talking to her was like being buried by an overfilled duvet. The soft down-filled cushion was absorbing Albertine's words in its copious warmth, allowing for no resonance or response. She suddenly missed the restrained conversation of the English, which although perhaps less overtly friendly was nevertheless more direct. She was also suddenly conscious that Ellen was the same age as Amanda, her daughter, who she began to miss, along with all the other things Amanda represented for her – her home, her grandchildren, her life.

At last Max and Bill returned, looking flushed and pleased with themselves. They had obviously had some success and probably also some rum to celebrate.

'Bill's found us a boat. We can collect it in an hour,' Max said.

'Ellen, can you take Albertine back? I'm going to take Max snorkelling and set him up with some dive lessons. He'll bring me home when he gets his boat. Don't wait lunch, we'll have some here.'

Albertine wanted to scream 'what about me' but instead said, 'That sounds very exciting.'

'You can't be here very long without learning to dive, that's for sure,' Bill said as this unlikely pair went off together, like boys playing truant, like men going off to war.

Ellen left Albertine at the dock. Alone in the house, she faced clearing up after the hurried unpacking of the night before. She found a dead scorpion on one of the shelves and shuddered with fear as she swept the hard crisp little body into the dustpan. What had the previous night seemed an intensely romantic little house, in which she had thought, Max allowing, she could be happy for ever, now appeared dark and impersonal. The chairs were uncomfortable, the primitive furniture, painted black, emphasised the gloom; the bare boards were scratched and already covered with sand. She wanted to swim but she knew that to do so would only intensify her loneliness; she felt that the first swim was something they should do together. She thought how much it was always like this. Max would be enjoying himself without giving her a thought; he would come back full of self-importance over his new skills and expect supper. She looked at the chicken wings in despair. She sat on one of the black chairs at the black table, prey to her imagination, which was always vivid especially when allied as it was now to self-pity.

For many years the image she had of herself was as a large lump of Cheddar cheese on a plate, dry and scaly in parts, shining with fatty drops of yellow sweat, liquifying inside as the outer scales hardened and parted in ever-widening cracks. Mice crawled over this unappetising mass, munching continuously, growing fat and lazy on her ever diminishing bulk. These she thought of as munchers.

Her munchers came in many categories: bodiless shapeless feelings of guilt and remorse, boredom and fatigue and responsibilities both real and imagined. Those responsibilities that were real she left unattended and thus they became fodder for the guilt. She nursed this guilt muncher as she would a sickly child. She nourished the imagined responsibilities on panic until they became giants in her tiny world, leaving her prostrate and exhausted from fighting such a ferocious enemy bare-handed. But there were also munchers who were real people: hungry people, hopeless people, who fed on her compliancy and poured out their despair into her ever-open ear. Her family called them Albertine's lame ducks and no one but herself knew that she was the lamest of all, that she needed these lame but living ducks as the only proof of her own existence.

Without the munchers, when she was alone as now, her mind was a dark and terrifying forest, peopled with ghosts and monsters, threats and cavernous holes. Tall black trunks of trees guarded her in their shadows; the soft fallen leaves, sodden with moisture, lying on the floor beneath impenetrable canopies, unwarmed and unlit by the sun, blanketed footfalls and silenced the heralds of desperation, leaving her unarmed and undefended against the poisoned darts of memory and against her dreams. Her screams of fear were silent screams and even if he had been listening, Max could not have heard her. But he did not listen. He was too occupied listening to his own voices which told him that his life too was wasted. He blamed Albertine for his disappointment, blame she carried willingly; his blame provided delicious meals for her munchers.

She wondered when it had gone wrong or when she had gone wrong. They had met when she was only 21. She had seen little of the world by then but had found it hard. She had discovered that retreat was safer than attack and she saw in Max someone who could provide the haven she sought. He was ten years older, and to her unsophisticated self he appeared glamorous. She could not see then that he too was in retreat and that he would not be retreating unless he was wounded – or that he would conceal his wounds from himself by wounding her. His arrogance and egotism she saw as power, a power she thought would protect not overwhelm her. She saw a man powerful enough to provide the family life she craved. It would be through the lives of her children that she would discover a meaning she had failed to discover in her own. Having died as a person she would be reborn as a mother. But after the birth of their daughter Max had said he did not want any more. She mourned her unborn children continuously without being able to see that Max had recognised her mothering desire and wanted it for himself. They had married without knowing that what they thought they saw in each other was only a reflection of their own needs; they could not speak to each other because only they could have given themselves the answers they wanted to hear.

The only child of rich parents, overindulged by his mother and ignored by his father, Max had a particularly sheltered and gilded youth. His slightly saturnine looks won him attention wherever he went, he had an enquiring and quick mind, a natural athleticism and an instinctive ability to lead. From school, where he had been head boy, he had gone straight to Sandhurst as a last desperate attempt to please

16

his father, who had been Colonel of the Coldstream Guards, the regiment Max joined. He would have preferred to go to Cambridge and read PPE as he had a vague ambition to go into politics eventually.

Four years into his military career his father had unexpectedly died of a heart attack. Max left the army and moved home again to support his mother, where he remained in part to please her but mainly to please himself. There was little for him to do. The small estate he had inherited was run by a good farm manager and the few local committees he was a member of did nothing to stimulate or engage his once active mind.

He had been used to succeeding without effort but had discovered that along with his many gifts he was cursed with an almost crippling inertia. The days of doing nothing slipped into years, and although at first his conceit protected him from the realisation that he was letting his life seep away, by the time he recognised it, it was too late and his voices became not only disappointed but embittered. Albertine was always the first target of his bitterness; to the rest of the world he appeared charming and urbane. Only to her was he distant, only her did he ignore. Only she would have held so tenaciously to the belief that their unhappiness was entirely her responsibility.

2

It took some time for them to adjust to their new life. The days seemed to revolve round the shopping trips to San Pedro. They swam, they read, they went onto the reef. In the afternoons they slept in the hammocks and walked up to a resort two or three miles up the coast, where they would have a drink and talk to some of the American tourists. They celebrated Christmas in the Catholic Church, where Albertine was enchanted to find that *Rudolph the Red-Nosed Reindeer* was one of the carols. They made their journey to the mainland, visiting Mayan sites and rainforests, looking for but failing to find howler monkeys and jaguar. They slowly adapted to the gentler rhythm of the days.

Max had become quite proficient at diving, which relieved his boredom to a certain extent. He and Bill would go off together, sometimes for the whole day. This oddly mismatched couple, who as far as most people would see could have nothing in common except their gender, seemed to have found a way of communicating that Albertine envied. When Max came back from one of these expeditions he was invigorated in a way she knew was not entirely due to the physical excercise; he was, for him, rejuvenated, as some men are rejuvenated by their adult sons. Albertine wondered how different Max might have been if Amanda had been a boy. Only slowly had she discovered in many ways, though culturally apart, Bill was a younger version of himself. Bill's father was a professor and Bill had a degree from Harvard in social anthropology. Having spent two years in New Guinea studying an obscure tribe for his doctoral thesis, he had suddenly and for no apparent reason abandoned the academic life. For what, Albertine could not help wondering; not, she was sure, for Ellen, to whom he was not married and with whom he appeared to have an entirely superficial, though obviously very sexual, relationship. But then she had never really been able to understand why Max had suddenly abandoned his career. Despite his outmoded way of life, Albertine realised when she saw them together that Max was just as much a dropout as Bill. Whatever it was that had driven them both to defy their fathers' expectations perhaps bound them in other ways as well.

Albertine had not succeeded in establishing any rapport with Ellen, so, when Max and Bill were together, she was left alone wondering more and more what she was doing there, what either of them was doing there, for that matter. She wrote often to Amanda but said nothing about her true feelings. She did not tell of her sometimes agonising home-sickness or of the boredom she endured on her own. She wanted Amanda to think that this uncharacteristic expedition was a total success and that her parents were branching out on an exciting new experience, as indeed she was still hoping it might turn out to be.

The end of the first month was unexpectedly upon them and they had to go to Belize City to register their intention to stay for a further 30 days. They decided to take the boat rather than the tiny aeroplane, both for a change and because it was cheaper. The Banana Boat – not, to Albertine's disappointment, named because it carried bananas to the mainland, but because it was bright yellow – was a canopied trimaran with seats all round the sides. The space in the centre containing a cold box for those purchasing perish-ables unobtainable on the island was fast filling up with the backpacks of five German students, already *Achtung*ing away to each other. Albertine had never been able to overcome her dislike of the Germans. Her childhood dreams had been full of jack-booted Nazis invading her bedroom and leading her to Hitler, a terrifying moustached figure with evil red eyes who was waiting to do indescribable things to her.

The boat was nearly full. As well as the Germans there was a middle-aged American couple, the man bearded and wearing a white linen cap, the woman muscular and trim despite her 50-odd years – Albertine could imagine her jogging every morning. They were both studying their guidebook with the gloomy intensity of people determined to enjoy their vacation. There were two older American men with shirts open to their protruding paunches and shorts tightly belted under them; they both wore heavy gold chains round their necks, one bearing a medallion and one an anchor. It was only after studying them for a while that Albertine realised that despite their different hair colour, one being grey and the other dark, they must be identical twins. Their hair receded to exactly the same point, their fleshy noses and thick lips under identically shaped moustaches were the same, their ears joined the top of their jawbone at the same place and were both lobeless. She wondered if the grey-haired one had suffered some trauma turning him grey overnight or whether the other resorted to Grecian 2000. They were talking quietly and companionably to each other.

There was a pregnant Belizian woman with a large shopping bag who continually stroked her bulge as if to reassure herself that it was all right and next to her two Carib men, one with the wrinkled face of a walnut, the other young and attentive; grandfather and grandson, she thought. There were two drivers, a young smiling thickset man with legs like posts and classic Mayan features; the other a somewhat dour-looking Carib with moustache and wearing a bright yellow cap bearing the words *Banana Boat, San Pedro.* They seemed to be waiting for someone, taking turns to look up the long wooden pier to the booking office and checking their watches. She could see now who they were waiting for was an old woman, 80 at least and even from a distance very obviously English, wearing a loose checked aertex shirt, the kind not seen in England for years but common at one time, thin navy blue cotton trousers and a large straw hat, limp and floppy with age, which would not have seemed out of place on Miss Marple. She was obviously a well-known figure on the island; surrounded by small eagerly chatting boys all carrying some part of her equipment – a cushion, a basket, a pair of steps – she was smiling warmly at them and calling them by their Christian names. The man with legs like posts was on the pier to welcome her.

'Morning Miss A. You make your visit today?'

'Yes, Armando, the time's come round again.'

The steps were set against the boat, the cushion was placed carefully in the corner and she was helped over the steep side. There was a lot of fussing, a lot of cheerful banter; this was clearly a regular ritual.

Miss A now seated, the boat was loosed from her moorings and roared into the calm lagoon. It was an hour and a half's journey to Belize City and they would make one stop, at Caulker Caye. Albertine settled down to enjoy herself. She knew the route as they had been nearly as far when they had gone on their fruitless search for manatees, those shy mammals, half seal, half dolphin who lived in the waters just outside the mouth of the Belize river; these animals had for some strange reason, since they seemed particularly ugly, spawned the myth of the mermaid. The sailors whose eyes had been so grossly deceived must have either overstepped their ration of rum quite considerably, or a year or two away from women had left them with an oddly distorted memory of what they looked like.

They had been going barely three minutes when her thoughts, which had been randomly jumping from one inconsequential thing to another – remembering the drum-like feeling of advanced pregnancy, wondering what it would be like to look at someone else and see onself, deciding that pelicans were like harrier jets both in their shape and the level at which they flew, low over the water in straight lines veering neither to right or left – when she became aware that there was a crisis in the German camp. She did not understand what they were saying but panic was written on all their faces, particularly on that of a blond curly-haired one in white shorts and singlet who was begging the driver to turn back. He was pointing to the shore and with imploring gestures was saying 'Just five minutes.' The driver shook his head and stared adamantly ahead. The boy returned to his seat and his companions all began turning out their pockets and counting the small selection of loose change, which to their chagrin only amounted to a few dollars. Albertine, whose curiosity was always insatiable, swallowed her reluctance to speak to Germans and asked what had happened. It transpired that he had left his money belt and passport behind, that there was no chance of turning back although they had at that moment been passing the hotel and that there was no other boat that day. She had to admit to feeling sorry for him, but was at the same time rather satisfied that the efficient German had been found to be so inefficient.

She turned and whispered to Max, who seemed quite uninterested in what was going on. 'He's left his money behind, can you believe it? No wonder they lost the war.'

'Very unlike them,' he replied and shut his eyes.

Miss A, in the back of the boat, seemed asleep as well. She had pulled her hat well down over her face, and her long fingers like knobbly twigs were folded in her lap. The American twins suddenly came to life. It would be best, they said, if the German telephoned the hotel from Belize City and asked for the money and passport to be put onto the aeroplane which went every hour. In the unlikely event that the hotel refused to do this, it would be easy, and not cost more than 40 dollars, to fly back himself and collect it. A solution so simple it left the Germans dumbfounded, and the journey continued without further incident.

Albertine was beginning to feel uncomfortable, a sinking sensation in her stomach spoke of dread, her enjoyment of the journey was suddenly overshadowed by a strong feeling of isolation. She wanted to wake Max up but knew that he would only be angry with her and she would not be able to explain her feelings.

Only the sound of the engine disturbed the silence that

22

had now settled on the boat. Max and Miss A slept, the Germans were subdued and the rest of the passengers gazed out to sea with dead eyes. Albertine knew that to them she would have the same look, that her vacant stare would not reveal the confusion of her thoughts. She knew this holiday was not a success nor was it likely to become one. She and Max had not, despite the days spent in closer quarters than they had ever been before, become closer in any other way. The difficulty they had always had in communicating any part of what they were thinking to each other had, in the absence of anything much to occupy them, become more acute. She felt sure that the otherwise inexplicable feeling of dread she was still experiencing was to do with the thought of the day ahead. What would they do after the registration, what would they talk about, how would they fill up the time? Would Max, who was always particularly irritable in crowded and unfamiliar situations, fall into a sulk or drink too much at lunchtime and become rude and aggressive? He had been drinking a lot since they had been in the country. Albertine knew it was because he was out of his environment, but found the knowledge no comfort and his bad temper no easier to deal with.

Their only other visit to Belize City had been by air when they had gone on their journey to the mainland. They had been led to believe from the guidebooks that it was a dangerous and devilish place where as likely as not one would be stabbed in broad daylight by a drug-crazed Rasta- farian or beaten and left for dead on account of a few measly dollars. From the air it looked just such a place. To call it a city seemed a joke; it appeared to be all shanty town. The densely packed, flat tin-roofed houses seemed to be sinking into a wasteland of reddish-brown, stagnant water and stunted scrubland, a town of playing-card houses, tilted, sloping and liable to fall with the slightest breath. They had stayed only long enough to hire a car.

Approached from the sea it seemed quite different. The first thing to stand out was a large and, if not beautiful at least imposing, bright blue building; three storeys high, it

23

towered majestically over the whitewashed houses on either side of it. It was almost certainly a hotel and almost equally certainly a new one. The boat took a right turn round a headland and slowed down into an unpretentious but colourful little harbour. There were a few yachts moored and a small cruise ship named *Caribbean Lady*. Young boys were diving into the muddy water from the jetty and as the boat came alongside men appeared from nowhere crying, 'Taxi . . . Taxi.' Facing the jetty was a perfectly proportioned pink and white colonial-style wooden building which Albertine was pleased to see was the Bellevue Hotel, where it had been recommended that they should have lunch after their registration.

There began an urgent scrambling for luggage. Albertine, bending to collect her bag, noticed with shame that, from the labels on their backpacks, the 'Germans' were in fact Swiss. Not after all the descendants of the murderous Hun, but no doubt delightful, industrious and peace-loving sons of cuckoo-clock makers and mountain goatherds, more accustomed to yodelling than shouting orders. No wonder they had made the easy mistake of leaving their money behind.

Miss A, waking from her snooze with a jerk, let her hat fall to the ground. Her hair was white, coarse and springy, short and brushed back from her long thin face into tight curls which fell away into a sort of Eton crop. She tapped the driver with her stick and was obviously asking him if he would pick it up for her. The smile she gave him was charming and persuasive; Albertine had seen it a hundred times, a thousand, a million.

How could she have possibly failed to recognise her immediately? Why had the strange feeling of dread she had experienced all through the journey not warned her? Her mouth alone she should have recognised, her smile she saw now was just the same, wide and large, revealing all her teeth. It was one of the very first things about her she had been conscious of. She had seen that face through so many moods, that smile had been directed towards her for so long that it had been for years etched on her memory; now she was drowning in a tidal wave of recognition. Superimposed upon or emerging from the old woman was Miss Armstrong. The fingers like twigs she had observed only half an hour before, she could see now tapping restlessly, urgently on the arm of a chair, a table or her leg. Perhaps it was for this reason that she had been able to look at her so closely without seeing her. In old age the frenetic energy was stilled. Miss A was not the driven Miss Armstrong of her youth. Even if she had not found the peace which passeth all understanding she had certainly found the peace which comes from the acceptance of herself as she was and all the intelligence, the anger, the charm, the desperation, the fear and the uncertainty which Albertine could remember so well had in her old age become synthesised into gentle warmth and generosity. She carried now the certainty that she could give and receive in equal measure with no fear of rejection. Her long narrow face had lost the rigidity which had made her look so formidable in the past and had settled into folds of tranquillity; her mouth, which had been so often drawn into a tight and downward dipping line, seemed now to be in a permanent and wide smile.

Albertine could see why she was so obviously loved and respected by the people here. The two images of past and present were fused together in her mind, and as she watched covertly a repetition of her embarkation, the steps, the smiles, 'Taxi Miss A?', 'I'll look after your cushion, Miss A', 'Don't forget your hat, Miss A', as she saw her helped out of the boat and into a taxi, she was overcome with terror and shame, with an almost overwhelming desire to run after her or as far away as possible. She was sick with apprehension, dread and an awful familiar feeling of despair.

'What on earth's the matter, Albertine? You look as if you've seen a ghost.'

This quite ordinary expression made Albertine want to cry and not, for once, because of the coldness in Max's voice. It *was* a ghost she had seen. A real ghost, the ghost of her youth, ghost of her dreams, the ghastly ghost of betrayal.

Not a ghost in a white sheet nor even a ghostly spectre, but a spirit beckoning her to the deepest and darkest long-hidden and denied corner of her heart and of her mind and of her memory. A ghost which through the years had tapped her on the shoulder, and she had run as she wanted to run now. A ghost she had thought was laid to rest, whose reappearance threatened the very foundations of her fragile psyche.

3

Norfolk, England, 1951

The sweet and heady scent of wallflowers coming from the beds on either side of the French windows of the school hall, the sound of bees – and of *The Merry Peasant*, played with many inaccuracies and hesitations, coming from one of the practice rooms – had lulled Albertine, who was sitting between the doors, into a state of semi-unconsciousness. It was a Wednesday, which meant that it was a half holiday. She was surrounded by girls working in their gardens. There were beds set either side of the paths running to Darwin, one of the two boarding houses, to the classrooms and to the gym ground. Each garden had a separate individuality; some were crammed with brightly coloured annuals, some divided into smaller beds by pebbles collected from the beach and planted in graduated shades of blues and greys and greens. It was usually this type that won the gardening prize, but there were also vegetable gardens, strawberries and runner beans battling for space with feathery carrot tops and tender peas. Each garden clearly reflected the character of its owner and, apart from providing a useful pastime for free days, gardening was a good exercise in compromise as every patch was shared and debates on where to put what could be heard ringing through the otherwise quiet summer afternoons. Sometimes debate would turn to passion and one partner would storm off in a rage at failing to have her way.

Albertine, until this year, had shared a rockery with Julia, her best friend, but Julia had left after taking O levels and Albertine, without her prodding and superior knowledge, had let it go. She could not now even weed it with confidence and, apart from candytuft, she had no idea what to plant; Julia had always done that so now it was overgrown and a mess. I'll have to give it up, she mused idly.

She was meant to be finishing an essay on the metaphysical poets and had managed to persuade herself that listening as she was to Benjamin Britten's *Holy Sonnets*, she would be helped in this. She had only recently discovered this piece of music and somehow Britten's phrasing and the passion inherent in Peter Pears' interpretation had made Donne's words more comprehensible; also the sonnets chosen by Britten all reflected her current obsessions. The imperative tone of 'Batter my heart, three-personed God' was exactly what she wanted to say herself since she had 'discovered' God the year before. She wanted to be submerged and subsumed by an 'experience' of God, to know for herself the ecstasy recounted by the saints; she wanted visions, and sometimes she succeeded in whipping herself into such a state of religious euphoria she almost believed she had experienced one and went about for days afterwards with a holy look on her face, hugging the knowledge that she was in some ways more spiritually advanced and aware than her fellows.

She had not yet had an 'experience' of love, but she felt the poignancy of the words 'Since she whom I loved hath paid her last debt, and her soul, early in the morning, ravished' as if she had. Today she was thinking of Julia as she heard the words, realising that now Julia was in the world and she was still at school she had probably lost her as surely as if she was dead. She was remembering the last holidays she had spent with her. Julia's was a proper family, a family Albertine longed for. She had five brothers and sisters, a benign father, a tolerant mother; they were constantly engaged in something – riding, boating, fishing, target-shooting with air pistols or driving rats from haystacks. Albertine was determined that when she married she would have just such a house, just such a husband and just so many children; she would be just such a mother. Her own family was fractured; her parents were divorced and she and her sister lived a small life with their mother. Albertine was not unhappy but the three of them lived their own lives which seldom touched.

The words 'solely on heavenly things my mind is set' confirmed the belief that the poem related to her intimately. Her mind was already set on heavenly things, which was not to say that she was not looking forward to the pain and the rapture of Anna's love for Vronsky, for instance, or even the nonsensical disaster of Juliet's for Romeo.

'Death be not proud' did not speak to her quite as personally; she was quite unable to imagine her own death, and the death of her grandfather two years previously had left her with only the rather uncomfortable feeling of being watched. Like Maria in *The Parasites*, which she and Julia had recently read, she had an idea that he was sitting on some heavenly cloud watching her every move and gasping with disbelief and shocked disapproval when she did something wrong. She was more concerned about what he would be thinking of her than of the punishment she would receive if she was found out, although the sins she was thinking about were less public than those for which she might be gated. She wondered what he would have thought of her inept and unsuccessful attempt, by pretending she had something in her eye, to get the boy whose photograph she had under her pillow to kiss her; or even worse, when she was sweet monitor, if he had seen her take a barley sugar from someone's box and put it into her own. This theft, carried out on impulse, made her blush still whenever she thought about it. She had tried to return it but her sweet parcels never had barley sugar in them since she liked Caramello and Crunchies and she could not remember which box she had taken it out of anyway. 'Stealing is stealing' her mother used to say but that theft had been nothing like stealing the bit of lined paper from a pad of Basildon Bond in the village shop or razor blades from the chemist, both of which she and Julia had done and which had left them both with an exaggerated sense of triumph and excitement since they did not want either of them. She did not want the barley sugar either, which is why her mother never sent her any.

'Albert, the Head wants to see you, now, in her study.' The girl who came with this message, Judy Whitelock, looked very smug. She did not like Albertine nor did Albertine like her. She was definitely one of the goody-goodies, always top of her form order, which was the weekly rating of academic success, and of house order, which was the rating of acceptability in the house, generally related to tidiness and general conformity. Albertine was invariably bottom of this. It was not that she was deliberately rebellious – she very much wanted to be acceptable and tried very hard to conform – but it seemed that no sooner had she learnt one rule than another reared its head and bit her where she was least expecting it.

'Oh God, did she look angry?'

Judy Whitelock did not answer but looked deliberately mysterious, as if to imply that she knew all about it and that Albertine was in for a serious and well-deserved punishment.

With the heaviness of nameless dread weighing on her, Albertine went over in her mind the various possibilities for this summons and could think of nothing; but that was always the way. Like the time she had innocently boasted to the old headmistress about her very fine collection of the topmost shoots of the pine trees round the school, which meant that she had been the first to climb to the top and thus have the privilege of naming the tree. She could not believe how quickly an expression of benign sweetness could change to one of speechless rage. She had no idea, botany not being one of her best subjects, that in the pursuance of her collection she had managed to deform most of the trees in the grounds. She had been nearly expelled for that. She was far from being the only one with such a collection but she took all the blame for the desecration and had been gated for the whole term. The whole school, including the head girl, was gated for a week. Old JPC believed in peer group pressure and peer group responsibility.

Albertine knocked on the door.

'Come in.' Miss Armstrong was at her desk but got up as Albertine entered.

'Ah, Albert, come in, sit down.' She was smiling and seemed excited, which was unusual; she never called her Albert either. It didn't feel like trouble; if it had been she would have stayed at her desk and Albertine would have been left to stand by the door. She sat on the edge of the sofa and waited.

'Don't look so nervous, I'm not going to bite your head off.' Her laugh was reassuring but Albertine felt that this might just be a subtle ruse to deflect any excuse she might think of on the spur of the moment.

'You know what we were talking about the other day' – Albertine tried to look blank but felt suddenly sick – 'that you should have a shot at Oxbridge; well, I've spoken to Miss Larkin, who agrees with me. She says you have a very real understanding and love of literature and that you have matured a lot over this last year. Have you thought any more about it yourself?'

Had she thought about it? Since Miss Armstrong had brought up the subject a few weeks before she had thought of very little else. She was not interested in Cambridge, which had a cold, scientific aura round it; all the people from school doing maths or physics and chemistry seemed to opt for Cambridge, and its colour itself seemed to represent its chilly nature. Oxford, however, was the cradle of all her heroes: Gerard Manley Hopkins, Sebastian Flyte, Oscar Wilde, not to mention Henry Newman and Ronald Knox. She had imagined herself sitting at the feet of Socrates and Peter Abelard, drowning in knowledge, drunk with learning and carried as if by an eagle through dreaming spires to Parnassus.

Apart from the obvious drawback of not being 'bright' enough Albertine had immediately seen two insuperable

31

obstacles. One was that she had given up Latin two years before and Latin at 'O' level was essential, the other was her mother. She knew that it was only with the greatest difficulty that she was managing to pay the fees as it was since her father made little if no contribution, and to stay on for a further four terms would pose a serious problem for her. Beyond that, she knew in her heart that university was not in her family's scheme for her. If her future had been discussed at all which it rarely was, she knew that what was in store for her when she left school at the end of this term was a Season in London, then some time in France to 'learn the language' and then some sort of undemanding and unserious job while she waited for real life to start. Real Life meant marriage (to some suitable man) and children. No-one, not her mother and certainly not her cold, unloving and unapproachable father would want a 'blue-stocking' daughter. She could see many battles ahead and in her heart of hearts she knew they could not be won however hard Miss Armstrong fought for her. She did not dare say this because she knew how much Miss Armstrong despised the frivolity of what she labelled indiscriminately 'upper-class parents'.

'What about Latin?' she said, naming the only difficulty she knew Miss Armstrong would understand or at least have any sympathy with.

'I've thought about that and have already spoken to Mr Harper and Mr Woods; they are both quite certain that they can get you through in a year.'

Mr Harper and Mr Woods were two local clerics who came every day, in Mr Wood's ancient and somewhat battered Alvis, to teach Latin and Scripture. Every girl in the school was half in love with Mr Harper who was a tall, very thin, romantic looking man with a magical smile and a beautiful voice. He seemed very holy and apart from the pipe which was never out of his mouth, very ascetic. Mr Woods was short, fat and plain with grey skin and thick purple lips. His grey suit was always crumpled and the trousers two inches too short. He was very jolly and before

Albertine had given up Latin she used to organise bets as to how soon and for how long they would be able to 'red herring' him. It was very easy.

'I say Mr Woods, just before we begin, you know where it says in the Bible ... what does that really mean?' and he would be away with passionate enthusiasm until the bell went.

'You are dreadful you girls, never mind, we'll make it up next time.'

He was also an authority on opera and any question about Mozart who was his favourite composer could absorb at least half an hour.

'The reason I have called you in today is to say that I have spoken to your mother and she is coming this weekend to talk about it.' Seeing Albertine's expression of shock, Miss Armstrong continued, 'It is what you want isn't it?'

It was what she wanted but the gulf between desire and fulfilment seemed unbridgeable; the lump in her throat which made it impossible for her to speak and which had brought tears to her eyes was created from fear, fear of the battle to come, fear of the challenge, but most of all fear of failing. She had never before wanted anything enough to mind very much whether she had it or not, which to a large degree contributed to her insouciant approach to life. At this moment all she could do was nod while Miss Armstrong said, 'Well, run along then,' and added gently, 'It will be all right, you'll see.'

She had seldom seen Miss Armstrong this friendly although she had noticed that this term she seemed to be more interested in what she was saying in class. Sometimes she felt her looking at her with a close regard she could not interpret and which made her feel slightly uncomfortable.

Albertine went upstairs to her dormitory, where they were not allowed in the daytime, and lay on her bed fighting the lump in her throat, the terrible dragging sensation in her stomach and the horrible thumping in her chest.

She decided to walk down to the cliffs; it was always here that she managed to feel calm. In all weathers the sound of the waves breaking, sometimes with a near deafening roar, sometimes with a barely audible whisper, could clear her head from the clanging confusion of boarding school life: the petty punishments, the intense relationships and the homesickness. This day the tide was out and the ridged expanse of sand shone as the sun caught fragments of its glittering grains. She climbed down the cliff, whose sandy face was eroding at the rate of six inches a year from the fierce, implacable winds coming directly from the North Pole, and ran towards the tremulous dribbling of the exhausted waves, rejoicing that hers were the only prints on this new land, kicking the piles of sand worms with her toes and feeling the hard ripples on her insteps.

She had said she wanted to try for it and, faced with Miss Armstrong's belief in her and in her imagination living in the groves of academe, she did. But here alone on the seashore, seeing the far horizon, it seemed that real life was beckoning her to walk down the shiny path of the sun on the water to the future. To try would mean four more terms of school, it would mean the terrible battle with Latin, it would mean failure and facing an army of 'I told you so's'. She would be nearly 19 years old and still a schoolgirl. But if she succeeded *she* would be able to say triumphantly, 'I told you so'. Perhaps she should leave it to fate in the shape of her mother: but supposing her mother said no, and supposing she had not fought for this her one chance to join her body of heroes . . . Supposing her mother said yes and then she failed. At the thought of failure her stomach took a sickening turn and set her whole body reverberating to the sound of 'fail' ringing in her head.

But to say no to trying would also be failure, failure of a worse kind. It would be failure of courage, said the voice of truth; if you don't try you can't fail, said the devil's advocate. To try would be putting off for such an age the grown-up world that Julia described and which she was longing to join. Nothing is worth having that does not come with struggle and sacrifice, said the puritan in her. And so the contradictory voices raged. Her mother was coming in three days; she would have three days of this turmoil and then it would be decided one way or another.

As she often did when she could not face school, she went to see 'old JPC'. Joan Pelham Carter, the founder of Hartwell, was well into her seventies. It was she who had agreed to take Albertine when she was 11 years old, despite the fact that she had already been expelled from two schools.

'I like the sound of her; term starts in two days; don't go to the black market for coupons, we have plenty of clothes here for her to choose from,' JPC had said to her mother.

She had arrived on a bitterly cold and rainy night, drenched and frightened, at the Junior House, which was in the village away from the main school and which was more like home than a school. Nine 11-year-olds were in the motherly care of Mrs Saunders, a widow whose children had left home. There had been a misunderstanding, due no doubt to her late and hurried acceptance. Mrs Saunders had been led to believe that Albertine was French and for the first ten minutes after her arrival attempted to speak to her in French. Albertine eventually managed to say 'I'm sorry, I don't understand,' but it was a poor beginning and repre-sented graphically the difficulty she had always had fitting in. For three years she had struggled to obey the incompre-hensible rules and to keep a low profile. This was hard for her, but JPC's mixture of firmness and affection had gradu-ally convinced her that this was not a hostile place and that if she did 'bad' things it did not mean that she was herself 'bad'.

JPC, retired now for over a year, lived across the road from the school and it was there that Albertine went, still tormented with indecision and fear.

'Come in, dear child. You're just in time for tea.'

'Oh, I'm sorry, I don't want to disturb you,' said Albertine untruthfully.

'Don't be silly. Get another cup from the kitchen and bring it into the garden.'

Albertine did as she was told. Tea with JPC was always a large meal, scones, cakes, watercress sandwiches, probably because she hoped that she would be joined like this and she very often was. For those who had been her pupils, her 'children' since she called everyone 'dear child', she had become in her retirement their favourite grandmother. Her home was a place of normality and peace; she would play croquet, snookering viciously and with great delight, and then present enormous plates of food as they gossiped about the ordinary day-to-day happenings of the place that had been until so recently her whole life.

'Well . . . are you going to tell me or not?'

Albertine, struggling with a spiky and tickling bit of cress in her throat, looked with gratitude at the kindly old woman who had always understood her. Had she come to talk or had she come to escape the thoughts that were driving her mad? Here in the garden with the roses just coming into bud, the flower beds stuffed with wallflowers and lupins, the strong, straw-hatted, wise and gentle figure of JPC had to a certain extent silenced the conflicting voices in her head, but had clearly not removed the anxiety from her face or the tension from her body.

'How did you know?' she stalled.

'Albertine, don't play with me, tell me what is wrong or eat up your tea and tell me how the play is going.' Albertine was producing *Romeo and Juliet* for the house play.

'Miss Armstrong says she wants me to sit for Oxford,' she blurted out.

The old face relaxed into an enormous smile. 'Hooray,' she said. 'Hooray.' And she clapped her soft white hands. 'I always knew it. Why so worried? Isn't that what you want?'

'I don't know what I want . . . No, that's not true. It is what I want; but suppose I fail,' she whispered.

'Now look here, Albertine, look at me, my dear child.' This was JPC at her most compelling. 'I have watched you since you first came here as a fierce, angry and unhappy child; I have watched you tame your temper, I have watched you fit in, though I know how hard it was for you, I have watched you give neither too little nor too much, but you never deceived me, and I have always known, known from

36

the beginning, that once you were doing what you were really interested in, you would be unable to keep up the pretence that you were a middler; once you were really engaged, you would have to give your best. And you must believe me – are you listening to me? – if you give your best it will take you wherever you want to go. Of course you won't fail.'

She was listening and JPC's words were charging her with hope and excitement. So she had known, this wise old woman. Had she known why, she wondered; had she known that at the last school from which she had eventually been expelled she had been moved up and up until at ten she had been in a form with 13- and 14-year-olds, so that she had been without friends at all, bullied by her form and ignored by her contemporaries. She had been expelled because no one could control her ungovernable rages, the only form of self-expression allowed her.

'You know I gave up Latin two years ago.'

'I know you did, and very silly of you it was too, but now you know there is a reason for you to do it you won't find it a problem. Does Miss Armstrong suggest you try in English or history? You could do either, you know.'

'She said English, I'd rather do English, I think, though I do like history.'

'Yes, more scope for you, I think. Well, well, well! What a day!' And she leant back in her chair, smiling.

'Miss Armstrong has still got to persuade my mother. She's coming this weekend.'

'Your mother is a sensible woman and she'll know that this is best for you. If there is any difficulty, send her down to see me; bring her anyway – I'd like to talk to her. Now run away, dear child, and take that look off your face. Take the tray as you go ... And don't forget to bring your mother.'

By the time Albertine had put the tray in the kitchen, washed up and gone back to say goodbye, JPC was asleep, still with the satisfied smile playing round her wrinkled mouth and penetrating the folds of her aged face.

4

The red and white checked tablecloths, the alpenhorn hanging on the wall along with the cuckoo clock and pictures of men in coloured braces and leather shorts standing below tall snow-capped mountains, declared defiantly that the restaurant Miss Armstrong, Albertine and her mother were now in was Swiss. Albertine was dressed in her grey Sunday frock, bought especially for her confirmation the year before, which had a wide white piqué collar not unlike a sailor's, coming to a tie just at the point of what might have been her cleavage if she had one. She had thought it very smart and grown-up the previous year but now it seemed drab and young. It was also rather tight and the permanently pleated skirt, once so sophisticated, was no longer pleated but more crumpled and too short. She had grown about two inches that year. She did not feel ready to have a serious discussion about her adult life.

The waiter, dressed in black trousers and scarlet waistcoat as if prepared to perform some cloggy type of dance, hovered expectantly for their order. Albertine was shocked to find how expensive everything was. Her only previous experience of going to a restaurant other than Lyons Corner House and Selfridges Snack Bar had been when she was much younger when her grandfather had had pantomime parties for all the grandchildren and they had eaten in a private room at the Connaught, where there had been no menu and therefore no prices. She was worried about who was paying. If it was her mother, as seemed most likely since it was on Albertine's account that they were there, she knew she would be horrified that there was nothing on the menu for under ten shillings.

'I think that as this is a Swiss restaurant we should have the fondue,' said Miss Armstrong, folding the menu and handing it to the waiter.

Albertine did not know what fondue was but glad to be released from the agony of making a decision.

'And we'll have a bottle of the number twelve, and three glasses of sherry. Do you mind your daughter having a glass of sherry, Mrs Williams? It is a rather special occasion.'

'I suppose it's all right just this once,' replied her mother, in a tone which indicated that she too felt subject to Miss Armstrong's authority.

Albertine had only had sherry once before, at Christmas. She did not like it, but realised that along with grapefruit and coffee it was just one of the things she was going to have to get used to if she was to be taken seriously in the adult world.

'Well, that's that,' Miss Armstrong said, leaning back in her chair. 'How was your journey?'

'Apart from a long queue at the Blackwall Tunnel it was fine.'

'I always come by train. There's a school car I can use during term time so it seems more sensible to leave the car for Maud, and the porters are so good at Liverpool Street it's really a very simple journey.'

In the holidays, Miss Armstrong lived with her friend Maud, who was a don at London University. They had known each other since they were students and had lived together for the last 20 years.

Albertine took a sip of her sherry. The sharp dry bitterness caught in her throat and she coughed and spluttered. Her mother looked embarrassed and frowned at her, Miss Armstrong laughed and said, 'Don't drink it if you don't like it.'

Albertine blushed furiously. 'It's delicious, it just went down the wrong way.' Resolutely she took another sip. She wondered when they were going to start talking about Oxford and which of them was going to bring the subject up. She was nervous that as it concerned her it was her job to start the conversation. She had not had a chance to speak to her mother alone and had no idea what her thinking about it was. Her mother had given no indication that she knew that this was the reason she had been asked to come. Albertine was beginning to feel very hot but could not take her cardigan off as there was a split under the arm of her frock which she had been meaning to mend for ages but had kept putting off. She was also beginning to wonder if she was going to faint. Fainting was very popular that term but pretending to faint in prayers in order to get out of lessons was quite different from the real thing. She wanted to ask if she coud go outside for a moment, but she did not dare. She had another sip of sherry, which made the floating sensation more sickening and the swimming vision worse.

The waiter arrived with a stand and a small paraffin flame, which he set up in the middle of the table. He brought two large bowls of white crispy bread cut into squares and some very long-handled forks. Her interest in what was coming next drove away the giddiness that had threatened to overwhelm her. A second waiter arrived with a black cast-iron cauldron full of bubbling cheese. It seemed an extraordinary meal.

'Have you ever had fondue before, Albertine?'

'No, I don't think so,' she answered and realised how idiotic she sounded; as if she could have forgotten a meal as strange as this, but she hated to admit doing anything for the first time, feeling that people would be looking at her, scrutinising her in the hope of finding her doing it wrong. She had no idea of how to tackle the cauldron.

'You take a bit of bread like this,' Miss Armstrong said, as if she had overheard her thought, 'and dip it into the cheese like this. Be careful, it will be very hot.' She speared a square of bread with her fork.

The cheese hung in long strands from the bread and in getting it into her mouth Albertine managed to leave a sticky trail across her plate, the tablecloth and the front of her frock. She forgot the warning in her embarrassment and succeeded in burning the roof of her mouth so badly she had to spit the bread out.

'Albertine, really!' her mother said reprovingly.

'Never mind, try twirling the fork round like this.' Skilfully Miss Armstrong twiddled the fork in mid-air over the pot, winding the threads into a perfect ball before blowing it and finally popping it neatly into her mouth, sticking out her lips in a pouting shape as she delicately chewed the molten cheese. Miss Armstrong had obviously done this many times before.

Albertine was pleased to see that, despite her strictures, her mother was not doing very much better herself, continuously losing her bit of bread and undecided whether to fish for it or start again with a fresh piece.

Having established undoubted superiority over the meal, a ploy Albertine now realised was probably carefully planned, Miss Armstrong said, 'What are *your* ideas for Albertine's future?' She used a tone of voice which implied very subtly that Albertine's mother's thoughts and plans were of no greater significance than anyone else's, as if Albertine's future was a ball to be kicked around by anyone who happened to be near it at the time; it placed Mrs Williams firmly on the defensive.

'I must say I was surprised when you rang. Although I realise Albertine has more intelligence than she has so far demonstrated, as all her reports have said "Could do better, if only she would try", it still seems a big jump to suddenly say she should go to university, especially Oxford. Isn't that very difficult to get into? Her O levels were very unremarkable.'

'Forget about O levels, they tell you nothing; as I said on the telephone, it is her work this year that is the indication of what she is capable of. In my opinion it would be doing her a grave disservice not to allow her the opportunity of trying. What do you want for her yourself?'

'Well, her father and I thought a time in France would be a good idea.'

'To live in a family, I suppose.'

'Well, yes, and they would take her to museums and art galleries and generally show her Paris, you know . . .'

It was very obvious that her mother had no clear idea at all, as Albertine had suspected.

'We would also like her to have a bit of social life, meet some people, smarten up a bit . . .' her voice trailed.

'So you want her to be dragged round French museums by unwilling paid bear-leaders and then dressed in ball gowns and presented to admiring nitwits.' Miss Armstrong was unable to keep the tone of scorn from her voice.

'No, no,' her mother said, although that was exactly what she wanted, 'it's just that I don't want her to be disappointed. The daughter of a friend of mine, a very bright girl, tried this year to get into Oxford and she failed although she had eleven O levels and was considered certain of a place by her school.'

'Mrs Williams, do believe me. I've been in this business a long time and I can recognise what Oxford and Cambridge want when I see it. They are not interested in the amount of knowledge their candidates have acquired but their ability to use and interpret it; your daughter, as she has shown this year, has that ability. I would not have invited you to this discussion if I didn't think she had more than a good chance of succeeding.' Miss Armstrong had dropped her aggressive tone and was now pleading Albertine's cause persuasively.

Albertine herself was beginning to be irked by the cloak of invisibility which had descended on her at the start of this conversation. Neither of them had even looked at her let alone asked her opinion. She wondered if it was always to be like this; whether forever it would be other people making decisions about her, for her, in spite of her. Whether what she wanted for herself would ever be more than an irrelevance in other people's view of what would be 'best' for her. She wondered why she was there at all. No doubt this conversation would go round and round throughout the meal and at the end, after pudding, she would be informed of the decision they had come to. Not being allowed to speak, she ate instead and was feeling rather sick. Whether she went to university, to Paris, to London or to the moon was suddenly unimportant; what was important but clearly impossible, was that in her life it should be she who made the decisions. 'Of course,' she heard Miss Armstrong say, 'she has a lot of catching up to do, particularly in Latin, but if she works she'll cope with that.'

'Will she work, though? That seems the point. She may be excited and enthusiastic at the moment, but I know her: she is lazy and changes her mind all the time. If she doesn't leave at the end of this term, what will happen if she decided in the middle of next year that it was all a mistake and too difficult and that she would rather be doing something else? She'll have lost a lot of other opportunities.'

'Albertine.' Miss Armstrong's gaze was firmly fixed on her. 'Can you convince your mother that you will work hard?'

Albertine felt it was the wrong question. It should have been 'Do you want to go?' She knew she had to work hard and to assume that she did not know this was treating her as a child. She did not want to say to her mother that it was doing the work that she was most looking forward to, because that sounded priggish and she did not want her mother to be part of the exciting world she was discovering. She did not want Miss Armstrong there either, but for a different reason. She did not want her to realise the intensity of her interest in case she failed to rise to her own high expectations.

With the spotlights of two eyes now firmly focused on her, she wished devoutly for the return of invisibility.

'I would like to try, Mummy.'

'I'm sure that is what you think you want, while you're in that atmosphere, Albertine; but school is a very small part of life – you'll realise that when you leave. I'm sure you don't want to be a teacher or anything like that, do you? So I can't see the point of you going to university. I thought you hated school and were longing to leave.'

'Yes, Mummy, I do want to leave, but it's only four more terms. I can stand that, I've thought about it a lot, honestly.'

She did not say she wanted to learn for the sake of learning. She had no concept of a career or even a job, and what she wanted eventually was what her mother wanted, to be married and to have a large family like Julia's; but before that she wanted an extension of now, she wanted academe, she wanted mental excitement, she wanted the sense of achievement she had when she wrote a good essay. She did not want balls or museums; she wanted the world, but not yet.

She did not want her life to be prescribed by her parents. She wanted it to be an adventure. She wanted to be an explorer, and while they were talking she was realising that the reason she wanted to stay on at school and to go to university was because if her life was to be a voyage of discovery she had to have a well-provided ship, and education was the chandler's store. She needed knowledge and understanding as much as a sailor needs spare sails and screws and nuts. And just as a sailor sailing off into unknown seas will only feel secure if he knows that the ship is fully provisioned, so she would need food for her mind and her imagination if she was to begin her life with any confidence. She knew very well that now she knew nothing; the only charts she had were ill-defined, or well-used and leading to such familiar places that to follow them could not possibly be called an adventure. She wanted her heroes to be the stars by which she set her course and then to embrace with wholeheartedness the destination to which they guided her. She thought that if she said this to Miss Armstrong she would understand what she was saying but that her mother, because her ideas of the way people behaved and the aspirations they should have were so firmly fixed by her upbringing and class conditioning, would not.

'I don't know what your father will say.'

She detected a weakness in the wall of resistance. She knew as well as anyone that her father, from whom her mother had been divorced for many years, had played no part in her upbringing and that although he would groan 'My God' and clasp his forehead at the thought of a blue-

44

stocking daughter, he had no authority or will to override her mother if she had decided on a course.

'Let's have some dessert,' Miss Armstrong suggested.

They all chose vanilla ice cream with hot chocolate sauce, always Albertine's choice of pudding on the last day of the holidays when she and her sister would be taken to Selfridge's before being put on the train. Miss Armstrong had clearly also scented victory and Albertine allowed herself a glimmer of hope. She was surprised that the question of money had not been raised.

'I don't know how much it will cost. Will you be able to afford it?' Albertine said, pre-empting a possible later objection.

'Let's wait for you to get in first before we worry about that.'

And Albertine knew they had won. She felt a sudden almost overwhelming love for her mother; so difficult to talk to, so unlike herself she seemed sometimes to have come from another planet, yet so much on her side. She knew that if her mother was really now convinced, she would fight for her all the way and she would find the money somehow and never mention the extra burden that she would surely have to carry. Albertine wanted to get up from her seat and go and hug her, but she was herself too diffident and she also knew that that was not her mother's style; she would be both embarrassed and unable to return such an obvious show of affection or gratitude.

Miss Armstrong gave her a complicit look of victory, which almost drove Albertine to say that she had changed her mind, so strongly was she now identifying with her mother, who in some way had become the defeated one. Albertine all her life had been on the side of the underdog and she very much disliked the feeling of being allied with the victor. She felt flat, deflated; she had won what she wanted and the victory was sour and stale.

It was Miss Armstrong who paid the bill. Unaware of Albertine's conflicting emotions, she was in triumphal mood. 'This deserves to come out of school funds. Don't worry, Mrs Williams, you won't be disappointed, I can assure you.'

Her mother smiled weakly and said, 'I hope not.'

The journey back to school was conducted in almost total silence. There was nothing more to say. Albertine wanted to ask about things at home but felt such questions would be rude, excluding Miss Armstrong, who was sitting in the front seat. She did not want to talk any more about school or Oxford, which would seem like rubbing her mother's nose in defeat. After such an evening, to talk about anything else would be irrelevant, and so the three of them sat wrapped in their own silence.

Albertine, who was sitting in the back seat behind Miss Armstrong, felt a hand on her knee and then a squeeze. She's saying we've won, she thought, and although still confused herself about whose side she was really on, she knew it would be churlish not to respond; she was grateful to her too, for her interest and her effort. She removed the hand from her knee and squeezed it back. The hand quickly returned, groping round her calf, her foot, fluttering over her knee. Albertine took it again and this time the squeeze was held for the remainder of the journey.

'Thank you very much, Mrs Williams, for coming,' Miss Armstrong said warmly as she released Albertine's hand and opened the door. 'I'm certain you will never regret this decision and that Albertine won't let you down.'

'Goodbye, Mummy. See you very soon, only about four more weeks . . . I'll write.'

She tried to say something meaningful and to do more than give her mother the customary peck which touched more of the air beside her ear than it did her cheek, but under Miss Armstrong's gaze and because anything more would be so out of character, all she could do was whisper, 'thank you.' It was so quiet she was unsure whether her mother had heard her. She did not respond in any way other than to say that she would give everyone at home her love.

Back in Miss Armstrong's study, Albertine waited by the door to say goodnight.

'Come in,' she said. 'Don't stand there, come in and tell me how you feel about it all.' She was still excited, radiating a nervous energy, walking round the room picking things up from tables and putting them back again.

Albertine remained by the door, saying only, 'It's very good news.'

'It's wonderful news, wonderful.' She advanced towards her. Like bat's wings, her arms were outstretched, the black cloak she was wearing hung in wide folds either side of her thin body. She pinned Albertine like a stuck butterfly against the closed door and kissed her, hard and on the mouth. She was muttering words which Albertine could not hear and despite her attempts to break through the dark embrace Miss Armstrong did not release her.

It was a most unpleasant experience, the worst aspects being the claustrophobic intensity and Alice in Wonderland-like quality of the interlude. She felt fear; something unknown and threatening was in that embrace. It was not just a kiss, it was danger. She had no idea how to respond so remained standing against the door until Miss Armstrong, with no explanation of why she had kissed her in that way, released her.

'You'd better go now, darling. Goodnight, sleep well.'

Albertine instinctively held out her hand. It was ignored. Miss Armstrong instead placed a chaste kiss on her cheek.

All three girls in her dormitory were asleep, humped bodies under red blankets revealed by the dim light of a full moon. She crept across the room to her bed and undressed. She knelt, as was the custom, for her prayers, which were a garbled mixture of thankfulness with a plea for explanation, of hope merged with *tristesse*. She felt an inexplicable ache of longing for what she was giving up and more than any sense of excitement for the future she felt dread.

The door opened and silently the black-clothed figure of Miss Armstrong entered. She knelt over the kneeling Albertine and, kissing her again, she whispered, 'Pray for me too.'

5

It is a fact that however degrading, loathsome, even terrifying the experience, constant exposure to it eventually inures the victim to the pain. If this was not so, no one would survive the horror of war or the soul-numbing deprivation of concentration camps or even the desperate daily grind of total poverty. The human mind has ways of severing itself from the body to a greater or lesser degree, and so it was for Albertine. Not that she would have put herself into any of these categories. As a first sexual experience, with nothing to compare it with, Albertine was confused rather than terrified when Miss Armstrong made the first advance towards her, and the relationship as it progressed was ambiguous rather than degrading. Nevertheless, it was only bearable because she did succeed in distancing her mind from what she was undergoing physically, and it was only gradually that she discovered that what she most disliked about it all was the feeling of powerlessness. Nothing that occurred between them was of her choice and there was nothing she could do to avoid her. Miss Armstrong was the Head, she was a pupil; and she could not alter that.

The evening in the restaurant had been the beginning. Now, some months later, the nightly prayers were over; this ritual always preceded going to bed and generally took the form of Miss Armstrong asking God to bless the great love they had for each other. They were now lying comfortably together, Miss Armstrong's arm round Albertine's shoulder, and a plate of banana sandwiches balanced precariously between them.

'You're looking happy today, darling. Has anything nice happened?' Miss Armstrong was hoping, rather too obviously, that the anything nice would have something to do with her. Albertine knew this and tried hard to think of something that would please her in this line but, failing, told the truth.

'I got an alpha for my essay on Hopkins' imagery today,' she said.

She did not add that she had also had a really lovely letter from Wilfred, mostly about his increasing success on the drums, but starting '*Ma plus chère Albertine*', which she realised was an exciting advance on '*ma chère*'. He had also signed it just 'W' which seemed more intimate than '*Wilfred*'. She was wondering if she could write 'darling Wilfred' back, but thought that she would wait a little. Miss Armstrong did not know anything about Wilfred and would have been horrified had she known how much of Albertine's time was spent looking at the now rather dog-eared photograph she had of him standing in pyjamas on a balcony playing the clarinet. Wilfred had aspirations to be a jazz musician.

Miss Armstrong, clearly a little chagrined not to be the cause of her happiness, nevertheless managed to sound pleased. 'Well done, I'm delighted,' and they continued to munch.

I wonder why it is that food in bed is so much nicer than food on a table, and why at this time of night (it was 11 o'clock) it should taste so much more exciting, Albertine was thinking. If all that was expected of her in this strange union was to sit up in bed eating and chatting it could all be quite pleasant. The praying was excruciatingly embarrassing, the sex was sometimes disgusting, sometimes disconcertingly interesting but the conversation was generally always, as long as she stayed away from speaking about her love, fascinating.

'Do you still keep a journal?' Miss Armstrong interrupted her thoughts. She knew that it was the vogue to keep journals at the moment. Girls of all ages could be seen scribbling furiously in hard-backed volumes, their arms curved round the page, guarding the secret entries.

Albertine felt trapped. If she said she did not, Miss

49

Armstrong would know she was lying and wonder why. But why was she asking? It did not sound as if it were a casual enquiry.

'Yes, sort of, I haven't written anything in it for ages though,' she lied. 'I don't seem to have time now,' she added, implying that the volume of work and her virtuous application to it kept her from such frivolous activities. She took another sandwich, hoping that Miss Armstrong did not suspect that she was worried by the question.

'I'd like to read it.' The tone of her voice was impartial and the smile with it friendly, as if she was asking for no more than that she should lend her the book she had just finished and enjoyed.

'Oh no, honestly, you'd be terribly bored. Anyway, I'm not even sure I know where it is.'

'How could I be bored by anything written by you about you? It's what I am most interested in. Can't you see that?'

Albertine could see that very well, which was why she was determined not to show it to her.

'How many volumes have you got?'

She had started keeping her journal in the lower fifth, in a red exercise book with a red shiny cover, and rather like Cassandra in *I Capture the Castle*, from where she had got the idea of a journal rather than a diary in the first place, she had progressed to the thicker hard-covered books, of which she now had three, two with dark red backs and the current one, which was green.

'I'm not sure, one or two, I think.'

'When did you start keeping it?' Miss Armstrong persisted.

'I don't know, about a year or two ago, I suppose; but I've told you, I don't bother with it any more.'

She felt herself struggling in deeper and deeper water; very soon she would drown. She should have said no emphatically, straight away, but Miss Armstrong never allowed her to say no. Many of the conversations that took place in this bed were like this. First there would be prevarication on Albertine's part and then submission. After the submission Miss Armstrong would spend time trying to make Albertine feel that she had not given in, merely agreed to do as Miss Armstrong wanted because she loved her.

'I can't see why you don't want me to read it. You know I love you; don't you trust me? Or have you written things about me in it that you don't want me to read?' She said this with an unpleasant and unnaturally coy expression.

'Of course not, no; how could you think that?'

'Well then, why don't you want me to read it?'

Albertine tried firmness. 'Well it's private,' and then rather feebly, 'You know . . .'

With the authoritative tone she still sometimes used with her, the strong implication behind the honeyed words being that she was in command, Miss Armstrong said that there should not be private things between people who loved each other. 'That's what love is, total sharing and giving; can't you see that?'

Albertine felt ticked off, a gamma or even a delta in the examination of loving. She capitulated.

'I'll see if I can find it,' she said, thinking that she could play for time, she could 'lose' it, or keep 'forgetting' to bring it. She did not know if what she was feeling was anger over the intrusion, or panic that she should read some or all of the things she had written, thereby discovering what a small part, if any, Miss Armstrong and their nightly capers played in the drama of her inmost thoughts. She did not write about it because she did not like to think about it; it was too hard and she always tried to forget completely what had happened the moment she left the room.

'Do you mind if I go now? I'm really quite tired and I've got an essay to write tomorrow.'

It was only very rarely that she managed to escape before the main activity of the night was under way. Sometimes if she had the curse she made that the excuse, she even occasionally, without knowing what a well-worn ruse for avoiding sexual intercourse it was, said she had a headache. Never before had she simply said 'I want to go.' She was surprised to find it was so easy. As it was early, she almost thought that, despite Miss Armstrong's insistence that she

51

should always climb over the broom cupboard to reach her room, she would risk the stairs and a possible meeting with Miss McClaren; the matron's room was at the bottom of the stairs which led up to the attics where Albertine and the other Oxbridge candidates had their own rooms.

Outside Albertine's room there was a small balcony which overlooked the cupboard where all the cleaning materials for the whole house were kept. Getting down was moderately easy; she just had to climb over the railings of the balcony and then, first crouching on top of the cupboard, she could swing herself slowly over the edge and drop quietly to the floor. Getting back was much harder and at four o'clock in the morning, which was when the climb usually had to take place, it almost seemed the last straw in an interminably ghastly night. She had to jump to grip the edge of the top of the cupboard and then pull herself up, hopefully high enough to get a little leverage from putting her foot on one of the many things inside the cupboard. She sometimes thought bitterly that the endless hours that she had spent on the bar in gym, which had obviously prepared her well for this climb, was no doubt introduced into schools for just such occasions. When else would this skill she had achieved ever be put into practice, or was adult life to be one long climb in and out of other people's bedrooms?

Miss Armstrong knew that she had upset Albertine over the journal question and wanted not only to placate her but also to reassure her that her demands were not insatiable.

'Yes, go now, my dear, but be careful.'

To read the journal had become an obsession with her. It was in that book that she knew she would discover what Albertine really thought about her and how much she understood about her own feelings for Albertine.

It had been so easy to get her into bed. She had simply suggested that she came to her room one night and that had been that. She had offered her a sandwich and said she would be warmer if she ate it in bed. It had been only about two weeks before she came every night. Albertine had not as yet exactly responded to her sexual advances, but she had not refused them. Miss Armstrong was sometimes surprised by her apparent innocence, which was almost frightening if it was real and not assumed for her benefit, and at other times she thought she saw in her expression an almost uncanny awareness of what was going on and of how much power Albertine had over her, not that she had ever attempted to use it. She was sure she would see the journal, it was a question of when rather than if: she knew she had only to put a bit of steel into her voice for Albertine to cede.

Miranda and Ruth and Judy were still up when Albertine got back to her room.

'Gosh! You're early. What happened?' they said together.

'She wants to read my journal,' replied Albertine, her voice charged with drama. They all appeared stunned. The privacy of the journal was sacrosanct; not even in the midst of the fiercest feud would any of them dream of stooping so low as to try to read even their worst enemy's secret thoughts. It was an accepted code that made the nearly intolerable lack of privacy of boarding-school life almost bearable.

'But that's private,' they said, genuinely astonished that Miss Armstrong should apparently not understand this most basic concept.

'What are you going to do?' said Miranda, ever practical.

'I don't know, I simply don't know. It's not just that it's private, it's what's in it ... There's hardly anything about her at all and if there is it's mostly about our conversations about her, or how awful she is, or what I can do about her ... She'd kill me if she read it, I know she would.' And as she said this the full horror of her commitment to show it to her finally hit her. 'I said I might have lost it, but I know she didn't believe me, and you know what she's like ... She'll get it out of me, I know she will.'

'Well, I think it's the absolute bottom,' said Ruth. 'Honestly, Albert, you must just say you won't and that's that.'

It seemed so easy, here in Ruth's room, surrounded by her righteously indignant friends. Why, oh why, thought

Albertine, can't I do just that, say no? But she knew it was impossible; even to these, her closest friends and confidantes, it was beyond her to describe the almost miasmic control Miss Armstrong had over her. It was as if, when she was in her presence, she was under some hypnotic spell. It was not that she was unwilling to hurt her, nor even that she was afraid of her. It was that she could not do anything but what was asked of her, from laying bare her body and apparently now her soul.

'It's really got to stop. We'll have to tell someone now,' Miranda said.

It was a great comfort to Albertine that what was essentially her problem was seen by her friends as theirs as well. They never said, '*You* must tell someone,' it was always '*We*', and that they could never decide who the someone should be was not for want of trying. The assault on her body, which really none of them could understand because it was quite outside any experience they had either had or read about, was impossible for them to imagine and so seemed less important in some ways than this assault on her privacy. This they could imagine and they revolted against it.

'I wouldn't show my journal to anyone, not even my husband,' said Ruth emphatically.

They often fantasised about their husbands, and what they would or not do for them. They gleaned much of their knowledge of married life from Mary Grant's Problem Page in *Woman's Own*, which they would read with a lot of giggling and a mixture of delight and horror of what was in store for them. 'Have you read this? "Dear Mary, my husband has been unfaithful again, even after he promised me that he would never do it any more. The trouble is that this time it is with my best friend and I can't forgive either him or her, signed Desperate." My God! I'd kill him if he was my husband. Honestly, the things some people put up with,' they would say with all the experience of their 17 years of more or less incarcerated existence.

It did once occur to them that they might consult the omniscient Mary Grant about Miss Armstrong, but as ever

54

they were defeated over the words to use, and after many weeks of scanning the letters they had not read one from a schoolgirl, let alone one on this subject.

'You can't do it. Honestly, Albert, you can't' Miranda insisted.

'I know . . . I'm going to bed. Perhaps she'll have forgotten about it in the morning.'

But Albertine knew she would not have done and that if it came to a battle of wills Miss Armstrong would win every time.

6

This is the private Journal of Albertine Williams.
Anyone reading it will be struck dead.
Hartwell school
Brampton
Norfolk
England
Earth
The Universe . . . Space

The word *Private* was printed in large red letters, ringed with stars and underlined three times. She could remember doing it and also remembered the sense of excitement as she started writing on the clean white page.

5 June. I have decided to start keeping this journal to record my private thoughts. I am determined to keep it up for the rest of my life so that when I am famous people will know what I was like when I was 15. At the moment I am sitting at my desk in the study. I am meant to be doing prep and I hope that horrible old Camilla who is taking it doesn't see me or she will confiscate it and there goes my private thoughts!!! I think I will be a writer when I grow up, or perhaps an actress. There's only half an hour till prep finishes so perhaps I'd better get on and do my Biology. I hate Biology, all that stuff about the pancreas which sounds disgusting, and blood. If I think about blood I want to curl my hand in until it hurts my wrist. I'm certainly not going to be a doctor. Ugh!!!

I can't show her that, thought Albertine, who was now lying in bed with the journals. It's so babyish and I hadn't even learnt how to do slopy writing. The letters were round and rather uneven. She could remember practising for hours to make her writing more grown-up. Even now it sometimes reverted, especially if she was in a hurry. She could also remember the rather terrifying feeling of having no very significant private thoughts to record.

6 June. It was a lovely day today. Julia and I decided that we were going to be friends forever. We found this poem by Byron where it says 'Friendship is love without its wings' and we decided we would always wear something, sort of like a wedding ring, to remind ourselves of our vow of friendship. We found these silver chains in the village, real silver! and we put them on each other, holding hands and swearing never to take them off. They cost 9s 6d, which is half a term's pocket money, but it's worth it. We are never going to tell anyone why we are wearing them, not even our husbands. I hope Mummy gives me some more money at half term. I've only got 2s 3d left to last until the end of term. I am looking at my chain now. It is lovely. It is wonderful to have a real friend. We are going to try and wear the same clothes too. I really want a Gor-Ray skirt like Julia's. We took photographs of each other sitting on the fence over the path leading down to the sea. We sat on the fence with our legs sort of sideways and there was nothing in the background except the sky. It looked very romantic. I can't wait for them to come out.

Albertine had had a letter from Julia that morning saying at the end 'I'm still wearing my chain'. She was still wearing hers too. It had broken twice, but she had managed to get it mended although the man in the shop had said the links were getting very thin and that they would not last much longer. Miss Armstrong was always asking why she wore it – in fact, one of the times it broke was when she was in bed

57

with her – but she had not told her yet. She did not want her to know anything about her feelings for Julia, which were private and special. She still missed her very much. She wondered if their friendship would last after the chains were broken for ever or if that would be an omen.

10 June. I have decided to be confirmed. We, Julia and I and Biddy, decided we would go to church at Mr H's church and so we left early as it is 12 miles. When we were nearly there I was pushing my bike up the hill past Billing Chapel. There was a field of mustard, least I think it was mustard, beside the road. It was very beautiful, bright yellow and sort of shiny and stretching as far as I could see. I stopped to get my breath and it suddenly seemed as if I was part of the field, sort of bathed in yellowness. I didn't hear a 'voice', but I knew for certain that there was God. It was like St Paul on the road to Damascus. I didn't tell anyone because it was too special, not even Julia. When I was in church I decided to be confirmed, and all the way back I was so excited about God. I really want to know everything about HIM. I think I might be a nun when I grow up. I'm going to tell JPC about being confirmed tonight when I say goodnight. I'll make sure I'm the last in so that I can tell her on my own.
    Later. I told her. She was very nice about it and said that I could start confirmation classes next term. The confirmation will be in March. I told Julia about my decision to be confirmed but I didn't tell her why. She said she might be confirmed too. Perhaps I might become a missionary.
    Prayer: 'Please God, help me to be worthy of being a missionary or a nun. Amen.

11 June. In prayers this morning we had the prayer, 'Teach us Good Lord to serve thee as thou deservest, to give and not to count the cost, to fight and not to heed the wounds, to toil and not to seek for rest, to labour

58

and not to ask for any reward save that of knowing that we do thy will.' I am even more determined to be a nun or a missionary. I might go and work for Albert Schweitzer in a leper colony. I would not mind getting leprosy if that is what God wants me to do. I have started reading *I Leapt over the Wall* by Monica Baldwin. It is about someone who stopped being a nun, but if I was one I wouldn't stop. This afternoon in free time I went into Brimpton Church and sat in the back pew for ages. It was very nice. The sun was shining through the window of St Francis. I wondered if it was God telling me that he wanted me to be a vet, or look after animals. I wouldn't mind doing that. I don't care what anyone says, I'm sure that Bonfire and Trudy have got souls. It was really embarrassing because Father Somerville came in and he asked me if I was all right. I wanted to ask him about being a nun or a missionary but I didn't dare. I just said, 'I'm OK, thank you, I'm just going,' and he said, 'Don't let me drive you away,' and he smiled really nicely. I think I might become a Roman Catholic.

Albertine could not stand it and turned the pages rapidly, blushing for her 15-year-old self.

20 Sept.   Today is the worst day of my life! There was a match against Norwich High (we lost 6–4). At half time JPC came onto the pitch while we were having oranges and she had an awful-looking woman with her. She was very thin and scrawny-looking with a horrible grim sort of face and very big teeth. She started talking to us. We couldn't think why because usually not even JPC comes onto the pitch at half-time. This horrible woman congratulated me on the goal I shot. Anyway in prayers tonight she was on the platform with JPC and JPC said, 'I want you all to meet Miss Armstrong who is going to be your new Headmistress.' I couldn't believe it. She looked so awful standing beside JPC, who is so wonderful. JPC looked warm and large and comforting, and this awful Miss Armstrong looked like an evil scarecrow. She grinned, baring her huge teeth, and said how much she was looking forward to next term and getting to know us all. Well! she's certainly not going to get to know me!!! She had awful hair too, sort of frizzy and black, not like JPC's bun which is always coming undone. It wasn't just me, the whole school seemed sort of stunned. Julia and I talked about her for ages and we vowed we wouldn't do anything she said. She's obviously going to be a 'real' headmistress and there won't be any fun any more, like when JPC gives half holidays if we can answer a question. Only last week she said at prayers, 'If anyone can tell me why Charles I walked and talked half an hour after his head was cut off there'll be a half holiday.' No one got it though Margaret Riley suggested that because he was a martyr he had been given special grace. JPC left the platform chuckling and said, 'Don't think of miracles, think about punctuation. I can't imagine this place without JPC. We thought we might run away when she comes. Almost the whole house was in tears. It is really ghastly. Apparently she is going to spend a week here to learn how the school runs. I am not going to speak to her if she speaks to me and nor is Julia.

   Later.   She was with JPC when we said goodnight. JPC said, 'This is Albertine Williams,' and the awful woman sort of grinned. I didn't look at her when I shook hands. She had horrid bony fingers. I washed my hands straight away to get rid of her horrid touch.

Albertine remembered that day so well. She could still remember the pain she felt on realising that everything was going to be different and the general hysteria in the school as slowly everyone took in the fact that JPC really was going. When she had announced at the end of the previous term that she was retiring, it had not seemed too terrible; she was very old, she was going to live nearby and no doubt everything would be the same and she would still be running the school but from a distance. That there would be someone else in her place had not really sunk in at all.

As she read her journal she found it hard to believe that only two years ago she should have been so young. It seemed as if she was reading the writings of a demented ten-year-old. What on earth had happened to her during that time? She could hardly bear to go on but it held a gruesome fascination. Of course, as she had known all along, she could not possibly show Miss Armstrong any of it; it would be far too humiliating and the bit about her would hurt her terribly. How extraordinary it was, she thought, that she should be lying here reading about having to wash because she had shaken hands and now, every night, those same hands were all over her. She flicked through the pages.

20 Oct.   Hooray, hooray. I've got the curse at last!!! It's a bit difficult because I was meant to have had it only ten days ago. I have pretended for over a year because I was so sick of everyone 'boasting' and saying they were better than me because I hadn't started. I have only got a few STs left from the last false time. I don't know how many I will need now I have really got it. I feel very excited; perhaps soon I'll be able to have a bra – my breasts are coming along quite well, definitely more like plums than walnuts. I can't tell anyone I've started because I told everyone before when I hadn't. It will be jolly nice to put down N/P in the games book without being frightened of being found out. Help! I've only just had time off games . . . Never mind, they'll probably not remember!

How devious she had been, going month after month to Miss McClaren for STs, which she solemnly wrapped in the sheets of newspaper hanging on the back of the door, and putting them, pristine, in the can beside the loo. If she had been in the middle of a good book and wanted to finish it she would put N/P in the book and go to Miss McClaren

61

with a pained expression and a request for supplies. There had been a time when she had gone so frequently she had been put to bed, which had been wonderful, though there had been one terrifying moment when the doctor had come on his usual weekly visit. She had heard him and Miss McClaren coming down the passage. 'Is there anyone in there?' he had asked, and Miss McClaren had said, 'Only someone having trouble with her periods' and they had gone away.

It was so strange that now what had become such a real curse should only so recently have been such an exciting and longed for event. It was strange too, she thought, that when she hadn't had it she could have asked so blatantly for STs, whereas now she had she found it really hard and had to screw herself up for hours before knocking on Miss McClaren's door and blushed ferociously at the mention of the word, preferring to use the trade name Kotex.

She could not possibly show her any of it; the whole book was just a catalogue of overdramatised religious fervour or disgusting bodily functions and had little or nothing to do with her. She wondered if the next volume would be any better and reached for the first of the hard-backed books. The writing was slightly improved; although it was still round it had an overall slope to it.

3 Jan. I have been to my first proper dance. It was to celebrate Camilla's sixteenth birthday but it was a proper grown-up dance with an orchestra, or I suppose it was really a band and there were not only grown-ups and children, but people of 18 and 19, not like the Pony Club dances. It was held in the library at Scot Hall, which looked amazing with flowers everywhere. Mummy made me a new frock specially for it. It is beautiful: white net covered with red circles and has got masses of layers and straps on the shoulders instead of the horrid puffed sleeves of my other one, which is pale blue net covered with sticking-out pink rosebuds and looks really babyish. I thought it was going to be ghastly because

after dinner when we went upstairs to the loo the
Grimley girls were there and they looked fantastic, both
dressed in very grown-up yellow taffeta frocks and their
hair was curled and I'm sure that they were wearing
make-up. They were wearing nearly high heels too.
Mummy won't let me wear high heels not even tiny
ones, because she says they will ruin my feet. They were
giggling in the bathroom and I was sure they were
giggling about me. I hate them. But anyway, there was
this wonderful French boy there, called Wilfred, he
pronounces it Vilfreed, who is the son of one of Aunt
Margaret's friends and who has come to London for a
year or two!! Aunt Margaret is sort of looking after him.
He is 19 and is really good-looking with dark curly hair
and huge brown eyes. He is meant to be learning how
to be a banker but he spends all his time learning how
to play jazz. I don't know anything about jazz. I must
learn!!! Anyway he was nearly the oldest boy there and
he spent the WHOLE night dancing with me except
when we had to do an awful thing called a Paul Jones
when we had to dance with whoever we ended up in
front of. I could see the Grimleys were livid because he
was by far the best-looking as well as being nearly the
oldest. He said he loved my frock. He is sort of serious
but very funny too. He says he is going to come and see
me tomorrow before he goes back to London AND that
he is going to write to me at school. I wonder if he will
be my 'boyfriend'. I asked him why, as he was French,
he was called Wilfred and he said that his mother loved
England and wanted her sons to have English names.
His younger brother is called Cyril. I don't know anyone
English called either Wilfred or Cyril, but I didn't tell
him that in case he was hurt.

She thought she could just show her that. It was still very
childish and banal but apart from the exclamation marks,
which she regretted, at least it was not too over the top and
she need not tell her that she was still seeing him, writing to

63

him and thinking about him. She could laugh about it and invite Miss Armstrong to acknowledge how far more grown-up she was now. It was funny; that night she had really thought she was going to have a 'love affair', but although Wilfred still wrote to her nearly every day, and had just begun to start his letters '*ma plus chère*', they consisted mostly of detailed descriptions of his day, his progress on the drums and his rows with his landlady, which were mostly related to his drumming. He also seemed to be trying to educate her. She had written to him saying how much she loved Elgar's cello concerto and had received pages back about Elgar being simplistic, over-romantic and not a serious composer. She had felt chastened and doubled her attention to Bach and Vivaldi. She, Ruth and Miranda had recently discovered Vaughan Williams, *Fantasia on a Theme by Thomas Tallis* and *Flos Campi* being their favourites, but it was still the third and fourth movements of Beethoven's Ninth that sent them into ecstasy.

She had never mentioned Miss Armstrong to Wilfred, nor him to her. This double deception, the juggling with her emotions, the lack of sleep and the increasing interest she was finding in her work was wearing her out. She thought that she would like Wilfred to kiss her, which so far he had not done; she felt sure it would be a far more exciting experience than the kisses she endured from Miss Armstrong. The relationship she had with him, though there was nothing sexual about it, it was far more real; the mental intimacy far more satisfying than the tumblings and the incessant and increasingly intrusive demands made on her by this woman who was old enough to be her mother.

7

She had not slept well. She had had her recurring nightmare where she had the main part in a play and had not learnt a single line. In the wings she desperately tried to scribble the next scene on her hands, her arms, on bits of paper in her pocket; she was surrounded by an infuriated cast, horrified by her negligence, and on stage she was so deafened by her fear she could not hear the prompter, not that it would have made any difference if she had. Eventually the curtain had come down to the slow handclap of an enraged audience. She woke up with the sinking knowledge that she had an impossible task to perform, and moments later she remembered the journal.

She decided that she had to be ruthless. She would cut out every page that would in any way be embarrassing; the trouble with secret thoughts was that they were by definition secret and therefore embarrassing if uncovered. Albertine had been ashamed herself by the meanderings of her 15-year-old self, but she was still furious that she should be compelled like this to destroy them. She was a hoarder of memorabilia. She had every programme of every play and concert she had ever been to; she had the newspapers of every main event during her life: the Festival of Britain, the death of King George VI, the birth of Prince Charles, the Coronation of Elizabeth – all these were saved for her old age and for her grandchildren. Her schoolgirl journals were part of this collection, along with her horse pictures, the relics of an earlier craze. She could imagine herself reading them when she was 'old and grey and full of sleep', when she was past embarrassment and in a position to look back with tenderness on her childhood self. She had not reached that stage yet; she was still too close to it and she felt no tenderness, she felt revulsion.

The first volume she could pretend she had left at home. She began to read the second one.

28 Jan. Gosh it's cold. I'm wearing two vests and my blazer all the time but am still freezing. It was gym today and although it was nearly snowing we still had to do it. The bar was white with frost and we couldn't hold on because our hands went numb, but we did a lot of horse and box things. I quite like doing them. I like the feeling if you get on just the right place on the spring-board, for a moment it almost feels as if you are flying. I am house gym captain this term and have got to work out a design for the marching competition. I am thinking of doing a Union Jack, but unless I can get different colours in somehow, it probably won't be very effective. I am in the first lacrosse team again, left attack. God I hate it, especially this term when it is so cold. The wind on the games field is unbelievable. JPC used to say that it came straight from Siberia and I can quite believe it.

For 'secret thoughts' it was not exactly riveting, but at least there was nothing much to hide apart from her immaturity. Albertine was struggling to be mature, which she interpreted as being serious and being only concerned with things of the mind.

30 Jan. I must say the work this year is much more interesting than it was in the fifth form. We are taken much more seriously and instead of things being either right or wrong we are allowed to give opinions and then have to say why we think that; and French, which I didn't want to do because I was always hopeless at it and it was so boring, is now really interesting. We are doing

French literature so it is just like English only in French. We don't have to do any grammar or dictées. I must say I still don't like Miss Armstrong, but she is a brilliant teacher; she concentrates more on what is 'meant' than the translation, although we do have to translate as well. We are doing *Le Misanthrope* by Molière at the moment.

3 Feb. I have had a letter from Wilfred!!! He said he would write but I didn't think he would. It is quite a short letter saying how much he enjoyed meeting me and how he is looking forward to next holidays. He sent a photograph of himself playing the clarinet. I don't know what I am going to write back; nothing interesting ever happens here. I had a letter from Julia too. She is having an amazing time. She is in Egypt because her father is in the army there. She sent a photograph of herself on a camel, and she has had a fantastic day when she rode in the desert on an arab stallion and galloped for miles and miles. It must have been incredible. I miss her terribly, not just to talk to, but I feel sort of lonely all the time. There is no one I really want to be friends with; anyway everyone seems to have friends. I hate school.

That must go, she decided and took a razor blade. Very carefully she cut out the page, close to the sewing. She could remember the feeling of desolation the first terms after Julia had left. Now she did not mind so much. She, Miranda, Ruth and Judy had become a companionable foursome, bound by their mutual ambition and propinquity, but most of all by the secret they did not know how to tell. Separated from the rest of the school, they had developed their own lifestyle. To all intents and purposes they were treated as grown-ups or at least as students; as they sipped their ginger wine out of TCP bottles they felt like adults.

She read two or three entries about the gym competition, which she left in, not that they were interesting but they were quite harmless.

10 Feb.   We have started doing Pascal in French. There is this wonderful Pensée '*Si vous ne me cherchez pas, vous ne m'avez pas trouvez*'. Somehow, since being confirmed God has seemed much more difficult. I haven't exactly 'lost my faith' but it all seems much less important than it used to be. I can remember when the Bishop preached at the confirmation he said, it was from Isaiah, 'Fear not, for I have redeemed thee, I have called thee by thy name, thou art mine.' It sent shivers down my spine and I felt really claimed and belonging to God, but now I don't seem to know. Pascal also had this sort of wager. If God exists, the atheist will never find him and the Christian will gain the infinite; if he doesn't exist, the atheist and the Christian are in the same boat, neither of them knowing anything; so it is much better to live as if he does exist, or something like that. In other words I must keep on *cherchez*ing, which according to Pascal means that I have already found him. Religion just seems much less exciting than it used to. I still go to eight o'clock every Sunday and I still get a bit of a shiver when Father Somerville says, 'This is my body', but the trouble is it doesn't seem to last.

She could not decide about that; on the whole not, she thought, and cut it out. She was still confused about God and did not want to discuss her confusion with Miss Armstrong. They were doing Descartes this term, and the uncertainty surrounding her very existence had made the idea of a personal God even more difficult to comprehend. She was prepared to discuss the whole problem intellectually, in a lesson, but she did not want to expose the panic she experienced if she contemplated a world without God.

12 Feb.   Miranda and I have decided we are going to go on a Pilgrimage to Canterbury next holidays. We are going to go on horses along the Pilgrims Way. It will be quite complicated to arrange as we will have to find places to stay that have room for horses, and we'll have to get things like saddlebags for our clothes and stuff, but it will be great fun. I haven't asked Mummy yet but I'm sure she'll be OK about it. We have worked out that it will take about three or four days.

Nothing wrong with that.

15 Feb. It was the Relay Race today. I was running down the Bump as usual. I really love it. It is very exciting standing at the top and wondering who will come first. Today it was really windy and I seemed to be there for hours getting more and more tense and colder and colder. It was Anne, from Darwin, who came first and a few seconds later Biddy. I grabbed the ruler and ran. I just thrust my body forward and trusted my feet to catch up and to avoid the rabbit holes. I passed Joanna about halfway down. I find that if I don't think at all my feet seem to know what to do . . . If I do think and start trying to find the best way down, I stumble. It's a wonderful feeling to get to the bottom without tripping or thinking. It is difficult to describe. In some ways I am never more connected to my body than then, but in other ways it is as if I am all feet and the weight (which is me) that propels my feet forward is something quite outside myself. That does not describe it at all well. It's very exciting being so out of control in one way and so in control in another.

Apart from being pretty illiterate that was OK too. Perhaps it was not going to be so difficult after all.

16 Feb. I have had a letter from Mummy about the Pilgrimage. She says we can't go with only two because if we have an accident someone must stay with the person who is hurt while the other one goes for help . . .

The bell summoning the school to prayers sounded through the corridors. Ruth banged on her door,

'Are you coming, Albert?'

She looked at her timetable and saw that she had two free periods; as long as she did not read every entry the whole way through she should be able to edit the whole thing in that time. She knew Miss Armstrong: once an idea had taken hold she would not let go until she had achieved her object. She would not be able to delay the moment of showing it to her for very long.

> *28 Feb.* We've got to go on bikes on our Pilgrimage, it is too difficult to ride. Susan H. is coming with us and we are aiming to get there in time for Easter Sunday, which seems very appropriate . . .

This whole term seemed to be occupied with planning the Pilgrimage; apart from one or two references to letters from Wilfred, which she cut out, there was nothing that she particularly minded her seeing. She rather regretted that there did not seem much that would be likely to impress her either. If she was to be revealed in this unpleasant way at least it would be nice to be discovered to be someone whose secret thoughts were thoughts worth having.

She read the long description of the Pilgrimage with interest. She knew Miss Armstrong would be bored by it and she left it in for that reason. The only relic she had of the experience that had taken so much planning was a tile she still had on her mantelpiece. It was of the Reeve, and she had bought it because for some reason she and Julia had always been reduced to helpless giggles when they read 'this reeve he sat upon a full good stot, that was all pomeley grey and highte Scot'.

> *7 May.* It's very strange this term. I have this horrible feeling nearly all the time. Nothing seems fun any more. I tried climbing a tree but it just seemed boring. I used to love getting really high up and seeing for miles and feeling very frightened at the same time, or getting really comfortable on a big branch and reading. No one

70

would know where I was and I felt very safe with the feel and the smell of the bark, rough and strong on my back. Julia and I used to go through the field of cows beyond the games field and lie down on our tummies and wait for all the cows to come and smell us and then we would try to grab their horns jump on their backs and ride them. I tried doing that today too, but without Julia it wasn't any fun. I feel sort of worried all the time too, but I don't know what I am worrying about. It's like having a pain at the top of my stomach, and the days go really slowly. I feel as if I want to be alone but when I am I feel lonely.

10 June. I think Fiona Campbell has got a pash on me. She sort of follows me around and blushes if I speak to her. It seems really strange to have someone having one on me. I can remember when I first came, Jenny W. A. asked me who I had a pash on and I didn't know what she was talking about because we didn't have them at St Catherine's. She said it was someone in the sixth form who you really liked and then you watched them and collected their things, like kirby grips or stones they had walked on. I didn't know anyone's name apart from Angela Walton's so I said I had a pash on her. When Julia came she decided to have one on her too and we used to hide in the bushes to see her walk through the gate to the games field. We really cried when she left. It was quite fun in a way. I must remember to smile at Fiona. When Angela used to smile at us we nearly died of happiness! Perhaps I should start wearing kirby grips!!!

12 June. My mother came yesterday to talk about going to university. We had dinner in the really posh Swiss Restaurant and had something called fondue, which was really difficult to eat. Miss Armstrong was most peculiar. All the way home in the car she held my hand and kept squeezing it. I didn't know what to do. When we got back to school Miss Armstrong took me into her study and I thought it was just to say goodnight, but she pushed me against the door and kissed me, horribly, on the mouth. It was disgusting and I didn't know what to say. She looked very strange, and when I was saying my prayers she came into the dormitory and kissed me again. Mummy says I can try for Oxford. I should be feeling very glad but instead I feel as if I don't know what I want. I think it is because of Miss A. I hope she doesn't do it again.

That had been the beginning. She could not remember the first time she had had to go to her bedroom but it had been very soon after that. She did not tell anyone until the next term, when they had all been moved up to the attics and she had become close friends with Ruth, Miranda and Judy. That had been a very nice term. They had discovered Noël Coward, and while the rest of the school were locked into the unvarying routine they had all sat in Miranda's room and listened to the ominous warning of 'bad times just around the corner', or were carried away by dreams of sailors in far-off places. It was in that comfortable and comforting environment that she had at last told them what went on when she was summoned to the Head's room. They had assumed that she was in trouble of some sort or in difficulties with her work, and were completely baffled by her expurgated description of what took place not only at night but at intervals through the day. They had been good friends, had never doubted her and tried their best to arrive at some solution.

She skipped through the pages.

31 Oct. We have been doing about the Hell Fire Club in English and reading a book about witchcraft. As it was Halloween we, that is Patsy, Jenny and I, decided we would try and raise the Devil. When everyone was in the hall playing games, bobbing for apples and things, we went down to Scripton Church. We chose Scripton because it is so isolated and no one would see us; the graveyard is very close to the cliffs so is really eerie. We went into the church and put on some choirboys' surplices. We read Our Father backwards, then we made a circle of hymn books and wound our way round them saying the Creed backwards. It was absolutely terrifying. The Devil didn't come, thank goodness. I can't imagine what we would have done if he had. After we had been in the church for quite a long time we went and sat on one of the gravestones and read *The Waste Land*. I think it is a wonderful poem but I don't understand it all. When it came to 'I think we are in rats' alley / Where the dead men lost their bones', I thought I was going to faint with terror. It was almost more frightening than in the church. Everything was so silent and still; I started imagining all the dead men coming from their graves and rats creeping round all the tombstones. We just managed to get to the end of it. We couldn't decide what to do next and Patsy said, 'Let's go and see Miss Larkin', so we did. We told her what we had done. We could see she was quite shocked but she couldn't be too angry as it was she who had given us the book to read in the first place. She gave us cups of cocoa and then read 'Ash Wednesday' to us. It was wonderful. She has got a fantastic voice.

> Teach us to care and not to care
> Teach us to sit still
> Even among these rocks,
> Our peace is in His will
> And even among these rocks
> Sister, mother
> And spirit of the river, spirit of the sea,
> Suffer me not to be separated
> And let my cry come unto Thee.

Miss Armstrong is away tonight so I don't have to go to her room, thank heaven. I don't think I could cope.

1 Nov. Something awful happened today. I had a letter from Miss Armstrong, unbelievable! She's only been away for a day. It was written in the train and it was very passionate, the sort of letter I get from her in the holidays. I read it outside because I did not want any one to know who it was from. People are so nosy. When I went back to my room I couldn't find it. I told Miranda and Judy, who were in. They were absolutely sweet; Miranda went through everywhere I had been and then said she would go and look. Judy looked after me, I was in a terrible state. I tried to imagine what would happen if someone found it. It was odd really because if it had been found I suppose that that would be like telling someone, something we have never known how to do, but when it came to it I could not bear the idea of her being in that sort of trouble. I don't want her to be ruined, I don't want people to know, I just want her to stop!!! Anyway, Miranda found it on the drive (so in fact anyone could have picked it up). I was so relieved I asked them if they would like to read it. I could tell they were not sure but they did and it was rather awful because they didn't know what to say. It was obvious that although I thought I had told them what she was like, they hadn't really understood. I can't blame them; if I was not having to go through it I wouldn't be able to imagine it either.

Albertine was despairing. With very few exceptions there was nothing in any of the volumes she could bear Miss Armstrong to read, although she was tempted to show her how incredibly careless it was of her to write to her in the way she did and also that her friends knew all about it. There was quite a lot about her work, which she decided to leave in to impress her, and a lot about Wilfred. She cut out the pages furiously, leaving less than a quarter in each book. She felt as desolate as if she had cut away most of her life. She could have saved the pages but she felt almost as revolted reading them herself as she would have done had Miss Armstrong read them. It was done, though, and however much Miss Armstrong tried, there was now no possibility of her probing into her thoughts. She still had only her body, and with that she would have to make do.

Albertine took the volumes herself that night without being pressured. She might as well get it over with quickly.

'I have brought my journals,' she said, handing over the pathetically thin volumes.

Miss Armstrong, whose face had lit up with the words, looked profoundly disappointed.

'What have you done to them?' she asked.

'There were some parts I did not want you to see.'

'It looks to me as if you did not want me to see anything. What have you done with the pages?'

'I've thrown them away. It was all rubbish, I promise you.'

She read them lying on the bed. Albertine walked round the room in agony and fury. Miss Armstrong's mouth was turned down at the corners; she was frowning and her eyes were fierce. When she had reached the last of the desiccated pages she looked at Albertine with an expression she could not interpret. After what seemed to her an eternity Miss Armstrong said, 'I had not realised you were so young.'

These words cut through Albertine like a serrated knife leaving torn and lacerated flesh and her nerves exposed. She had deliberately left in the parts she considered showed her at her most mature, the intellectual parts, the parts she considered indicated her brain, her powers of deduction, the parts she thought would have raised her in Miss Armstrong's estimation. Having felt nothing but anger, she now felt belittled and undervalued. It was a feeling that was to stay with her for a long time, but the memory of where this feeling began faded swiftly until she began to feel that it was Miss Armstrong who gave her confidence rather than the one who had taken it away.

8

It was dark in the cupboard. The clothes surrounding and half burying her had a faint smell of dry-cleaning fluid and felt rough on her face. Miss Armstrong wore mainly tweeds, severely tailored coats and box-pleated skirts in checks or herringbone, in dark colours, browns or greens or greys. There was little room for Albertine's feet; whenever she tried to shift her weight she seemed to tread on yet another pair of shoes, which were all in much the same style, patterned brogues with fringed and pierced flaps over the laces, which jumped up and down as Miss Armstrong walked. These were in brown and white and dark green, with slightly raised Cuban heels. Each time she trod on one she nearly lost her balance; she was very nervous of tumbling in a disorganised heap into the bathroom. She wanted to sit down but when she tried this the discomfort was even greater; she would find a heel digging into her bottom, and having her knees squashed against her chest for more than a few minutes gave her cramp and somehow the clothes hanging above her seemed more claustrophobic and threatening. The two or three evening dresses she had, black silk, felt shiny and sinister, like wet seaweed. Each time her arm brushed against one of these dresses she had a shock as if she had been touched by a drowned man.

Miss Armstrong was at a Governors' dinner. Governors' meetings took place once a term, but once a year the business aspect of them was combined with a social occasion in the evening. This time it was dinner with the Chairman. The Governors were all local worthies, apart from the school solicitor, who came up from London and stayed overnight at one of the hotels in Cromer. Miss Armstrong always dreaded these meetings. Albertine would know when one was due as Miss Armstrong became more tense than usual and more angry. It was during the week or two before a meeting that she would talk about her childhood, which had been quite deprived, anyway by the standards of the girls in the school. She would tell of the times her father had hidden in a cupboard, leaving her, as a 13-year-old, to tackle and dismiss the bailiffs. She had won her education, through fierce competition, to a grammar school in the North-East, which was at that time enduring the worst of the poverty which culminated in the Jarrow March. She had gone on to London University on a scholarship and then to increasingly prestigious teaching jobs in London day schools. This was her first boarding school appointment.

Albertine had no experience with which to compare her story, but she could empathise with her anger and took personally the diatribes against the spoilt, unthinking girls she was meant to be teaching who did not know how fortunate they were and who frittered away their chances; and against a government which allowed to them to continue in this privileged position whilst other, in her eyes more deserving, candidates for academic success had little or no opportunity. Albertine felt the attack was unfair; it should, she thought, have been directed towards the parents, who made the choices, rather than towards the children, who would anyway have preferred to be somewhere else. She also thought, though did not dare say so, that if she despised them all so much, why was she in that job? At the same time she felt that what Miss Armstrong was saying was true and felt guilty for her undoubted happy existence. To be a socialist was beyond any sort of pale for someone brought up as she had been on a diet of 'How could they have got rid of Winston Churchill after all he has done for the country?', but she was certainly a communist, having been inspired by a book called *I Believe* by Douglas Hyde. She had secretly written applying to join the Communist

Party and felt determined, when in the world, to fight for Justice and Equality and most of all for a Classless Society.

What Albertine did not understand was that most of Miss Armstrong's anger, which intensified as the meeting drew near, was misdirected fear, and that probably a great deal of the fear was that she should be discovered to be abusing the sacred trust between parent and teacher. Albertine did not understand this because she did not know that this complicated though in some ways interesting relationship was abuse. She did not know that the disgust and fear she experienced was a right and proper reaction to Miss Armstrong's misuse of her position to gain her way, and that the interest she felt was an interest Miss Armstrong aroused deliberately in order to keep her in her power.

Earlier in the evening Albertine had been summoned to the study. Miss Armstrong was ready to leave, dressed in one of the black silk tubes which clung to her jutting hip bones and hollow sunken chest. The high padded shoulders and full back of her Persian-lamb jacket made her look like a black vulture. She smelt strongly of eau de cologne and her face was rigid with tension, or terror.

'Do I look all right, darling?' she asked.

'You look fine, very distinguished.' Which she did, in a gaunt sort of way. She wore no jewellery apart from the pearl studs in her ears which she always wore.

'Please ... please be there when I get back. I couldn't bear to be alone tonight.'

Albertine, who had been rather hoping to have a night off, said, 'Of course I'll be there. What time will you get back?'

'Oh, I don't know, about half past ten, I should think. Be there at ten and you'll be in no danger of bumping into Miss Brunt.'

Miss Brunt was the cook, who came every night to turn down her bed and leave the plate of banana sandwiches, which were ostensibly meant for periods of night starvation but which had become an intrinsic part of the night's ritual; a midnight feast or a wedding breakfast, a prelude to the

78

main feature, a sort of B movie. Years later, at children's parties, when banana sandwiches were the staple fare, along with Marmite, a picture of sitting up in bed, munching sandwiches and chatting idly, would flash across her mind. Those times were the best times; it was then that Miss Armstrong would talk happily about her childhood, about her father, whom she had loved, and Eric, the man who had loved her, and about her life at university when she had become inspired by Pascal, Racine, Alfred de Vigny and Beaudelaire, an inspiration she managed to pass on so brilliantly to those she taught.

'Hide in the cupboard in the bathroom in case anyone else should come in for any reason,' she added.

And so Albertine had made the perilous descent over the broom cupboard, getting into the wardrobe only just in time to miss Miss Brunt, who seemed to take an inordinately long time dealing with the bed. She could hear her banging away next door, drawing the curtains; she seemed to be moving furniture. Supposing she should come to the cupboard to put away some clothes? Albertine felt sick with terror and that she would die soon if she could not stretch or cough. She had a suspicion that Miss Brunt was one of the people who suspected what was going on; that suddenly the order for sandwiches should be doubled was in itself suspicious, that they should always all be gone must have aroused some questions; and sometimes, when she had been in the passage waiting to go into Miss Armstrong's study, Miss Brunt had given her a very unpleasant, knowing sort of leer. She was a fat, grey-skinned, woman, with short black greasy hair, and her white overall was always spotted with fat from frying, or with red from tomato ketchup, or brown from the thick gelatinous gravy which came with nearly every meal. She made it her business to know what was going on everywhere in the school. Albertine suspected that she was at that moment going through Miss Armstrong's desk, which she used for her private correspondence. She was the sort of woman who would enjoy having secret knowledge about people. Not that she would ever use it; the knowledge would be enough to give her a sense of power. When Albertine had said as much to Miss Armstrong, all she had said was, 'Don't worry about old Brunt, she's all right really.'

When she heard Miss Brunt leave, she wondered if she dared leave her prison, but she had been told to stay there and so she did. She was cold and very tired. She wanted to cry and to be back in her own bed in the attic, where she was safe and normal, where her only concern was whether she would get her essay in on time and if she would ever really understand Descartes or the complex mingling of imagery and philosophical thought in the metaphysical poets. She wanted to be excited by 'the bracelet of bright hair about the bone' and to work out why quite ordinary words like 'bright' should take on such special meaning when in conjunction with particular words. Why 'it's a bright day today' should sound so pedestrian and 'Where hang in shades the orange bright, like golden lamps in a green night' should be so powerful. She did not want to be alone in a dark cupboard, she did not want to have to face Miss Armstrong when she returned, or the climb back to her safety, or the complicated story she would have to tell if she was found mid-climb. She could never understand why Miss Armstrong insisted on this way of getting to her. Yes, she would have to go past Miss McClaren's door, but she could always say she was going to the loo; it would be far more extraordinary to be discovered dangling from the shelf containing Gumption and Vim.

She could not see her watch but she felt sure it must be after half past ten. She was paralysed physically and emotionally; she felt numb, cold and desolate, as if the only comfort she would ever have for herself would be from limp lifeless objects like the limp lifeless clothes around her now, which did not even give her the warmth she needed. She wanted to rip the slimy dresses from their hangers and wrap herself in them but did not dare. Although she half wanted to destroy them as she half wanted to destroy Miss Armstrong, she was afraid of the consequences, so she shivered instead as she endured instead the probing, poking fingers.

She wondered too why it was that she was so necessary to Miss Armstrong, that just by existing she seemed to comfort her, whereas all she felt from her so-called 'loving' was an increased sense of loneliness and separation. Perhaps if she could call her Gerda, as she wanted so much, it would feel different; for her she would always be Miss Armstrong or the Head. Since she had asked her to call her Gerda – indeed pleaded with her, 'I want to hear you call me by my name' – she had been unable to call her anything, making the times when she was lying naked in her arms even more extraordinary. In some ways it was during French lessons, when she could call her Miss Armstrong, that she felt most intimate with her; when she saw her eyes light with enthusiasm and tenderness – 'Yes, that's right, Albertine, you've got it' – and she would feel stimulated and rewarded, pleased that she had again proved to her that her faith in her was not without ground.

This morning had been just one of those times. They had been told to translate a long passage from *Phèdre* into English verse. Most people had put it into rhyming couplets; Miranda had condensed it into a sonnet; some had cheated and put it into blank verse. She had chosen sprung rhythm, Gerard Manley Hopkins being one of her heroes. She had wanted her translation to please Miss Armstrong, certainly, but mostly she had wanted to do justice to the original, so she had worked harder on it than on anything she had done before, and her work had been rewarded.

'You have chosen a perfect form to render the tension of Phèdre's forbidden love, and not only that, you have made a poem in its own right. Well done.'

The piece they had been asked to translate was where Phèdre is soliloquising on her love for her stepson. Albertine had been so interested in the play and so absorbed by her task that she had made no connection between that forbidden love and the forbidden love that had kept her in the cupboard for so many hours. Her relationship with Miss Armstrong the teacher and Miss Armstrong the lover were two completely disconnected things. There were four people in this relationship. Whilst she was the pupil she had absolutely no knowledge of the lover, and when she was the lover she had no memory of the teacher. She did not even wonder if Miss Armstrong, when she reprimanded her for sloppy work, at the same time was thinking of the few hours before when she had reprimanded her, in almost the same tone of voice, for her failure to call her Gerda.

Albertine knew that her particular relationship with Miss Armstrong had nothing to do with the excitement she always experienced in her lessons. They all felt it. It was Miss Armstrong's great gift that she could break through the hierarchical barrier between teacher and pupil without losing control. She could draw out of the most unpromising material hitherto undreamt perceptions. Lessons with her were nothing about imparting knowledge, though knowledge was imparted imperceptibly; they were a voyage of discovery and they always came away from them talking about what they had discovered. They respected her and felt that she respected them and learnt something new from them too. Whereas after most lessons the conversation, if any, would relate to the personal idiosyncracies of the particular teacher, after one of Miss Armstrong's, arguments could rage for hours if not days over the rivalry between the Jansenists and the Jesuits or the relative merits of Beaudelaire and Alfred de Vigny. She achieved the interest by a combination of strictness and encouragement. She did not tolerate either careless work or sloppy thinking. She praised often but always expected more, and it was everyone's desire to live up to these expectations, for their own sake as much if not more than for hers. She was a mentor rather than a schoolmistress, and for this reason she succeeded and for this reason they all felt something like love for her, as perhaps there is always love for the person who brings out the best in one, or who sees something that no one else has seen before.

Albertine was not loving her now; she was filled with a cold anger and a sense of powerlessness which trapped her as closely and darkly and remorselessly as the cupboard walls. It was in this mood that she eventually fell asleep.

It was nearly midnight when Miss Armstrong returned. Albertine woke to feel fierce arms hauling her up from her crouched sleep. Miss Armstrong was sobbing in her ear.

'Oh my dearest, dearest love, how can I do this to you? How could I have made you wait? Why didn't you go back to your room? Oh, thank you, thank God you're here. It was so awful, and all the time I was thinking of you and praying that you would still be here . . . but you shouldn't have been, I shouldn't have asked you . . . oh darling, darling Albertine, what am I doing to you? Come to bed, my darling love, and take this terrible night away from me. They are awful people, awful, smug, pompous people who wouldn't know love if they stepped in it – they would trample and destroy it. Oh my star, my darling bright and glorious star.'

Miss Armstrong was crying and laughing insanely in turn, words tumbling from her mouth in disorganised patterns. She dragged the still sleepy Albertine to the bed, where she tore off her clothes and Albertine's pyjamas, ripping a button off in the process. The intensity of her words and the manic look in her eye frightened Albertine. Miss Armstrong had never been like this before; her lovemaking had always been gentle and calm, perhaps even sensuous, and Albertine, although knowing perfectly well that she was not feeling the same emotion as Miss Armstrong, did occasionally, when she was not disgusted, quite enjoy it. To be caressed all over, to feel the tingling of arousal and the sweet heaviness of satisfaction was sometimes very pleasant. She did not like being kissed; she found Miss Armstrong's tongue in her mouth embarrassing and she did not know what to do with her own. She did not like it at all when it was 'her turn' to do it to her. She found it revolting when she was asked to 'hold me there, touch me there'. She knew she was not doing it right when she felt Miss Armstrong strain and groan 'more, more'. Sometimes Miss Armstrong would grab her hand and with a firm grip move it up and down moaning, 'Yes . . . yes . . . yes . . . oh yes,' but this did not often happen. It was usual for Miss Armstrong to do it to her, and she would fall asleep seeing the gentleness in her eyes as she said, 'There, my love, you see you do like it, don't you?'

But this time it was different. She seemed to be everywhere at once. Albertine, fresh from sleep and cold and anger, felt herself being devoured and flailed. She could not breathe, she was suffocated by the pressure on her mouth and Miss Armstrong's tongue seemed to be down her throat. Her hands were not gentle but fierce and invasive; desperately she seemed to be trying to annihilate her, to remove her flesh and become bone to bone, she writhed all over her, twisting her breasts round until they hurt and all the time sobbing in deep gasps, 'Albertine . . . Albertine . . . Oh my God, Albertine.'

The onslaught passed. Miss Armstrong lay back, not as sometimes at peace, but tormented and twitching.

'I'm sorry, my darling, I frightened you, didn't I? I need you so badly, so terribly badly. You don't understand, do you? It was those awful men, they despise me, look down on me from their ghastly upper-class bastion, and I was so afraid for you. I was so afraid you would have gone. I shouldn't have done that to you; say you forgive me, darling. Say it . . . go on, say "Gerda, I forgive you"'.

Albertine felt too battered to know whether she had been frightened or not or whether she forgave her. If she had known about such things, she would have known she felt raped. She felt numbed, bruised both in body and spirit. She wanted to sleep and forget the whole awful night.

'Show me you forgive me. Love me, please love me, I want to feel your hands on my body, I want to hear you say "Gerda". Oh darling, I'm so sorry.' And she turned towards her, weeping again, and laid her head on Albertine's bruised breast.

Albertine reluctantly put her arm round Miss Armstrong's bony shoulders and helplessly patted her. She knew that the sooner she did what was wanted of her the sooner she would be able to get away, but she was so exhausted, and the little pity she felt for her was not enough to overcome her distaste for the thin, empty breasts she was meant to be caressing or the white skin of her stomach, which was stretched between her protruding pelvic bones and puckered round a wide dark scar down the centre of her body, almost reaching the thick tangled mat of dark pubic hair, so unlike Albertine's own, which was fine and sparse and silky.

'It's all right, I understand,' she said, though she did not at all, and then she whispered because she could not bring herself to say it aloud, 'It's all right, Gerda, I promise.'

'Show me you mean it. Kiss me, please kiss me.' And Miss Armstrong tried to pull her on top of her, but Albertine was asleep, the arms of Morpheus stronger than those of her assailant.

It was nearly dawn when she was forced awake by an urgent shake. Miss Armstrong was saying. 'Wake up, darling, I'm afraid you must go now.'

She rolled over, pulling the blanket over her head.

'Albertine, quickly, come on . . . wake up. You must go . . . now.' Her voice was her Headmistress voice and Albertine responded to the note of authority. Like an automaton, she found her pyjamas and groped her way to the door. Miss Armstrong came with her and, giving her a perfunctory kiss on her forehead, she checked the passage to see if it was clear.

With legs like tombstones and her arms like wrung-out tea towels, a head which felt as if it was not only stuffed with cotton wool but also bound in plaster of paris, she attempted the assault on the broom cupboard. After three attempts to gain a bit of leverage from the handle of the Hoover, she gave up. Not caring what anyone would think when they found a chair in such an unwonted place, she got one from the bathroom and hauled her way up and over the balcony to her room.

She felt that it should look different after such a night, but her room was the same. It was her haven and her

85

anchorage. It was more 'her place' than even her room at home, which had to be kept as her mother wanted it kept, with clothes in the 'right' drawers and folded. Her mother made periodic drawer inspections, and if they were found to be not to her liking, the clothes would be emptied onto the floor and Albertine would have to put them back in good order. Her bed had to be made before breakfast and nothing had to be left 'lying around'. 'There's a place for everything and everything has its place,' her mother was fond of saying. She had an electric fire, but was only allowed to have one bar on in the morning to dress with and for half an hour at night 'to take the chill off'. 'Money doesn't grow on trees' was another of her favourite sayings. Whenever she said this, Albertine had an image of an enormous oak tree with leaves of furled notes and bearing fruit of clustered coins, which fell in delicious golden showers whenever anyone passed.

Her room in the attic was all hers. Everything in it was 'lying around'. Her desk, or table it was really, was covered with books, some open, some in piles. The floor round it was white with crumpled balls of paper from failed beginnings of essays, her cello, out of its bag, leant against a wall and was also surrounded with sheets of music, her bed was covered with clothes, as was the 'comfortable' chair by the fireplace. She was allowed a real fire in the tiny grate as long as she looked after it herself, which meant carrying buckets of coal from the coal shed behind the kitchen and taking out the ash. It was worth doing this to go to sleep in firelight and to roast marshmallows listening to *Saturday Night Theatre* on her little, treasured Marconi portable wireless, the result of five years saving, or to Noël Coward on the red wind-up portable gramophone, which was also on the floor, surrounded by piles of records out of their brown and torn paper covers. She had photographs cut from newspapers and magazines of all her current heroes pasted onto the walls. Laurence Olivier, his hair died white for Hamlet, standing with Vivien Leigh on his arm outside the gates of Buckingham Palace; Richard Burton, whom she had seen playing Prince Hal and Henry V at Stratford the previous summer, and Denis Matthews, whom she had heard playing at the Hastings Festival and to whom she had been introduced. No one ever came into these rooms. They, the Oxbridge students, were expected to keep the rooms clean themselves, and occasionally she did have a blitz on it and swept and dusted and rearranged the books and the precious things on the chest of drawers and the mantelpiece; photographs of her dog and her horse, large and perfect fir cones, bits of driftwood from the beach, the delicate bleached white skull of a seagull and golden stones, which might or might not have been amber. She also had a kitten called Tamburlaine, who was both allowed and not allowed. In other words, everyone knew she had him, but since animals were not 'allowed', no one mentioned it. He never saw the world outside her room, and the ash from her fire largely went into his tray, making the floor even more gritty and messy than it would otherwise have been.

As she climbed into bed, under the car rug, which was stained with the remains of fungi from leaving it damp too long when she had slept out one whole summer, and which had a large hole in it where the mushrooming growth had eaten away the fibres, Tamburlaine jumped onto her chest and kneaded her breasts rhythmically. It was as much an assault in a way as she had just suffered from the kneading fingers of Miss Armstrong, his loud purring was not unlike the whispered plea 'Albertine', but it soothed her lacerated senses. She drifted into sleep wondering why it was that the simple, uncomplicated, speechless love of an animal should be so comforting and if there was something wrong with her that she should find stroking Tamburlaine, as she was now, dreamily, so much more to her taste than stroking the frizzy wiry hair of Miss Armstrong.

For Gerda, what little of the night was left was spent mulling over its horrors. Tossing and turning as the dawn broke, she reviewed the whole terrible evening, from the patronising insincerity of the Governors, through the interminable meal,

87

during which all she had been able to think about was Albertine shut in her cupboard and how soon she would be able to leave, to what she could now see was an inexcusable violation of the one person she so desperately wanted to protect. She was divided between remorse for her lack of control and terror that she had destroyed any feelings Albertine might have had for her. She could not get out of her head the look of petrified disbelief she had seen in Albertine's face during the violent lovemaking.

Was the love she had for her wrong? She knew the world would say it was, but the world was often mistaken. How could God, who presumably had made her as she was, have made her something that was bad? If this love was wrong, why did it give her such joy? – not lustful pleasure, she persuaded herself, apart from tonight, but joy, joy in giving, joy in seeing her beloved grow in mind and strength and beauty. She knew that one day she would have to give her up, but meanwhile she could give her so much of her wisdom and so much of her love.

How could she repair the damage she might have done tonight? How could she reassure Albertine that it would not happen again? How could she be sure herself that, as her passion increased – and she recognised that it was increasing, that it had become an obsession – it would not happen again? She wanted to awaken in Albertine the same desire that was in herself; she was sure that it was only a matter of time and patience before she would. She had gone too far tonight, she knew that. She would make it up to her.

Suppose that from now on Albertine refused to see her, refused to come to her room; worse still, suppose that because of this night, she should tell someone. She did not know that Albertine did not realise that she could 'refuse' a summons to the Headmistress, nor did she know that Albertine, even if she had known which adult to tell, did not know what to tell them. Miss Armstrong had no idea that this was one of the endless discussions that took place in the attics almost every day. She wanted to believe that the love she felt was shared and that therefore so was the secret.

Her last thought before she slept was that she would give her something; something precious, something Albertine would know was precious. She would give her the *Letters of Abelard and Heloïse* that Eric had given her so many years ago. She would know from that that she had indeed given her all that she could. She imagined the look of understanding and forgiveness on Albertine's face as she received it. She would inscribe it simply *To A from G, with love,* and the date. It would be all right.

9

'Albert, wake up! Wake up! The bell's gone and you've missed breakfast . . . Come on . . . Oh do come on . . . Wake up, it's nearly nine o'clock.'

Albertine was in the middle of a dream. She was riding her horse over the downs, which had become a strange and wondrous place illuminated by a golden light which burnished the clumps of gorse, making them seem like so many burning bushes, heavy with portent. There seemed to be no horizon; the golden landscape merged imperceptibly with the bright sky, in which hung a blood-red sun. From this sun streamed scarlet rays, like rivers in the sky, and she knew that if she could reach one of those rays she would be purified. 'Wash in the blood of the lamb,' the golden light seemed to be saying to her. Her horse suddenly developed wings and she was Bellerophon riding the mighty Pegasus, but as she approached the cleansing stream, it vanished and she was flying over a limitless sea in an empty sky. She knew she was free but that the freedom had been dearly bought, leaving her alone in this now pale and lifeless space. Beneath her, patterning the glass sea, she could see little islands of emerald green. Each island had on it one tall tree, taller than any tree could possibly be and not looking as if it were growing, rather carved from wood and painted, like toys placed on cardboard grass.

The vision, for the dream had a visionary quality to it, smashed into diamond-like fragments as she became conscious of Miranda's continuing plea, 'Wake up, Albert.'

Seeing she was now awake, Miranda said, 'You must be

90

quick, it's nearly prayers. What on earth time did you get back to bed last night? I'm sure I heard you and it seemed to be morning, or nearly. Honestly, Albert, she is the limit. How can she expect you to do any work if she never lets you sleep?'

Miranda, though nice and probably now Albertine's best friend since Julia had left, had not yet managed to shake off the correcting attitude which she had no doubt acquired when she was head of house, before being released to 'do Oxbridge'. Or perhaps she had been made head of house because this trait in her character was recognised. As she left the room she said, 'Have you remembered you're reading the lesson?'

Although she was no longer responsible for drawing up these rotas, she was still able to remember more accurately than the people themselves what each individual was meant to be doing and when. Albertine had forgotten, as usual, and whilst trying to unearth her tie from the pile of clothes on the floor, she was also trying to find her Bible, in which was the slip of paper telling her what she was meant to be reading. The already chaotic state of her belongings was rendered even more so by this search, but she eventually discovered it, not on the floor but, surprisingly, in the bookcase where it belonged.

She just made it to the hall in time. As she ran through the dining room, knocking over a chair in her haste, she heard the head of school say, 'All ready,' and the sound of Miss Armstrong's footsteps hollow on the bare boards of the passage.

It was Ecclesiastes, Chapter 12, that she had to read. It was one of her favourites, which she almost knew by heart, and although she had no idea what it meant, the resonance of the words 'Or ever the silver chord be loosed or the golden bowl be broken or the pitcher be broken at the fountain, or the wheel broken at the cistern. Then shall the dust return to the earth as it was, and the spirit shall return unto God who gave it' vibrated in her head and took her mind off to some far place where words in apparently meaningless juxtaposition were able to create a healing stream, not unlike the stream of light in her dream in which she could bathe.

Prayers were long that morning – it was Form Order day. Miss Armstrong, in a monotone, read out the names of all the girls without once looking at the lines spread out in front of her. First of all came the subjects: lower fourth maths, and then the order for that week and after all the subjects had been gone through came the average, the Form Order, and the girls would shuffle smugly to the top or shamefaced to the bottom; this was the order in which they had to stand all week. In most forms there was little variation at the top or bottom. It was in the middle that most of the change took place. Albertine no longer had to suffer this public display of triumph or disaster. Apart from today when she was reading and therefore standing in front of the lectern at the end of the row of staff who lined the side wall, she and Miranda, Ruth and Judy stood right at the back of the hall in any order they wished. There was a radiator and hot pipe at arm level running the length of the wall. This was the only heat in the large room and in the winter they would fight for the radiator, but holding onto the pipe was something. 'You'll get chilblains if you hold onto that pipe too long,' Miss McClaren would say, or, 'You'll get piles if you sit on the radiator like that,' but she never said what piles were, and they all suffered from chilblains for most of the winter terms anyway. All the form rooms had one radiator in them, and before every lesson there was a struggle to reach it first. A row of girls would sit like crows on a branch warming their bottoms. 'Come on! You'll get piles. Give me a go. You are mean!' and the shoving and pushing would continue until the mistress came in and ordered them back to their desks.

Lower fifth English ... The dirge continued. Albertine thought of the hymn they had just sung which was also one of her favourites:

And soul by soul and silently the shining hordes increase
And their ways are ways of gentleness and all their paths are peace.

That seemed a far more satisfactory description of death than Shakespeare's in *Measure for Measure*, which she had just been reading:

'Aye but to go we know not where,' Claudio had said. 'To be imprisoned by the viewless winds and blown with restless violence round the pendant earth.'

That was very scary. The previous summer term Corinne Summers' little brother, only eight years old, had been killed in his first term at prep school by a cricket ball. Corinne's father was a vicar and Corinne had accepted her brother's death more easily than a lot of others in the school, Albertine included. Corrine must, she thought, be seeing him now as one of a silent shining horde; Albertine could not help thinking that he might be imprisoned in viewless winds . . . viewless, unseeing, blind wind of fate that should so arbitrarily pick off a child with something so seemingly benign as a ball. She looked at Corinne, who was as usual top of the fifth form, and wondered if the hymn had encouraged her or if she was so convinced that he was in paths of peace that she needed no encouragement.

Miss Armstrong had finished Form Order at last and was announcing that there was an away match that afternoon and would the team gather outside the front door at 1.30. She had not looked at Albertine at all throughout prayers nor did she now as she swept passed her and the staff, who turned in her wake and followed her out of the room.

The school broke from its serried lines amidst sounds of congratulations and commiserations: 'I knew I'd done awfully in that Latin test,' . . . 'Well done. Seventy-eight per cent. Fantastic!' The girls who came bottom tried inevitably to look as if they did not care and thought the whole business of Form Order a frightful bore, and the girls who came top likewise assumed an air of indifference. There was a competitive element, especially among the top people, but competition was bad form and to win was even worse; the winners had to demonstrate in some way that they had succeeded by a fluke. It was priggish to try, and prigs were the *bottom*.

Albertine knew she had two free periods and had already decided to sleep through them. She made her way through a group of giggling fourth-formers who were assembling their cleaning apparatus and arguing about their tasks. No doubt started during the war through lack of domestic staff, and no doubt continued to save money, the first period of the morning was devoted to housework. Both houses were entirely cleaned by the girls. It was never acknowledged that this was a form of child labour, it was sold to them – and no doubt to their parents if they ever enquired – as good training in household management.

Albertine in later life was never able to clean a tap without remembering the grey gritty texture of Gumption or to polish a floor without seeing in her mind's eye the great tins of thick yellow wax which they sometimes stole to get the study fire going and which had a peculiar smell she had never met since. She had enjoyed doing the dormitories and looking at the photographs on the dressing tables and stuck into the corners of the mirrors, giving so much away about the other lives they all had but of which they so seldom spoke. She had no idea who cleaned the form rooms; perhaps they were never done or perhaps when they were playing games in the afternoon an army of ladies with mops descended and scoured the place from top to bottom, like good fairies. They were never allowed into the form rooms in the afternoon; perhaps this was why.

The last day of term was devoted entirely to housework. The whole school swept and polished together. Each window was cleaned with newspaper, even the games rooms; the little rooms full of lacrosse sticks and smelling of vaseline and sweaty feet were emptied and scoured. Everyone greased their own stick for the last time, leaving great globs of vaseline on the triangular nets so that the next term they would still be soft and spongy.

Back at last in her room she found to her horror that Miss Armstrong had been there before her. On her pillow was one of the notes she was accustomed to leaving. Sometimes they were little letters: 'I am thinking of you and missing you, my love, and counting the minutes until tonight ... G'; sometimes, like now, they were a command. 'Will you come to my room at break. I need to see you ... G.' She tried to sleep but it evaded her; she would have liked to talk to Ruth and Miranda but they both had lessons that morning; if she could not sleep she would have liked to get on with some of the work which was piling up dangerously but she was too tired and too anxious about what Miss Armstrong was going to say to her at break. She was experiencing a depth of loneliness she had not encountered before and was engulfed by panic which dragged her deeper into isolation. She would have liked to run away but knew she could never run far enough to escape the radius of Miss Armstrong's power.

The bell rang announcing break and she dragged herself from her bed and down the stairs to Miss Armstrong's study. She knocked on the door.

'Come in! Ah, Albertine, could you wait outside for a moment or two. Miss Patcham and I have nearly finished.'

Albertine could see the school secretary collecting letters into a bundle and returning files to the cabinet against the wall. She waited. Miss Patcham came out and walked past her down the corridor to her own office, her high heels clicking; Miss Patcham was the only member of staff, if her job could be so defined, who wore high heels; she also had dyed blonde hair and her fingernails were painted scarlet and so long the girls thought they must be false and wondered how she could type with such extrusions. Her bow-shaped mouth was painted scarlet too, or rather her lips were painted into a bow shape, and all through the day she could be seen through the window of her room adding yet another layer to the thick shiny coat of colour.

'You can come in now, Albertine.' Miss Armstrong was using her headmistress voice, no doubt for the benefit of any other passers-by. Once the door was closed and the light in the passage which indicated that she was not to be disturbed was turned on, she took Albertine in her arms and pulled her head onto her shoulder. 'I'm so sorry about last night. It was terrible of me to leave you in the cupboard like that. You must be very tired this morning.'

So there was to be no mention of what had followed after her return. 'It was OK. I went to sleep for a lot of the time,' Albertine replied with as much distance as possible.

'No, no, it was inexcusable of me. I'm afraid I had no idea that the dinner was going to last as long . . . I have a present for you, to make up for it. I hope you will like it . . . I think you will.'

She handed her what looked like a slim volume wrapped in white tissue paper and bound with scarlet ribbon.

'Go on, open it.' Her voice and expression were tense with excited anticipation. It was always like this. Something would happen that would make Albertine think, This is enough . . . Absolutely enough! and she would be seduced back by gifts she was too polite or too inexperienced to refuse.

Reluctantly and slowly she unwrapped the parcel. It was *The Letters of Abelard and Héloïse*; on a previous occasion Miss Armstrong had shown her this very book and said how precious it was to her, the only memento of Eric, with whom she had once been in love. Albertine had coveted it then but now she knew that if she accepted it she was accepting her apology. She wanted to refuse but did not know how.

'Thank you . . . I must go now, I'll be late.' She tried to sound polite but only succeeded in sounding ungracious. The bell had not yet rung.

'Not yet . . . don't go yet . . . Look, I've written in it.'

Albertine opened the book and on the flyleaf she saw that Miss Armstrong had written: 'To A from G, with love' and a date. It was yesterday's date and Albertine thought sourly that it should have been today's. It was after midnight that had been the worst part of the night, it was for what had happened after midnight that she should have been apologising.

'That's very nice. Thank you again. I really must go, though,' and without waiting for her dismissal she returned to her room.

Well, at least she accepted it, Gerda thought. I knew it would be all right. She could have refused . . . Which was an indication of how little she understood, or perhaps how little she wanted to understand.

Of the four attics, Miranda's was the largest and it was in her room that they would gather for what they called their sessions.

'You look as if you could do with a session this afternoon,' Miranda said to Albertine at lunch.

'What I really want is some sleep but I think I am too angry.'

'Why don't we meet in my room at about four. Is that OK with you, Ruth?'

They were very observant of each other's need for silence. Their rooms all adjoined each other and it was difficult to work if there was anyone talking in any of the rooms. They did not work to a timetable but as and when they felt like it. Judy went all day to Bowlby's, the local boys' public school and would sometimes come back in the early evening to find them lying on Miranda's floor surrounded by the silver foil wrappers from Lyons chocolate cupcakes or Caramello bars, slightly drunk on ginger wine, from a session that had been going on all afternoon.

'A session! How lovely, what have I missed?' And without going into her room she would sit down with them, then if they remembered they would save a cupcake for her, or often she would come bringing their favourite chocolate marshmallows which they could not buy in the village but which Judy would buy in Holt on her way home and the session would continue until suppertime. It was when they knew that they had been going on too long that they played 'There are bad times just around the corner' and, giggling, they would have some more ginger wine and invite the bad times to come. The bad times were, of course, their failure in the exams ahead.

We're going to unpack our troubles from the old kitbag
And wait until we drop down dead

A likely story, Land of Hope and Glory
Wait until we drop down DEAD

they would shout in unison.

At four o'clock Albertine carried her gramophone and the records into Miranda's room. Noël Coward was as intrinsic a part of a session as Mary Grant.

'Was it really six o'clock when you came back this morning?' Ruth asked. 'Miranda said she heard you – I don't know how you cope.'

'I don't know either. Last night was terrible.' Albertine never really felt she could tell them how terrible it was. Modesty forbade her from going into explicit details about what Miss Armstrong actually *did* to her when they were in bed and she doubted they were able to imagine it.

'It was the worst . . . And what's more, at break today she gave me a book, Abelard's letters to Héloïse. She knew I'd coveted it – it was just a bribe really – but I didn't know how to refuse it.'

'I really do think we should tell someone, you know,' Miranda said. 'I'm quite sure it should be one of the Governors.'

'There was a Governors' dinner last night. That's why I had to hide in the cupboard for about three hours.'

'You what!' they both said.

'I had to wait in her bathroom cupboard till she got back. I went to sleep in the end and when she finally got back she seemed completely *mad*. It was quite frightening, actually. She was crying and grabbing at me and thrusting her tongue all over me . . . Ugh, it was awful.' She paused, remembering again the horror she was unable to describe. 'Still, at least she didn't pray.'

'Did you say *pray*? What on earth do you mean?'

'Haven't I told you about that? Every night, before getting into bed, we kneel and she says prayers.'

'I can't believe it. What sort of prayers does she say?'

'Oh, I don't know, she just rambles on about love and

how precious it is and how precious I am ... And how grateful she is – stuff like that. She doesn't say "Lighten our darkness" or anything; it would be better if she did. The sort of things she says are really embarrassing. Sometimes she holds my hand while she's doing it and sometimes she asks me to pray too, but I say I can't. That's generally when she holds my hand, as if she is making her prayer mine.'

Ruth and Miranda were as stunned by this revelation as they had been when Albertine had told them about the journals, and for much the same reason. For them all, praying was an important but an essentially private activity. It was not something they talked about to each other and it was something that they would not have dreamt of doing out loud, except, of course, at prayers when the set prayers were recited by rote. If anything, this was an even greater invasion of privacy than the journals; at least she had been able to tear out most of the contents, but to be expected to talk to God in public and, even worse, to hear someone else doing so was unbelievable.

'It's all very well, but it's getting beyond a joke for poor Albert, so close to exams ... Honestly, Albert, I don't know how you bear it,' Miranda sympathised.

'If we tried to tell anyone now, people might not believe us. They might say why didn't you do something sooner,' Ruth said. She had a feeling that it might end up with her being the one to tell as her father was a friend of the Chairman of the Governors.

'How about telling Mrs Grover?' Miranda suggested. 'She's always very reasonable.'

'But what could we say ...? Suppose she said, "What does she do?" It would be so embarrassing having to go into details. I couldn't bear it. And if she told one of the Governors then I would have to describe it all over again.'

Ruth and Miranda were very aware that Albertine had never told them very much about what she actually did. They had not asked, partly because they respected her obvious disinclination to tell them and partly because they

99

did not want to sound as if they did not believe her. Sometimes, when they were alone, they would say to each other, 'I wonder what she actually *does*?' Even when they were told about the prayers they had tried not to sound as shocked as they were.

'If we told a Governor, or even Mrs Grover, I'm sure they would tell my mother ... I'm certain they would ... And what would happen to her and to the school? What would JPC feel if everything became public? Other parents might take their children away in case it happened to them as well.'

They all felt a strong loyalty to the school; it had been built into them from the moment they arrived. JPC's ethos was that trust was at the centre of independence. She had allowed a lot of freedoms denied to other schools because she trusted her girls not to 'let the side down'. It was a point of honour with them not to betray that trust. They were not able to see that loyalty to the school did not mean that they should suffer abuse.

'Perhaps you should tell your mother but ask her not to tell anyone – get her to tell Miss Armstrong to stop it or she'll tell a Governor.'

'I couldn't. Honestly, I couldn't. You know what she's like. She wouldn't understand, and even if she did I'm sure she'd never say anything to Miss Armstrong. I think she is a bit frightened of her. She'd just take me away and I would have wasted all this time and not even have a chance to take the exam ... It'll be all right. There's only about five months left and most of that's holidays. I can cope with that ... Last night was particularly grisly, but it'll be OK. At least this term is nearly over.'

This was the circular argument that had been going on for over a year. It always ended thus. Albertine wanted to stay at school and she knew that she would be removed if anyone knew what was going on.

'Lets have *Sail Away* just once more.' Albertine went over to the gramophone.

The bell rang for supper before she had time to start. At

half past ten they went downstairs to say goodnight to Miss Armstrong. When she shook Albertine's hand she pressed a piece of paper into it which read, 'Come at 11.30. All my love. G.'

10

The months rolled by, bringing them closer and closer to November. The pressure of Miss Armstrong's love was lying less heavily on Albertine as the pressure of the exam grew closer. She was more worried by the lack of sleep than she was by either the furtive climb or the intrusion of her body, which she had learnt to detach herself from to a certain extent. She had also learnt to use her power over the Head in small ways, such as gaining extensions of bedtime if they wanted to listen to a particularly good concert or play; she even managed to wheedle a visit to the cinema for herself, Ruth, Judy and Miranda – an unheard of treat. Miss Armstrong collected them from Sheringham after the last showing with exhortations not to tell anyone where they had been.

The summer holidays gave her some respite. Although she had two or three letters a day from her and had to spend a week with her and Maud in their house in Surrey, for seven long weeks she was free, and she was counting the days until her eventual total freedom with even more dedication than she counted the days left before the exam.

She hoped that her mother would not allow her to stay with Miss Armstrong; that there would be something else planned or that she would consider it unsuitable in some way. Without telling her the truth, Albertine was unable to persuade her mother that she should not go.

'I think it is very kind of Miss Armstrong to be prepared to give up some of her time for you,' her mother said. 'It would be very ungrateful of you to refuse and it shows how concerned she is that you should pass.'

And so she stayed with them, and was astonished to discover that Miss Armstrong lived in what looked like a workman's cottage in a somewhat seedy terraced street on the outskirts of Esher. The houses backed onto each other, there was no garden, only a concrete yard, and the only view was of other people's washing. The inside of the house was very cramped and dark, overfurnished with heavy oak and uncomfortable chairs. It was very clean, though, which Albertine soon learnt was entirely Maud's doing. Miss Armstrong seemed to play no part in the domestic arrangements.

It was a very uncomfortable week for Albertine. At school the times Miss Armstrong could have her to herself were limited. Apart from the nights there were only odd periods of ten minutes or so when she would have to go to her study. At her home in Esher there was not ten minutes when she did not have to be with her. At school Miss Armstrong was always very much the Headmistress; even when they were in bed she still exercised a magisterial power. In her home she was relaxed and seemed in many ways almost a contemporary. She lay about in a deckchair in the yard wearing shorts and an aertex shirt, she smoked continuously, she wanted to make love at all times of the day, she was giggly and, in an embarrassing way, girlish and flirtatious. Under these circumstances Albertine found it even more unnatural to call her Miss Armstrong but was still unable to get her tongue round Gerda.

Her friend Maud was very difficult too. Albertine sensed a profound hostility towards her which she was unable to account for. She helped her wash up and prepare vegetables, she helped her lay the table, she tried to make conversation with her, which as she was an English don she thought would be easy, but Maud barely looked at her let alone spoke. Miss Armstrong had told her not to worry about her and that it was not personal. Albertine had no idea at all that they had been lovers for years. Although she was crippled by embarrassment at going to bed in Miss Armstrong's room, she assumed that Maud would think she was sleeping on the floor as there was no other room but

103

Maud's. She did not know that Maud had been turned out of her bed to make room for her.

They visited Hampton Court, where Miss Armstrong flirted with her in the maze and where they were discovered kissing by a family of father, mother and three children; they sang French songs together, Miss Armstrong playing the piano while Albertine sang and Maud prepared the meal. They scoured second-hand bookshops for more presents for Albertine. They talked neither of school nor exams nor of the future. They certainly did none of the work which Miss Armstrong had promised Albertine's mother was the purpose of her visit.

When she went home at the end of the week Miss Armstrong's letters became even more frequent, with many references to the time they had spent together. Albertine only answered one in ten, some of which she battled with as if they were compositions in which she tried to emulate the lover-like tone.

'It must have been ghastly for you staying with the Head,' Harriet, her sister, said on her return. 'What was she like? Did you have to do masses of prep?'

'Harriet, you mustn't say that. It was very kind of Miss Armstrong to have her,' her mother admonished.

'It was OK,' Albertine said.

She had one letter which worried her to such an extent she felt permanently in pain, unable to eat from the constriction in her stomach.

My Dearest Love,

Since you left I have been desolate. Without you the sun does not shine neither does the rain refresh. You and you alone are the only source of my being, you are my life and I am counting the days – no, the hours – until we can be together always. I have been imagining what our life together will be like; it will be like it was last week, it will be like Heaven and I continually thank God for the great gift he has given me in you. Of course I know that you will be away for some of the time (I

104

hope) and so will I (alas!) but the holidays will be long for both of us and I will see your dear sweet face and have your lovely presence with me all the time. Your only G.

She carried the letter with her and read it over and over again. It had not occurred to her that Miss Armstrong was hoping to keep her for even one day after she left school.

Dearest Gerda. [She managed to write what she was never able to say aloud.]
Thank you for your letter. Yes, it was very nice staying with you and I miss you too.

She felt as obliged to respond to her letters as she felt obliged to respond to her embraces, with as much reciprocation as she could muster.

I think my parents have plans for me to go to Paris when I leave and then I've got to be presented and all that stuff so I am not sure that I'll be able to come and live with you, fun though it would be.
We are going to Stratford next week to stay with some cousins and go to the theatre. We go every year. I have been to quite a lot of Proms. I am really glad that term doesn't start till after the last one. I went last year and it was wonderful, we slept out after the Ninth and had a terrific day singing and chasing balloons down Queens Gate. This year Ruth and Miranda and Judy are coming too. [She added that in case by some dreadful chance Miss Armstrong would take it into her head to come too.] See you quite soon, Lots and lots of love, Albertine.

My Darling Girl,
When you have left school you will be far less in your parents' hands. I know you will not be 21, but you are not a child any longer and you can say no. You know

what I think about the Season and I would be horrified to think that you would be prepared to do it just to please them.

Your letter sounded rather cold. Has anything happened to you? I hate not being able to see you and talk to you, I feel as if you might be being taken from me. Oh my dearest, I love you so much I can hardly bear to think of anyone speaking to you but me. I long for you every minute. Please write and say that you love me. I am glad you are going to Stratford, but most of all I want to know what you are feeling about me . . . Please Albertine, don't leave me burning. Forever, G.

Dearest Gerda,
Of course I love you, it is just that I have not much time for writing letters; there are so many things I have to do but they are quite boring things so I don't know what to write about. I think they have started to organise the Season thing so I don't think I can get out of that. I promise you I don't 'want' to do it. It sounds awful and I think you are quite right to disapprove of it – so do I. I *do* want to go to Paris, especially I want to go to the Russian church to hear that magnificent music, like the record I have got of the Creed which was recorded there. It is not long till term starts again, so I will see you soon. Don't worry about me, no one is trying to take me away from you. Lots and lots of love, Albertine.

Although she wrote about going to Paris so confidently, she knew the strength of Miss Armstrong's power of persuasion and was still frightened that in some witchlike way she would snatch her up to fly with her.

'You don't honestly mean you had to stay with her in the holidays . . . How frightful!'

They were back at school. It was mid-September and there were six weeks left. All four girls were becoming increasingly nervous and excited in turn. Albertine made a quotation book, which she carried with her wherever she went; Miss Larkin had emphasised how important it was to illustrate her points with quotations and she had selected some for every possible contingency that she could think of and learnt them at every available opportunity. Their sessions became less frequent but when they occurred they lasted longer. They were prepared and they knew it and the waiting became the greatest pressure they had to endure.

Two weeks before the first exam Miss Armstrong summoned them all to her study.

'I want you to bring all your books, all your essays, all your notes to me, here. From now on you are to do nothing.' She had a pile of books on the table by her desk. 'These are all you are to read in the next two weeks. Go for walks, go for bicycle rides, sleep, have fun . . . above all, relax. I want you all fresh when the time comes.'

The books she had selected were all Victorian novels of enormous sentimentality about dying children, orphaned children and bad people turning into good people through the influence of good children. They loved them and laughed as much as over Mary Grant, and cried as much as they had over *Black Beauty* and *My Friend Flicka* when they were young.

Albertine found the nightly ritual, though still a trial, bearable as she could sleep in the mornings. They went for long walks on the beach, they bicycled as far as Norwich; they became bored and longed for the moment when they could stretch their muscular minds, and at last that moment came.

'I don't want you to come tonight,' Miss Armstrong said. 'Have a really early night and a good sleep.'

Albertine had raged inwardly. She had made it sound as if not only she but Albertine as well was making an enormous sacrifice, but she was also admitting that for 18 months she had knowingly deprived her of the sleep she needed if she was going to be capable of her best performance.

*

During the weeks up to the exam Miss Armstrong had made no mention of her proposal that Albertine should live with her when she left school. Albertine herself, naturally, did not raise the issue, but it hung in the air between them like a gauze veil. During the period of waiting to hear if she had an interview, with the nights returned to normal, as Albertine was eating the last of the banana sandwiches, she raised it again.

'I'm sure you have passed, but if by any chance you haven't, what are your parents planning for you after France?' She made the words 'planning for you' sound like a mortal sin.

'They haven't said anything. They're waiting, I suppose.'

'You do know, don't you, that you won't have to do what they want?'

'Just as I suppose you think I don't have to do what you want,' she thought, but said instead, 'It's difficult.'

'It needn't be, my love. You can live with me. I'll look after you and find you something interesting to do.'

'Let's wait and see what happens.'

Their summons for interview all came together, Judy to Cambridge, the others to Oxford.

'One more hurdle, my darling, and you've done it.' Miss Armstrong was radiant. Albertine felt that she was celebrating her own triumph rather than Albertine's, but forgave her, believing that without her she could not have done it. In fact, she was beginning to fear she was so much Miss Armstrong's creature that without her at the interview she would be seen to be an empty vessel, a fraud, that she would be 'seen through'.

'I wish you were going to be there too,' she said one night, and for the first time meant it.

'I wish so too, darling, but I will be with you in spirit. I am always with you in spirit, you know that.'

When they all passed it seemed an anticlimax. So much time, so much effort, so many hopes, so many fears dissolved in an instant. They were left with only apprehension for the future, faced with the sudden realisation that what had seemed an end was only a beginning, that what they were leaving was safe because it was known and what was to come was unknown. Apart from university, which was alarming enough on its own, there was the world, there was adulthood, there was Life.

It was in one of their very last sessions that they began to contemplate what Life was going to be in reality. The immediate future was to be the same for all of them: presentation, balls, cocktail parties, dressing in grown-up clothes and wearing make-up – all things strange to them and very far removed from their ideals, from what they had worked so hard for and what had seemed so overwhelmingly important.

'What do you think we say to boys when we meet them?' Ruth said. 'I bet they won't be interested in the causes of the Reformation.'

'I'm most frightened of the dancing,' Albertine said. 'I'm always made to lead so I don't even know what to do with my arms if I have to be the girl.'

There was dancing every Wednesday evening. It was compulsory and was, apart from cookery classes in the lower forms, the only acknowledgement the school made to the fact that when they left there would be other things they would have to know about apart from academic work. They were taught the fox-trot, quick step and waltz, they rhumbaed to *There was a Rich Maharajah from Mogador*, they learnt Scottish reels and how to strip the willow. No one enjoyed it, though occasionally some became quite sentimental over the treacle tones of Charles Trenet singing *La Mer*, with which dancing always ended.

'Do you think it's really true that we have to curtsey to a cake?' Judy asked. 'I mean, I don't mind curtseying to the Queen, that's only right and proper, but a cake!'

They were talking about Queen Charlotte's ball, which was one of the first major events of the season.

'And why do you think we have to wear white? I look perfectly ghastly in white,' Ruth said.

'Because we're virgins, stupid,' Miranda answered.

'The whole thing is totally disgusting. It really is a marriage market, they might as well come up and feel our flanks and look at our teeth.' Albertine had been to a thoroughbred sale with her father. 'And why does wearing white necessarily mean we're virgins? Do you think they examine us first and say to some people "black for you, I'm afraid"?'

'Well, we haven't had much chance to be anything else, have we?' Miranda said, and wished she hadn't when she looked at Albertine.

Albertine, despite years of biology lessons, was very ignorant about her body and its various functions. Was she still a virgin or had Miss Armstrong taken that away from her too? Would she have to tell her husband about her when he discovered that she was not what he had expected her to be? She thought that virgins had the hole that men put their thing into closed, but then how could girls use Tampax, which she knew some did; perhaps it was true that if you rode a lot the skin covering the hole got worn away. She felt a sudden and acute surge of envy for the others, who could go dressed in white, like nuns making their first vows, or virgin brides. Queen Charlotte's was all at once not a revolting marriage market but a glorious array of purity and she alone would be somewhere in the background among the 'soiled goods'. She wished they would stop talking about virgins.

'Well, it seems an awful thing to say, but you know I'm not sure that I really want to leave,' Judy said.

She had voiced what they were all thinking; they had thought that they would go out into the world as free people, to live their own lives based on all the things they had talked about which had not been only about men or marriage but about political action, about how they could help change the world . . . serve their fellow men.

'I know, it's mad, isn't it, all these years ticking off days and now it's here . . .'

They all knew what Miranda would have said if she had finished her sentence; after all the years of incarceration,

110

what they had to face was more of the same; they would be living by other people's rules and up to other people's expectations; they would not be free in the sense they had thought they would be and at least here they knew what the rules were and how to make the best of them, but out there . . .?

'What do you think goes on in night clubs?'

'I've no idea . . . I don't suppose anyone will ask me to go to one.'

This was another fear that none of them had really wanted to own up to. To have to do the Season was bad enough, to be a flop would be the final humiliation; but it was difficult for them to appear to each other to despise the whole thing whilst at the same time wanting to be a success.

'Well, at least we'll have each other. Let's drink to that. Is that the last of the wine? Come on, what did the Musketeers say? "All for one and one for all!"'

They drank the dregs and played, for the last time, *There are Bad Times Just Around the Corner.*

It was on the train to Liverpool Street that Albertine knew what she was going to do. Miss Armstrong, while saying goodbye to her had whispered, 'I'll see you in three days' time . . . We'll meet in London. Oh my darling, how wonderful it's going to be!'

Albertine had only grunted at the time but as the train trundled slowly through the flat Norfolk countryside she decided she was not going to see her, she was not going to speak to her or answer her letters. Miss Armstrong could not force her, Miss Armstrong would not be there. She was free from her, and it was over. It was finished. She would go to Oxford and she would study and when she had finished she would write. She would spin words, weave them seamlessly, glittering and bright words, dull muted words, words heavy with meaning, translucent words lightly brushing the edge of meaning. Already she sometimes heard them in her head, sonorous, alliterative, onomatopoeic. She would make heavy tapestries of words, dense and dark but full of lighthearted dancing figures, prancing deer and falling leaves and flowers, and as she imagined the dancing figures free among the trees she knew that she was starting a life that would be exciting, that would be free and that would never again be subject to the darkness she felt she was emerging from, just as the train was emerging from a tunnel into bright sunshine.

11

'A thousand ages in thy sight are like a moment past'. The words of the hymn made a mockery of how Gerda was feeling. For her, every moment of every day was like a thousand ages. By ten in the morning she was so tired even the effort of lifting her pen seemed too great. She sat at her desk in front of unopened letters and unmarked essays. She looked out of the window and watched the life of the school pass before her as if on a screen, feeling as detached from it as in some ways she felt detached from her aching body. Sometimes the pain in her legs and the sensation of being bound round her ribs by an iron band made her wonder if she was really ill, if she was suffering from a heart condition, but the breathlessness and the palpitations would pass and she would lie for a while on the sofa, exhausted, and slip into a deep but always short sleep. The days were interminable and the nights worse.

Although she was so tired she could not sleep and, as it is said of drowning men, fleeting pictures of her life passed before her eyes. Small incidents were magnified and distorted into major catastrophes in which she always played the guilty part. She blamed herself for her mother's death and her father's despair, his drunkenness and his anger. She never consciously thought of Albertine but, like the pain in an amputated limb, her absence was driving Gerda crazy and she could do nothing to alleviate it. She paced the confines of her room, afraid to sleep and afraid not to. She could not contemplate the past or the future. She was paralysed in a present which held nothing but terror, not only by the nameless dread which threatened so often to suck her into its bottomless depth but also by what would happen when the inevitable discovery was made that she was not doing any of the things that she was paid to do. This thought produced a new dread, a real dread of the future. If she could not work, how could she live?

Thin as she had always been, she was becoming thinner. She could not eat; it was as if her epiglottis had grown to the size of a ping-pong ball and all food turned to cotton wool in her mouth and stuck in her throat in a large coagulated mass. She was also drinking secretly from bottles of gin she kept behind books in her study and in a drawer in her bedroom. She rinsed her mouth with eau de cologne. She was so closed away in her own tormented world that she did not realise that she was deceiving no one. The school secretary, who came every morning, was sent away on the pretext that there was nothing for her to do. She cancelled her lessons, saying that she had an attack of laryngitis. She was so convinced that she was the cause, either directly or indirectly, of all the evil and all the suffering in the world, it was only the thought of Hell that prevented her from taking her life. She eventually took to her bed, worn out by pretending and the effort to stay alive.

It was while she was in this state that the senior staff held an unofficial meeting. They were not sure what was happening but they did not want to involve the Governors. They were fond of her and respected her brain and her courage. They understood what she was fighting and wanted to help her in any way which would preserve her dignity if they could. They were also concerned for the reputation of the school, which they could see would be badly damaged if it was discovered that the Headmistress was incompetent. There sprang to life an institutional loyalty which overrode any personal resentment they might have felt for having to cover for the cripple at their head, and they also, although nobody admitted this, felt responsible for turning the other way when the Albertine affair had been at its height. They had been torn between doing their duty towards Albertine

114

and at the same time recognising that it could have happened to any of them. Nobody was prepared to admit that
they knew just how far it had gone. It was Mrs Grover, the
Housemistress of Darwin, who suggested the solution.

'I think we should send for Maud,' she said.

Maud came on the first train and Mrs Grover met her at
Norwich Station.

'How long has this been going on?'

'I think more or less since the beginning of term. We
didn't notice anything at first but gradually we realised she
wasn't doing anything, and about three days ago she went to
bed and no one has seen her since. Perhaps you'll be angry
that we didn't tell you sooner, but we didn't want to cause a
fuss.'

Maud *was* angry, and also worried, but managed to say
quite calmly, 'Has she seen a doctor?'

'She won't see one.' And they both knew that this was
outside the expertise of Dr Forest, who had difficulty diag-
nosing measles. Maud was certain that it was to do with
Albertine. Gerda had come home for the holidays radiant,
and Maud had known, though nothing was said, that she
thought that now Albertine had left school the love affair
would be in the open. Maud had watched with agony as
Gerda waited for the post, and she knew that the reason
Gerda barely left the house was in case she should miss the
call if Albertine telephoned. Slowly, as nothing happened,
she watched her assume a horrible brittle brightness. She
could not say, as she wanted to, 'I told you so', nor could
she comfort her. She knew that if she had tried Gerda would
say, and she would be right, 'This is what you wanted, isn't
it?' Maud did not know if the affair was known in the school
and did not feel that she could ask in case it wasn't.

Mrs Grover, who was also certain that Albertine was at the
root of it, did not like to mention it to Maud for fear of
hurting her. She did not know that Albertine had stayed
with them and did not know whether Maud even knew
about her. And so they skirted the issue.

'It could be overwork. Gerda has never been able to give less than her all, and she isn't physically strong,' said Maud.

'Could it be something to do with the "change", do you think?' said Mrs Grover.

Maud had come because she had been asked to and because she wanted to save Gerda from the inevitable dismissal and reverberating scandal which would destroy her career for ever if anything of the last 18 months should ever be known; but she did not know what to do, and she was not at all sure that she was the person to do anything. She was both the closest and the furthest away. For the rest of the car journey she tried to compose her thoughts and to keep her burning hatred of 'that little bitch', as she thought of Albertine, at bay. She knew very well that if she was to help, nothing of her own feelings about the girl must come through. She felt in her bones that as it was love that had destroyed her, it would only be love that would save her. This time it would be her love.

'How much do the girls know about all this?' she asked, as much to make conversation as anything.

'They obviously know she isn't well, but you know girls, they're not really interested in anything that doesn't immediately concern them and we've managed to cover for her.'

She knows, thought Maud suddenly, but bless her, she is too loyal and too tactful to say anything. She felt the strong wave of sympathy enclosing her, though Mrs Grover was looking straight ahead and saying very little.

'Does she know I'm coming?'

'No, we felt that surprise might rouse her as much as anything else. Were we wrong, do you think?'

Maud thought that it might make her feel plotted against but answered, 'I think you were right,' and hoped that she was.

Maud had only been to the school once before. She had come to give a lecture on Shakespeare during Gerda's first term. Gerda had tried to introduce a school lecture which would take place once a term and Maud had been the first. It had not been a success, which was perhaps the reason the

116

idea had been abandoned. Talking to an age range of 13- to 18-year-olds was quite outside her experience. She was used to lecturing to university students. She had tried to keep her talk light and anecdotal, but it was not her skill and she knew that she had failed to interest anyone. Gerda had been tense and nervy, tapping her fingers more than usual. Maud had been concerned at the amount she was drinking, and also that she did not appear to have a friend among the staff. Knowing that Gerda would need someone to confide in, she had not been surprised when the Albertine thing began, though she had tried to warn Gerda about where it could end.

It was summer when she had been before and the place had seemed quite pretty; there had been flowers and freshly mown lawns and the sun had shone on bright, laughing girls as they moved cheerfully, like flocks of starlings, from place to place. Now it was winter, the trees were bare and the passing groups of children were wrapped in cloaks, bent double against an icy wind, blue-faced and silent, their books clasped close to their chests.

'I'll show you to your room, then we'll have a cup of tea before you see her,' said Mrs Grover. Maud felt that she should go straight to Gerda but accepted willingly, ready to postpone as long as she could the likely painful and unsatis-factory visit.

She felt almost comfortable in the warm, book-lined, chintz-curtained room which was Mrs Grover's sitting-room – a stark contrast to the room she was to sleep in, which she understood was the sickroom, a bleak little place with an iron bedstead and unlined narrow orange curtains and, she had noticed already, no bedside light.

'Are those your children?' she said, pointing to a display of photographs on top of one of the bookcases.

'Yes,' Mrs Grover replied warmly. 'All sons. We didn't manage a daughter, and all, like their father, in the navy. This is my husband.' She showed a photograph of a hand-some, smiling man in the white uniform of an officer serving overseas. 'He died ten years ago. I don't know what he would think if he could see me now!' she said, with the laugh of someone who has changed their life completely but accepted the change with humour and risen to the challenge without resentment. 'The boys think it's quite funny that I'm here, but they're glad in a way. They were worried that I would be lonely if I just stayed at home. I manage to see quite a lot of them in the holidays when they are in England, and it's quite fun to teach again. Girls are so much more emotional than boys, which, having no daughters, I find interesting – though sometimes, I must say, their intensity can get quite out of hand.'

Maud wondered if she was going to talk about Albertine, but she went on, 'I expect you find that with your students, don't you?'

Maud said that at university the students tended to keep that sort of thing for their private life, which she had little to do with, 'Fortunately,' she said. 'I think I would be very bored and irritated if I had too much to do with adolescents.' As she had been bored and irritated, as well as hurt, by Albertine.

'Nice though this is, I think I'd better go and see her,' said Maud, rising.

'Would you like me to come with you?'

'If you would just show me the way, and perhaps be not too far away in case I need help.'

'It's a good time now. It's prep and there'll be no one around till seven. Good luck!' she whispered as they reached the top of the stairs. 'I'll be just below you, in her study.'

Feeling exactly like a terrier sent down to unearth a hunted fox, Maud knocked on the door.

'Gerda, it's me, Maud. Are you awake? . . . Gerda?'

Silence. Maud wondered what she would do if Gerda did not answer at all. Would they have to break the door down?

'Gerda, do open the door, darling.'

There was no sound. She felt helpless and then suddenly frightened. Supposing she was dead. Supposing they had all left it too late and she in her despair had killed herself. Supposing she was unconscious . . .

118

'Gerda, please . . . it's Maud and I have come all this way to see you. Please let me in.'

Nothing. She did not dare raise her voice for fear of it reaching the room where prep was taking place. She did not want a drama if it could be avoided.

'Gerda, I know you can hear me. If you don't open the door we'll have to break it down.' She tried to sound more confident and authoritative than she was feeling. If Gerda was conscious, it was obvious that she did not want to see her.

'Gerda, if you don't open the door I'm going to get someone to help me.'

'Go away, Maud. I don't want anyone. Please, please, go away.'

At least she was alive, but she sounded more than weak; she sounded entirely defeated.

Gerda's first feeling on hearing Maud's voice was one of relief swiftly followed by an increase of panic. If she had managed to rise from her bed and take up the reins of her job she could have passed off these last few days as a severe bout of flu, but Maud's presence had turned it into an emergency, making that excuse no longer possible. She wanted to let her in, to experience the comfort of her well-known and much-loved face, but she dreaded seeing the one person who knew why she was there, whom she could not deceive and whom on top of everything else she had betrayed. She knew Maud well enough to realise that if she said she was going to break the door down, she would. She wondered vaguely why she had come and realised with a sweaty flush of embarrassment that someone must have sent for her. She knew neither what day it was nor what time. Since she had been in her room she had not taken off her clothes and had barely moved from her bed. Like the wounded animal she was, she had lain in a foetal position, drifting in and out of sleep, only dimly aware, from the sound of the bell summoning the school to its regular daily rhythm, of the passing of time.

119

'Maud, are you still there?' she whispered.

'Yes, I'm here.'

'Wait a minute, I'm coming.' She crawled from the pile of bed-clothes and groped her way in the dark to the door. Seeing Maud standing in the doorway, so familiar and in this setting so strange, brought her to a full and horrible realisation of her situation. She pulled her into the room and, resting her head on her shoulder, she wept. She did not sob, she howled; she fought for breath through a hurricane of tears and clung to Maud as if to the only rock on a devastated shore.

Maud was terrified. Nothing that Mrs Grover had said had prepared her for this and she felt powerless and paralysed by the onslaught, as if she too was in the eye of the storm.

'There, there,' she said, stroking her head. 'There, there.' She was only too aware of the inadequacy of her response.

At last the gale subsided and Maud was able to take in the sight that met her eyes. She was shocked by Gerda's appearance. That she had not removed her clothes for days was obvious by their crumpled state and by the smell, which was a mixture of stale sweat, nicotine and gin. She saw three empty bottles fallen on the floor by her bed, which was like a shipwrecked vessel, sails draped loosely across the bows. Gerda herself, ravaged by tears, seemed little more than a skeleton; from the hang of her head and the stoop of her shoulders, she seemed to have lost all power to hold herself erect. Maud was brisk. Alarmed though she was, she could see very clearly that only by taking full control in a calm and forceful way would she be able to overcome further resistance.

'You get undressed. I'm going to run you a bath.'

'I can't, Maud. I can't . . . I can't cope, honestly I can't . . . I can't cope with anything. You should go . . . Please go . . . I just want to be left alone. Please.'

Maud, afraid of a further outburst of weeping, ran the bath. She emptied into it an almost full bottle of pine essence, and the sharp clean smell swept through the rancid room like the Meltemi after a long hot summer. She began to undress her; ignoring her pathetic whimpering, she led her to the water and closed the door. 'Lie there, darling, and relax; I'll be back soon.' She took the key of the bedroom with her and went to find Mrs Grover.

'It's worse than I thought,' she said. 'I've left her in the bath. I need some clean sheets, and would it be possible, do you think, to have some soup or something? I think she's very ill.' It was hard for her to keep a note of reproof from her voice. She was secretly horrified that nothing had been done sooner and she could see no way that Gerda's incompetence could now be covered up. She would have to take her home as soon as she was fit to travel; recovery would take weeks if not months. The Governors would have to be told what had happened and the best outcome could only be that they would never have to know why.

In the bath, the silken skeins of misery which had wrapped Gerda in so tight a cocoon that she had been almost protected gradually loosened and floated away. She was once again exposed naked to the harsh and piercing reality of her thoughts, which tumbled in her head like so many acrobats, leaping, somersaulting, swinging from one bar to the next. But the tent in which they played was the certainty that she could not go on. What 'going on' exactly meant she was not sure, but it had something to do with putting one foot after another and one word after another, neither of which she could do at the moment. She felt vaguely comforted by the presence of Maud so miraculously translated into her nightmare. She could hear her nextdoor moving about, she heard her open and shut the window, she heard her open the door and say 'Thank you, that's perfect.' She did not want to move in the bath and ruffle the thick dense greenness of the water and she did not want to speak; she wanted to stay forever in the amniotic fluid of her dark green womb.

'Are you all right in there?' Maud's voice was brisk and

kind, like a hospital nurse. 'It's time you got out; your bed is ready and there's some delicious-looking soup here. When did you last eat?'

The familiar lump in her throat prevented her from answering, but obediently she climbed out of the bath and, wrapping herself in a towel, she crept into her now ordered bedroom. The sheets on her bed were clean and pressed, the bottles had gone and dear kind Maud was standing firmly by the table on which was a tray laid with a crisp white cloth, a bowl of soup and a plate of thin brown bread and butter.

'How did you get here?' she whispered.

'Never mind that now. Where are your night things?' She was looking through her drawers and produced a pair of blue striped pyjamas. 'They look a bit thin but they'll do for now.' And very gently she removed the towel from Gerda's emaciated body and dressed her. She led her to her bed with the same delicacy as she would a somnambulist who might go mad if woken too suddenly to the real world; she sat her on the edge of the bed and lifted her legs, she pushed her back onto the piled pillows and drew up the bedclothes, she kissed her as she would a sleeping child. 'There you are, darling. Now here's your soup. Would you like me to feed you?'

And spoon by spoon she did that. Gerda's eyes were still those of a hunted animal but she swallowed the soup, and by herself she ate the bread and butter.

'When did you come?' she said, her voice almost normal.

'Ssh now. Mrs Grover rang to say that she was worried about you. I hope you don't mind. She's a very nice woman.'

'I got myself into a bit of a state, I'm afraid.' Maud was relieved to see a very slight, very rueful smile flick the corners of her mouth. 'I'm glad you're here.' And she closed her eyes.

'I'm going to leave you to sleep now but I'll be back in an hour or so and we can have a talk.' But she did not think she was heard.

*

'It must, I think, be handled in three different stages,' Maud said to Mrs Grover when they were together again. 'The first problem is what to do now. I hope I'm wrong, but I don't see this going away overnight and I think I should take her home as soon as possible. What do you think?'

Mrs Grover was clearly profoundly relieved. 'I must admit it would be difficult to carry on with the flu excuse for very much longer and I agree with you that she's not going to recover quickly. I'm sure, though, that she'll be better at home, but if she goes with you now I'll have to tell the Governors. There must be someone who is officially in charge. What do you think I should say to them?'

This was the moment that Maud had been dreading. She did not know Mrs Grover, and although she seemed vey sympathetic and although Gerda had always spoken very highly of her, she knew that they had not been friends. She did not know if she could trust her, did not know how much she knew, did not know if she could risk talking about it; but the weight of the pain she was carrying was such that she felt forced to.

'It is Albertine, isn't it?'

'I think so.' And there was silence.

'How much did you all know at the time?' Now started, she wanted to know it all; she wanted to talk about it as if it was someone else, she wanted to scratch as she would an insect bite, gaining a little relief with each scratch, knowing all the time that the wound would be more painful later.

'At first, nothing. We realised she was interested in her, but so were we all in a way. You could say that she had been one of our success stories. She was very difficult when she first came here but she was always an interesting girl, one of those we all felt had far more potential than she had shown, but few of us managed to gain her trust. It was Patricia Larkin who first got through to her, apart, of course, from old JPC, who had seen it from the start, and then Gerda. It was only after the lower sixth that I thought she was getting too close, too involved, and when I began to suspect that it might have gone further, I'm ashamed to say I did nothing, mostly because I didn't know what to do. I didn't feel that I could say to Gerda, "Are you sleeping with Albertine?" Even if she had admitted it, what would I have done? To go to the Governors would have been terribly bad for the school, and I also thought bad for Albertine; she seemed to be coping, her work was excellent. I'm afraid I put my head in the sand and hoped the problem would go away. I'm sorry.' As she spoke she knew how pathetic her excuse must sound.

Maud felt sorry for her. She had done no less than Maud herself and with higher motive. Maud could also possibly have stopped it and had not done so out of a mixture of cowardice and dread; that by interfering she would lose Gerda completely. She had played a waiting game which she knew was in her own best interest with no thought of the consequences either to Gerda or to Albertine, whom she still could not refrain from thinking of as 'that little bitch'. They had all been to blame. By a complicit inaction they had all helped her to this. That Gerda's career was over seemed certain; whether she would recover her emotional stability was questionable but only time would tell that.

'How many of the staff suspected, do you think?'

'I'm not sure. We never talked about it, but no one could have avoided noticing something.'

Maud and Mrs Grover sat again in silence, contemplating the enormity of the obsession that had put so much in jeopardy.

'What about the girls; did they realise what was going on, do you think?'

It was not only that she could not resist scratching the itch, could not resist talking about what had been for 18 months the big unmentionable, she also needed to know how public the affair had been so that she could exercise some form of damage limitation.

'I don't think so. They are a strangely naive lot, and if Albertine had told anyone I'm sure it would have spread; you know the strength of the grapevine.'

Whilst recognising the potency of the grapevine, Mrs

Grover had grossly underestimated the loyalty that exists in a subgroup; in this instance the group that was below the staff but above the rest of the school. However, she did feel a sudden horror, held in check at the time, for her lack of concern at what it must have cost Albertine not to tell anyone, if that had been the case. As a housemistress and second head of the school, it was to her that Albertine should have turned. She wondered why she had not done so and blamed herself for not allowing, even offering, her the opportunity. How grievously she had avoided her pastoral role, which she knew only too well was as much, or even more, a teacher's job as the imparting of knowledge.

'Is it possible to tell the Governors that she has had a sort of breakdown, without much risk of them finding out the cause?'

Mrs Grover, for the first time confronting her own culpability in the story, was becoming irritated by Maud's persistence but she was sensitive enough to realise that she was doing it as much for her own sake as to discover the answers.

'It's possible, and I think that's just what I should do. I don't believe that if she comes back it will happen again.'

From the tone and the slight lifting of her voice at the end of her sentence, Maud knew that she was wanting to know, but had too much delicacy to ask outright, if it had happened before.

'I'm not sure that she should come back, in fact. This, as you probably know, was her first boarding-school appointment. I think she has been very lonely; she is extremely highly strung, very emotional and expends a great deal of nervous energy in concealing that fact; she is also strangely dependent for someone who seems so strong. I think it could happen again here, but not in a day school, where there is far less intimacy between teacher and pupil, and with me at home in the evenings. Her great gift as a teacher is that she has both the interest and the ability to penetrate the minds of her pupils; at a day school I'm convinced that that would be as far as it would go. If any of this comes out she will never get another job in the teaching profession, which would be a tragedy not only for her but for the hundreds she could teach in the future.'

Mrs Grover thought how fortunate Gerda had been to find someone so understanding and so strong, and she felt a renewed pity for her in her struggle to do a job she was clearly not suited to without the person she was used to relying on. She was conscious of letting not only Albertine, but also Gerda, down badly. Gerda had needed a friend and without one she had been forced to take a lover. Why had she not been a friend? Jealousy must have played a part, Mrs Grover was unwillingly forced to admit. She had applied for the job herself and had been fairly confident of getting it. She was familiar with the school's rather idiosyncratic tradition and she knew she was a good teacher. After Gerda had been there a term, Mrs Grover recognised qualities in her that she herself did not possess. Gerda had an energy she did not have, she had a charisma which drew the best from both the staff and the children. She was not just a good teacher, she was that rare thing, an inspirational teacher. She was also a good administrator. Mrs Grover saw that she herself was in many ways too comfortable, too maternal; she could never have been an inspiration, though she was now beginning to wonder if inspiration was such a desirable quality in the hothouse of a girls' school. She had learnt to respect her, but she had not learnt to be her friend. She admired her but she did not like her, and had not been able to see the vulnerability behind the prickly shell. Sometimes when Gerda smiled it was as if the sun had emerged from behind a cloud. But there was never a cloudless day; no sooner did the sun emerge but it was hidden again, as if it had been exposed in error and had swiftly invited a denser, darker cloud to cover its mistake.

'So what do you want to do now?'

'I'll take her home tomorrow if she's fit enough to travel. She was quite calm when I left her so I think she'll be all right. Of course I should have driven here; I don't like the idea of taking her on a train. Is there a car I could borrow?'

'I could drive you both if that would help at all.'

126

Maud thought of the journey and the inevitably forced conversation, so she said, 'I think it would be better if I took her alone, though thank you. Would it be possible to get someone to collect the car the next day?'

'I'll come myself. The fewer people that see her the better.'

They were both silent again, contemplating the tasks that lay ahead. Mrs Grover thought about the Governors and what she was to say to them. She knew that they would ask her to act as Head for the time being: if Gerda did not return they might this time offer her the permanent head-ship. Maud thought about what she should do to restore Gerda's shattered self-respect, her competence and her broken heart and whether their own relationship would survive the restoration. She would have her back; but the future, which for this reason should have seemed light and airy, was weighted with a heavy darkness. It was as if she was starting a low crawl down an endless tunnel and the weight that bowed her shoulders, that forced her to crawl not stand, was the weight of Gerda's broken body and the silence in the damp and sinister tunnel was the silence of words that could never be spoken.

'I'm not going to inflict school supper on you,' Mrs Grover interrupted her thoughts. 'I must go and take prayers now, but stay here, have a drink, and I'll have something sent in for us both to eat in about half an hour. You must be exhausted. Do you want to go up again and see if she's all right?'

'I'd better do that . . . thank you for being so kind.'

Mrs Grover touched her shoulder. It was only a brief touch not a caress but even so it made Maud want to cry.

'Don't worry too much. I'm sure that when you get her home she'll be all right. There's too much here to remind her.'

'Why doesn't she answer my letters? Do you think she's ill? I've written to her and written to her, I've begged and implored her. Why, Maud, why? I don't understand it . . .

She loved me, I know she loved me. Do you think they've sent her away? Have they locked her in so that she can't write? They must be stopping her from seeing me.'

Gerda had been at home for three weeks. For the first two she had lain in bed for most of the day. She had barely spoken. She ate her meals, she slept, she lay with her face to the wall. She did not cry again but she was like a baby, and Maud treated her as such. She washed her and changed her clothes, she fed her and let her sleep. This was the first time she had spoken of Albertine.

'Didn't you say she was going to France almost immediately?'

'Well, she was certainly going sometime in the spring, but she hasn't written at all. Why didn't she write at once? Why didn't she answer my letters? Maud, I'm so worried about her . . . there must be a reason.'

'You don't think it's possible that she has decided to end it and hasn't the courage to tell you?'

'Why should she end it? I know that you didn't like her, but she wasn't like that. She loved me and we were so close. She wouldn't just stop like that unless someone was forcing her. I know her, Maud. You don't understand, but I know her.'

'I think you've got to accept that she's not going to write, and you'll probably never know the reason why.'

'I don't think I can survive without her, Maud. I don't even want to.'

A few days later she was sitting downstairs.

'Do you think you could ring her mother and ask where she is and if they are stopping her from seeing me?'

'No I don't. Gerda, you're crucifying yourself. You have to let go. I think you should get right away. Resign from Hartwell and go away, for a long time. Why don't we ring Geoffrey and Patricia and see if you can go and stay with them for a bit?'

Maud had had this possibility in her mind for more than a week. She had already telephoned Gerda's brother, who was in the Colonial Service, serving in British Honduras.

'No, I want to stay here, I don't want to go away.'

But a few days later, when Geoffrey rang her she put up very little resistance to his pressing invitation.

'Just for a month,' she agreed.

'Stay for as long as you like,' he said.

'I'll come and see you in the Easter holidays,' said Maud as she watched her disappear into the departure lounge, her back ramrod stiff and only her hesitant smile as she turned to wave goodbye telling of the courage this long walk was costing her.

12

Belize, Central America, 1993

Albertine had always felt that one day she would meet Miss Armstrong again. There had been odd times in her life when she had thought she had seen her; once on a beach in Italy, once in a crowded street and again at the other end of a large restaurant. She had sometimes thought that she would try to find her. She had asked people who had still been at the school after she left and had discovered that suddenly, in the middle of the following term, she had gone, and with no explanation, other than that she was suffering from strain, a new headmistress had taken her place. She had sunk without trace; no present had been given on her retirement, no portrait of her hung on the wall. It was as if those three or four years, Miss Armstrong's years, had never been.

When she was old enough to fully understand what Miss Armstrong had done to her, she understood more clearly the burden of guilt she must have carried. The frightful prayers before getting into bed became more explicable and she began to have pity for her. With pity came a strong need to forgive her, but beneath the need to forgive lay an even stronger need to be forgiven. She was certain that her breakdown, if breakdown it was, had been due to her, to her callous refusal to see her or even write. She experienced Miss Armstrong's guilt as if she herself had been the abuser, as if in forgiving her she could herself be redeemed. She wanted to show herself to her, unharmed, and to be able to

130

say, 'Look, you see, you gave me more than you took and I'm sorry I let you down, I'm sorry I couldn't love you as you loved me, I'm sorry I destroyed your life.' She did sometimes feel an executioner, a murderer, and she wanted absolution.

'You're being very quiet, Albertine. What are you thinking about?'

Max's question was asked more as a conversational gambit than because he wanted to know the answer. They were sitting on the balcony watching the sun go down, drinking rum and pineapple juice and recovering from the day's exertions in the city. Albertine had spent the whole day feeling as if the old woman on the boat had turned her to stone. She had not been able to think or speak and she moved as if by some mechanical device she was not consciously aware of.

Albertine had never told Max anything about the relationship; she had never told anyone. When, as custom dictated, she had flung her school hat, the grey mushroom-shaped, blue-ribboned insignia of her schooldays, out of the window of the train as it slid slowly into Liverpool Street station, she had thrown out everything that went with it. Not only the 'Latin and French, the hard school bench' but the unreality of the bedroom sessions, the dark and pervasive intensity of the whole relationship; she had thrown away the Albertine that had been and had stepped onto the platform determined to create a new Albertine. She had not realised then that people are like plants, that pruning creates new and healthy growth but pulling a growing thing up from its roots leaves the whole plant to die. She did not know that an unlanced boil spreads its infection silently and slowly throughout the whole body, its deadly influence poisoning the whole organism. She should have told.

'I think I saw my old headmistress on that boat.'

'You can't have done, she must have died years ago; didn't you say she retired when she was over seventy?'

'Not JPC, Miss Armstrong, who came after her. I've probably never mentioned her. I didn't like her very much,' said Albertine, trying to sound indifferent.

131

'How interesting,' he said, sounding bored. 'Are you going to try and see her?'

'I don't know. I might,' she answered, knowing that she would. 'What would you like for supper?' she added, in an attempt to change the conversation.

This obvious attempt to divert him paradoxically stirred his interest. 'Which one do you think she was? It can only have been the old woman sitting in the back, the one they were making such a fuss about. Why didn't you go and speak to her then? She looked more interesting than most of the people here.' What he really meant was that she looked English and therefore by definition more interesting.

'I could have done, I suppose. But it might not have been her, it just looked rather like her, that's all; it gave me rather a shock.'

'Well, she shouldn't be too difficult to track down, she's obviously very well-known.'

'I'm not sure I can be bothered; I don't know what we would talk about after all this time.'

'Well, you could fill her in with news of your friends; I should think she'd love to see you and talk about school. It can't be all that often that she sees any of her old pupils.'

Max was suddenly interested. He was increasingly bored by the quiet, uneventful days, and was missing not only England, but conversation that did not solely revolve round the small day-to-day happenings of the community that he did not feel part of. With not much to do, he was beginning to discover an interest in the country. Their visit to the mainland had stirred a curiosity about the early Mayan civilisation but he was also interested in the more recent past, whether colonisation had been good for the people or if some intrinsic sense of their own identity had been taken from them. The country seemed stable so he assumed that the British rule had not been too damaging. As far as he could tell, the democratic political system left by the British was still intact and worked well. He wanted to discuss what it was like when the country first became independent with someone who had been here then, who had seen it before and after, and to discuss why it had been such a peaceful transfer of power. If Miss Armstrong had lived here a long time she would know more about it than the Americans they had met, who had only been here a few years.

'We'll see,' she said, determined that if she met her, it would be alone; but anxious too, knowing that if Max wanted something he invariably had his way.

Had Miss Armstrong recognised her? she wondered later in bed. She had given no sign of having done so, but neither, Albertine thought, had she. She knew she must have changed far more than Miss Armstrong, and as soon as she was sure who it was she had turned her back on her; it was only when Miss A was engaged in the business of getting out of the boat that she had allowed herself a longer look. Miss A had seemed asleep during both parts of the journey and interacted only with the people she knew, paying scant attention to the tourists. But on the other hand she could be going through the same fluctuating indecision as Albertine. She could be deciding whether to try to find out where they were staying. At any moment a letter could be handed through their door and she would see again the strong slender writing; would she sign herself 'Gerda', 'Miss Armstrong' or, as before, simply 'G'.

She thought of those last letters she had had from her; letters she had found so painful to read she had eventually stopped opening them. She had never replied, and slowly they stopped coming; as if the blood from an open wound which flowed so freely at first had at last formed a clot and only occasionally, when knocked, had emitted a dark sticky seepage, an agonized plea for rescue. The last of these letters, which came long after she thought they had stopped, read simply, 'Please Darling, Please. Your Gerda'. Albertine had been ruthless, and it was for that ruthlessness – or had it been cowardice? – that she now wanted forgiveness. What reparation was possible after inflicting so much pain she had no idea. Perhaps Miss Armstrong could tell her that. With

133

these thoughts, and with a mixture of fear and anticipation for the morning, she went to sleep.

'I'm going into the village. There's not much to get, you needn't bother to come,' Albertine said brightly the next day as she washed up the plates from the night before. 'I only want some fish and I'll go to the post office to see if we have any mail.'

'Are you sure? I don't mind coming.'

'It's fine,' she said. 'Is there anything you want while I'm there?'

'No, I don't think so; you might get a bottle of whisky if it's not too difficult, and try and get another pineapple. I don't like that papaya, it tastes like sick.'

Albertine was not going to attempt to see Miss Armstrong today. She was going to find out where she lived, and as much about her life as possible. Where she lived should be easy; she would enquire at the post office; what she did or had done, what she was like, who her friends were, why she was there – all questions she wanted answered – would be more difficult. She was glad to find that Max's interest in her old headmistress had at least temporarily fallen into abeyance. He was already preparing himself for a pleasant morning's read in the hammock.

She was not aware that he was surprised by her sudden unexpected display of independence. Max had never been in the habit of considering what Albertine did with her days; he never asked her and did not expect her to enquire into his. If she had done so, he might have been forced to wonder if he could possibly spend his own time more usefully or if the slight feeling of ennui which was his constant companion might have something to do with the fact that he filled time rather than used it. He had to admit that his days were much the same as they ever were. He had substituted diving with Bill for shooting, he was reading books rather than *The Times* or *The Field* and he was sleeping in a hammock rather than in the chair in his study, which is what he mostly did when Albertine thought he was attending to his 'paperwork'. Seeing so much more of her through the day meant he was forced to wonder what sort of life they had that they could spend so much time doing so little and that it was hardly surprising that they had nothing to talk to each other about, making their marriage more of a burden than the mutually supportive structure he could recognise in other unions and which he had expected of his own. He was as much surprised by the sense of purpose she was displaying over this unnecessaary visit to San Pedro as he was by her independence. She was nervous of driving the boat and never did so unless he forced her to when he wanted to fish.

The post office of San Pedro was no more than a room five foot by eight, divided by a counter behind which sat Angel, a sallow-skinned, taciturn young man, surrounded by piles of parcels. He had a peculiar resistance, for one in his position, to handing out mail and insisted that no one should collect theirs more than twice a week. He had never been seen to smile and only very seldom, when correcting some customer for the sin of looking at 'his' parcels, to speak.

It was therefore with some trepidation, having asked for their mail, that Albertine said, 'I'm sure you must know a Miss Armstrong; do you know where she lives?'

'Why you want to know?' was Angel's unpromising reply.

'I think I saw her yesterday. She used to teach me years ago, in England, and I would like to visit her if she lives on the island.'

The transformation that came over Angel at the mention of Miss Armstrong was extraordinary. He put down his letters, usually clung to like a security blanket, and with a smile, so unfamiliar it seemed as if a rock had suddenly opened, he leant forward. Albertine thought for an alarming moment that he was going to hug her.

'You know Miss A? Miss A taught you? Miss A taught me.' His voice rose with excitement as he contemplated the coincidence.

135

Albertine found herself infected by his enthusiasm; she was beginning to feel, as he obviously did, that their close association with Miss A made them in some deeply spiritual way blood brothers.

'Miss A very wonderful lady . . . very wonderful. Where you living?'

To be addressed like this by Angel, to be suddenly visible, the mantle of foreigner removed, was a great honour.

'We're living at Tres Cocos,' she said.

This was almost too much for Angel. 'You living Tres Cocos! Miss A, she living just one mile Tres Cocos!'

He was ecstatic. The queue of hopeful letter collectors was building up behind Albertine as Angel drew a map, marking all the houses she would have to pass on her way to Miss A's house.

'You not miss it. On the beach, painted green; Miss A, she live there long time, very fine house. You tell her Angel send you.'

Albertine was increasingly embarrassed by the now angry mutterings behind her, of which Angel seemed oblivious. 'Thank you very much, you've been extremely helpful. I'm sure I'll find it.'

She could in fact remember the house well. It was unusual in that it had two storeys, and sometimes when she and Max had walked past it she had seen just the top of a straw hat through the dark mosquito screen and above the boarding of the balcony, and they had wondered who lived there. It was certainly painted green but it must have been many years since it had last had a new coat. The paint was peeling and faded, the steps up to the balcony were uneven and in parts rotten. It had probably once been the 'very fine house' of Angel's description, but it now appeared to be almost derelict. She had thought it was owned by a Belizian family. There were usually a large number of smiling, laughing children gathered round the dock, fishing, swimming or just standing. Albertine had, in her imagination, created a picture of a fat motherly figure standing permanently in a dark kitchen stirring enormous pots of rice and refried beans for this her large family; the straw-hatted figure on the balcony, whose face she never saw, she imagined to be the grandmother or grandfather sleeping the sleep of fulfilled old age, surrounded and honoured by his or her many descendants. Now she realised that those children must be a new generation of Miss A's acolytes, who in years to come would talk of the Englishwoman with warmth and affection and admiration. Angel had said that she had taught him. Taught him what, she wondered. Surely not Pascal, not Montaigne; she could hardly imagine him and his friends sitting round the dock or on her balcony translating Racine and discussing with juvenile passion the forbidden love of Phèdre for her stepson Hippolyte. But perhaps they did. She realised she was being astonishingly racist in assuming that because they had dark skins they would not be infected by Miss Armstrong's enthusiasm, as she had been, as so many were; that dark skins were immune to the contagion of charm or unable to respond, as they had, to her and her stimulating method of teaching.

Leaving the post office, she decided to go to Fido's. It was here, in a thatch-covered square, that many of the inhabitants of Ambergris Caye would meet for a drink or lunch after their business in the town. If she waited long enough she felt sure that someone would arrive who would know Miss Armstrong. She and Max had by now made quite a few friends among the locals and she knew it would not be too difficult to discover someone who knew her well. She sat at a table in the centre of the square and ordered a beer rather than the rum punch which she had grown to enjoy. She wanted to be sure of remaining clear-headed if she had to wait for a long time and as she had still not decided what she was going to do with the information once she had it, she wanted any enquiry about Miss A to sound as casual as possible. She did not want Miss Armstrong to know that she was asking about her and certainly not that she was on her tail.

It was nearing 12 o'clock. The tables were filling up with tourists, bare-chested youths in bright shorts with bum belts cutting weals into their burnt red skin, and bored-looking girls in Guatemalan cotton and tee shirts emblazoned with messages of hope or decorated with colourful depictions of local scenes. The noise was becoming deafening and Albertine was beginning to lose hope of any permanent residents entering what was fast becoming a mixture of a McDonald's hamburger joint and a London pub at lunchtime.

She was on the point of leaving when a couple she had met only once stopped at her table and asked whether she would mind if they joined her.

'We've met before, haven't we? Tony, and my wife Melissa. You're Albertine, is that right?' Tony held out his hand.

'How clever of you to remember,' she answered.

'I see you're drinking beer. Will you have another? Melissa, for you?' Melissa sat down while Tony fetched beers for all three. 'This place is becoming a nightmare, bloody tourists everywhere you go,' he said as his arm was jogged by a drunken-looking backpacker.

Albertine was delighted he apparently did not consider her a tourist. She did not feel a tourist but she often reflected on the fact that tourists, like capitalists or 'bloody' drivers, were always other people.

'Is it always like this as this time of year?' she asked.

'The trouble is that Belize has been discovered by the backpackers. They "do" Mexico and stop on the Cayes for a bit of diving before taking on Guatemala. Every year it gets worse.'

Albertine, who had very definitely wanted to see a bit of Guatemala herself before they left, gave a sigh indicating her total identification with the resident against the itinerant visitor, and made an instant decision to cancel the arrangement they had made to visit Tikal the following month.

'How long are you here for?' Melissa asked.

'We're not absolutely sure – about two more months, I think,' she answered, further distancing herself from the tourist who would have a fixed date on his return ticket. 'How long have you been here?'

They both laughed and Tony answered, 'We came for six

months about three years ago. We were at a bit of a loose end, a crossroads I suppose you could say. The kids were off our hands and we wanted a change. We fell in love with the place, and by chance the man who owned the *San Pedro Sun* had just been gaoled for murdering his mistress. We'd both been in journalism so we jumped at the opportunity to buy it. I think it would be difficult to live here with nothing to do; too easy to slip into the booze trap – I've seen it happen only too often. So we think we're very lucky, doing what we enjoy in a wonderful environment. Who could ask for more?'

'How interesting, and what fun . . .' Albertine felt sick with excitement and apprehension. She could not have possibly found a more suitable person to ask and was surprised that she had not thought of going to the newspaper office herself. The paper was full of local gossip; she might already have read something about Miss A and thought nothing about it.

'Shall we have something to eat?' she suggested, determined not to let her quarry escape.

'What an excellent idea. What would you like? Shall we share a pizza?'

Tony took charge and very soon they were presented with a pizza almost as large as the table.

'When we went to Belize City yesterday I saw a fascinating old woman on the boat. She seemed a great character; Miss A, they all called her; do you know who she is?'

'Good God, yes; everyone knows Gerda. I'm surprised you haven't come across her already – she doesn't live far from Tres Cocos.'

So it really was her. Even as she set off to the village, even when Angel said she was a teacher, she had not been absolutely certain that her eyes had not deceived her, that perhaps a vague similarity had worked on her imagination and triggered her memory. The name she had never been able to say herself, Gerda, used so easily by these strangers, made her real. She felt cold and hot at the same time and could not tell if it was excitement or fear which was draining strength from her limbs. She wondered how her voice would sound coming from her strangulated throat.

'I assume she's English,' she said, hoping that Tony and Melissa would think it was her nationality that had attracted her interest. She had been surprised at how few English there seemed to be in a country which had so recently been a colony. With the odd exception, all the foreigners they had met were American.

'Oh yes,' said Tony. 'As English as they come. She's lived here for years. She's eighty-five, you know. Amazing, isn't she?'

'Do you know what brought her here?'

'I don't, but you do, don't you, Mel?' answered Tony. 'Didn't Peggy fill you in when you were going to write an article about her?'

'Yes, I know a bit about her,' replied Melissa. 'Apparently she had a sort of breakdown, years and years ago, and came to stay with her brother in the city. He was something in the Colonial Service, I don't know what. She'd been a teacher, or even a headmistress I think, in England. Anyway, she stayed with this brother till he was posted back to England, and then she came here. She built that house she lives in now. In those days it was the only house up there north of the river; it must have been very lonely. After a bit a friend of hers from England, Maud she was called, came to live with her. Maud went senile apparently, a year or two before we came, so we never actually met her, but the stories about her wandering naked all over the island and marching into the school in full academic regalia, behaving as if she was the principal, were still rife when we arrived. In the end Gerda simply couldn't cope and she's in a sort of home somewhere in the city now. Gerda still visits her once a month, which is jolly good of her considering her age and that Maud never recognises her. That's probably where she was going when you saw her.'

'They were an amazing couple by all accounts,' Tony continued. 'Of course there were the usual stories about them being lesbians, but you always get that when women

140

live together; I never believed it myself, not that I think it matters if they were; they did an awful lot for the island, especially Gerda.'

'What sort of things?' Albertine asked.

'Well, the library, for one. Have you been into it? It's not much, I suppose, by American or British standards, but for San Pedro it's amazing. That was all Gerda's work. She got hold of the building – I suspect she put some of her own money into it. She bombarded the British Council for funds and she set up a trust called Friends of the San Pedro Library, to which nearly everyone on the island contributes. She chose all the books, and if you go there you'll find it's astonishingly comprehensive. Until fairly recently she spent a lot of time there herself, and she trained the girl who works there now. Incidentally, she's Angel's sister – you know, from the post office. An interesting family that. There are seven of them. They've all done remarkably well; mostly due to Gerda, who sort of took them up. Two of them went to university in the States.'

'She's wonderful with the young,' Melissa added. 'They all adore her. I think she used to teach a bit in the school when she first came here, but it was outside school hours that she did the most. She would have them up to her house, talk to them, tell them stories, educate them, I suppose you could say. There are so many people in San Pedro who stayed on at school entirely because of Gerda. I suspect, though I don't know this as a fact, that she paid for some of them. Even now she always has a troupe of children round her, and talk to anyone under the age of forty and they will have stories about Miss A.'

So she could still weave her magic, Albertine thought. She was suddenly overwhelmed by nostalgia. She knew what Miss Armstrong had given these people because she had given it to her. She had not 'taught' them French literature, as she had so naively thought only a few moments before; she had given them an enquiring mind. Albertine wanted to weep for the years she had wasted, for the years she had ceased to enquire, for the years that were lost to anxiety and boredom.

141

The years she had lost to the locust had not been spent in dissipation. Albertine knew that for her the locusts had been the opposite, they had descended on her and destroyed her spirit of search.

'When she was on the boat, you would have thought by the way people behaved that she was the queen or something.'

'She is, in a way, to the people here; they still feel very proud of their connection with Britain and I suspect that the Pedranis, if they were asked who they thought the Queen was like would immediately say Miss A. You should try and meet her,' said Melissa. 'She's quite something.'

'I'll try and do that. Look, I must go now, Max will be wondering what on earth has happened to me.' She felt she could not stand any more. 'How much do I owe you, Tony?'

'That's OK, have it on me. It's been good talking to you; we must all get together sometime.'

'Thanks a lot, that would be great. Bye now.' And Albertine left. She had found out what she wanted to know and in a daze she walked the sandy street to the boat, forgetting both the fish and the whisky.

'Where on earth have you been?' Max was furious.

'I'm sorry, I got caught up with Tony and Melissa – you remember them? They own and produce the *San Pedro Sun*.'

'I don't bloody well care what they do. I didn't know where you were . . . I haven't had lunch . . . I didn't know if you had crashed the boat . . . I thought you said you weren't going to be long . . . Do you know what bloody time it is?'

'Calm down, Max, for heaven's sake. I said I'm sorry. Why didn't you get yourself some lunch?' Albertine tried to sound reasonable but Max was clearly beyond the reach of reason.

'If I'd known how long you were going to be I'd have come with you. What on earth were you doing?'

'I've told you; I met Tony and Melissa and they asked me to have some lunch with them.'

'I was waiting for you. How would you like it if I went into

142

San Pedro and didn't come back for hours? I was worried about you.'

She knew very well he was nothing of the sort. He was bored and wanted lunch. Trying to remain calm, she refrained from reminding him that he very frequently went into San Pedro on his own and very frequently stayed there all day. She got some lettuce and cheese from the fridge and set them on the table.

'Is that all there is? That's great,' he said. 'What did you have? Chicken, I suppose, or perhaps lobster. Thanks a lot. Anyway, where's the bloody whisky? If there's nothing to eat I may as well get drunk.'

'Oh God! I'm sorry, I forgot to get it.' She remembered then that she had forgotten the fish too.

Max looked at her in amazement. 'I don't understand you, I simply don't understand you . . . I'm going for a walk.' And he strode out of the house.

'What about your lunch?' Albertine cried after him.

'I don't want any lunch!'

In fact, he had already helped himself from the fridge, but he wanted her to feel guilty at neglecting him.

It was a relief to have him out of the house. Feeling drained by his petulant anger and by the revelation that Miss Armstrong was only one mile away, Albertine lay on the bed and fed a tape into her machine. *Libera me, Domine, . . .* Fauré's haunting prayer exactly expressed her need. But freed from what, she wondered; freed from an ache which pressed on her, that weighed her down, that had always weighed her down and which she had spent nearly 40 years trying to ignore.

13

It had been easy when there was no possibility of it happening to think that she wanted to see her again. Now that it was not just a possibility but almost inevitable, Albertine did not know whether she wanted it or not. It did occur to her that she could do nothing. They had been here for more than a month without bumping directly into her, and Miss Armstrong obviously did not go out much. They could take definite steps to avoid her; they could stop their walks past her house, although she would have difficulty explaining to Max why she did not want to go up the shore any more, and they could, if they were invited somewhere, ask who else would be there, although it would sound a bit strange to do so. She knew in her heart that however much she thought of avoiding her, they would meet. How the meeting would occur and what she would say to her when they met she did not know, but meet they would. She wanted to see her again, needed to see her again, but *why* was the question that was tormenting her.

She had wanted to forgive her – or had thought she wanted to forgive her – to release her from the pain of guilt which Albertine was sure she must still feel, and to receive forgiveness for her betrayal; but was that really the whole truth? *Libera me, Domine.* Was it, in fact, not her own guilt, not her own betrayal that she wanted to be freed from, but rage? She was beginning to remember the nights of helplessness in Miss Armstrong's bed . . . Was it possibly not that she wanted to forgive her or to be forgiven, but rather to destroy her finally – not to offer thanks for what she had done for

144

her mind but violence for what she had done to her body, not to offer forgiveness but to mete out revenge? Was she angry that Miss Armstrong had gone on with her life, had made a new beginning, was free, whilst Albertine was still shackled to a past she had not been able to speak of to anyone?

She let her mind roam back to the nights she had negotiated the broom cupboard, cold, in thin pyjamas, her arms aching from the strain of hauling herself up over the balcony; back to the hypocrisy of the terrible prayers, to the indecency of her penetrative fingering, her probing tongue, her emotional demands. Those were the facts she remembered, but she also remembered the dark confusion, the secrecy, the shame. She remembered the awful feeling of powerlessness, the sensation of being trapped in a place she did not understand, caught in a country where the laws she was familiar with no longer applied, where the language spoken was not hers, where friends were enemies and enemies friends, a nightmare country from which escape was impossible. She was right to be angry. Her adult self knew that, her adult self could look back and see that she had been a victim and her adult self felt that victimisers should be punished, her adult self also admitted that if she had been a victim it was unlikely that she had been unharmed; victims suffered, and where else but in Miss Armstrong's bed had she learnt her uncertainty, her doubts about her self-worth and her confusion about where she 'fitted in'? Where else but in that bed, where she had been mesmerised like a mouse before a stoat or like a cobra dancing and weaving to the tune of the snake charmer?

But yet . . . *Libera me.* Did she dare examine her feelings when she heard about Angel's sister? Was there just a frisson of something like jealousy, or was it something more? The thought that perhaps she had not been the only one but just one among many was intolerable; but why, if the relationship had meant nothing to her, should she mind if there had been others? If she had not been important in Miss Armstrong's life then she had not had any power over her when she abandoned her, after all. All these years she had derived a small but secret satisfaction from the thought that her refusal to see her or write to her was punishing her, hopefully for ever. Had that not been true? Had Miss Armstrong immediately, once the crisis had passed, taken others into her bed, into her heart? And although the sexual part of the relationship had been disgusting, had she really enjoyed what was her first experience of being loved and was she afraid to discover that it had not been love after all, but a distraction for Miss Armstrong, that she had been replaced immediately, that Miss Armstrong's breakdown had been nothing to do with her and that she had felt guilty all these years for no reason? What had she really felt all those years ago? Was it her main fear that when she walked up those rickety stairs and stood face to face with Miss Armstrong, that she would not even remember who Albertine was?

The more Albertine battled with her thoughts the less she understood them. The story she had rehearsed, though only in her mind, had become crystallised in a form she could accept, a form which if known by the world would portray her as the victim – but was she? Perhaps all along she had been the seducer, perhaps she had deliberately and brutally manipulated Miss Armstrong's emotions to gain an easier and more pleasant life for herself, a more exciting year than was on offer in the sterile and institutionalised routine of boarding school. She was swept again by terrifying confusion. She felt her identity disappearing down a cavernous hole, into a well of dark glue; submerged in stifling stickiness, she was nearly paralysed, nearly silenced.

She often had dreams like this. Dreams in which she was no more than an amoebic blob of matter, armless and legless, with a tiny raised head like cartoon drawings of an octopus, with large eyes which saw only the feet of the giants around her that would trample her, so small and so powerless, so nearly completely invisible. Dreams in which she saw her body floating, drowning down a fast river, and from the bank she watched and knew she was just a piece of flotsam

146

not worth rescuing. She was not dreaming now, and she was going to fight, who or what she did not know, but she was not going to drown.

She did not want to be in the house when Max returned. She knew from experience that he would still be angry and she knew that he would continue to sulk until she offered him some placatory gesture. Her head was too full of Miss Armstrong to be able to enter their marital game, in which it was always she who in the end submitted. She hated the smug look on his face when he contemplated his victory, but it was easier. One day, she thought, I will not let him get away with it; but not today. Today she would avoid confrontation completely until she had at least satisfied one obsession. She would go and see Angel's sister, and test her feelings if, as she suspected, she too had been one of Miss Armstrong's lovers.

She found the library easily and was surprised that she had not noticed it before. It was an old building, wooden like all the old houses, sturdily built against the ferocious winds which battered the island in November and December. Hanging between the pillars supporting the balcony was a freshly painted sign, *Public Library*. Albertine went in.

The contrast between the street, bright with sunlight and vitality, and the calm stillness of the book-lined room gave Albertine her first true appreciation of Miss Armstrong's achievement. Through the small windows all that was visible was the sea; muted shafts of light striped the polished boards and in two of the three armchairs long-legged, dark-skinned teenagers sat deeply absorbed in their reading. The room was so like the library at Hartwell, which too had been an oasis of tranquillity in a frenetic world, she immediately felt at peace.

The librarian's table was set between two protruding sets of shelves. The woman seated behind it, reading herself, was about 30; she had the pale brown skin always referred to as olive, though why this should be so since olives are green or black was a mystery to Albertine. Angel's sister seemed

147

gentle and serious. Her long thin fingers played with a small gold cross at her throat and she was dressed all in black. She was more like a nun than a siren and Albertine knew at once that her desire to see her had been merely a whim, acted on solely to delay meeting Miss Armstrong. She was immediately more interested in the books themselves than in their guardian.

She went first to the French section and was not surprised to find all Miss Armstrong's old favourites, many of which she saw bore the letters *G.A.* on the title page. The English literature section was equally well endowed and most of these had the initials *M.S.* So this, thought Albertine, was where Maud's collection of books had found their last resting place. There were many inscribed *M. from G. with love*, just as so many of Albertine's had *A. from G.* She noticed with amusement that many were the same: *Harold's Leap* by Stevie Smith, George Moore's *Heloïse and Abelard* and Traherne's *Centuries of Meditation*. She wondered briefly if Angel's sister had the same books in her collection. She passed over the history section quickly, noting that the histories of the various conquests of Central and South America were well covered; Prescott on Peru, the letters of Cortez to the King of Spain and many others that she had not heard of. She would have to tell Max to come here if he wanted to know more about the country. She passed on to fiction. Here were all the English classics – Dickens, Thackeray, Jane Austen, the Brontës – and she found to her delight the Victorian novels, the actual books which they had all been made to read as relaxation in the final two weeks before the Oxford exam, when all their serious reading, all their notes, all their essays had been removed so they could approach their test with clear minds. Here was *Eric, or Little by Little, The Heir of Radclyffe, Little Lord Fauntleroy*. . . She was fascinated by the idea of the children she had seen playing in the sand round Miss Armstrong's house being exposed to just such an education as she. That they responded with the same enthusiasm was clear from the respect in which she was held but she wondered what possible connection they could make with their lives from such reading. She took *Eric, or Little by Little* from the shelf and advanced towards Angel's sister.

'I'm not a permanent resident, but I wonder if it's possible to have temporary membership?'

Angel's sister looked up from her book. 'Yes, ma'am. What is your name and where are you staying?'

'My name is Albertine Stevens and I'm staying at Tres Cocos.'

Angel's sister took a card from a tin box on the table and filled it in in neat copperplate.

'I gather all this' – Albertine swept her arm round the room – 'is Miss Armstrong's creation. I used to know her, in fact she taught me when I was young ... Are you Angel's sister? I've heard that he has a sister who works here.'

Her response was not as exuberant as Angel's had been but she paused in her writing and looked at her with interest.

'Miss Armstrong taught you in England?'

'Yes, a long time ago.'

'Miss Maud, she taught you too?'

'No, but I did know her. Did she teach you?'

'Not in school, but Miss A and Miss Maud, they both teach many things many people. Miss A, she very special lady.' Her eyes betrayed nothing but admiration. 'You go see Miss A?'

'I hope so, yes.'

She could not think of anything further to say. She took her book and left, nodding briefly to the two youths in the chairs who had interrupted their reading to listen to her conversation.

The brief respite from anxiety that she had experienced in the library was past. It had been a meaningless and fruitless journey. Angel's sister was obviously an irrelevance as far as meeting Miss Armstrong was concerned and all she had achieved by her visit was a further inevitable stoking of Max's anger, an opportunity to get the fish and whisky, and the lovely discovery of *Eric, or Little by Little*.

After buying two large kingfish steaks from a man cutting the freshly caught fish on the beach and, to make up for her stupidity in forgetting it the first time, two bottles of whisky, she went to Fido's bar to read and to postpone for a little longer the moment she would have to see Max again.

While drinking a rum punch she suddenly remembered a scandal which had erupted just before they left England, concerning the famous abbot of a well-known monastery. He was especially famous for his piety, and it was even suggested by his admirers, who were numerous, that sanctity would be a more accurate description of his closeness to God. He had been arrested for making sexual advances towards a 17-year-old novice, presumably in his charge, although this had not been stated. People who knew him, and Albertine knew some of them from the days when she had been given to piety herself, did not believe it; many others, those who had seen him on television and been captivated by his undoubtably charming smile and gentle voice, expressed shock but no great surprise. The general view was that if he had done it, the boy must have led him on, that a man in his position would not be so out of control of himself as to make an unwanted advance. Wrapped snugly in his fame, the abbot was seen as the victim of a spiteful and vindictive youth whose own advances to the abbot had been spurned and who had therefore gone to the police in a spirit of revenge. It was also being said that no doubt the boy was going to make a lot of money from selling his story to the press.

Albertine, when reading about it at the time, had surprisingly made no direct connection with her own relationship with Miss Armstrong. After his fall, she knew she was sorry for him. To be so public a figure and to experience such a very public humiliation was a terrible punishment for what might or might not have taken place. He had been temporarily relieved of all his duties, and was awaiting the result of further enquiries as to his guilt or innocence. How it was possible to test that Albertine could not see; it could only ever be one word against the other. Although the power of the abbot was probably in his favour, what was certain was that the abbot's career as saint or wise man was over. Always, for the rest of his life, would hang the question 'Did he?'

150

'Did he what?' was also a question that had interested Albertine. The papers had just mentioned sexual advances. Perhaps he had only put his arm round the boy, as a form of comfort or encouragement, and the fevered or sex-starved imagination of the adolescent had leapt to a conclusion, which if the abbot had been a revered mentor, an admired symbol of everything that was pure, would have seemed the grossest and most disgusting betrayal of a precious relation-ship and a hallowed ideal. Or perhaps he had had to go to the abbot's bed night after night until finally he had snapped. No one would probably ever know what really happened but Albertine knew that in this particular case there could be no winners. The novice would almost certainly feel betrayed in his vocation, the abbot might even yet commit suicide.

Now, sitting drinking alone in the bar, the picture of the aged Miss Armstrong vivid in her mind, she thought what would have happened if she, like the novice, had gone to the police. However, it was not an option she had considered at the time. Although she had thought that Miss Armstrong's carrying on had been strange and unpleasant, she had not known it was criminal. She was not even sure now.

She tried to imagine herself in the position of the novice. At house order, when they had to say what they were doing in the afternoon, she would have said, 'Go to Cromer, please.' She imagined herself bicycling the four miles, trying to form the sentence she would eventually have to repeat to the police. She would not be able, like the novice, to say, 'She made a sexual advance.' The papers then, unlike now, were not full of sexual advances, rapes or interferences. She would have to say something like, 'Miss Armstrong, my headmistress, makes me go to her bed every night and then she does things to me.' She found that she was blushing even at the thought of the imagined conversation. She could see the policeman, a mixture of Trevor Howard as Scobie – and their local policeman.

'Yes, miss, and what exactly does Miss Armstrong do?' He would be writing it all down in a large blue-lined exercise book.

'How many times do you say this has happened?'

'Why, in that case, have you only now decided to come with this very serious complaint?'

She would be stuttering, blushing, forgetting some details, repeating others. The Scobie character would be looking over gold half-rimmed glasses, while she back-tracked furiously, even denying what she had said, intimidated by his penetrating gaze.

'Well . . . perhaps it was only just once or twice.'

'Don't you think you are possibly just making the whole thing up?' he would suggest and she could imagine Scobie saying to one of his colleagues, after she had left, probably in tears, 'Who would have anything to do with adolescent girls, eh? I've just had a right one raving on about Miss Armstrong – you know, the Head of Hartwell School – screwing her every night for the last six months . . . Unbelievable, isn't it? Still, a complaint has been made and we'll have to investigate it. I don't fancy the job, but I'd better go myself, I suppose.'

A police car would have driven up to the school. 'One of your girls has made a complaint,' he would have said to Miss Armstrong. 'Of course I know there is nothing to it, but we have to follow it up, I'm afraid. I'm sorry to trouble you, but could you come to the police station – only to make a statement, you understand.' Miss Armstrong would have been calm, confident and extremely rational, knowing that no one would believe Albertine's story. She would just have to say that it was 'of course absolute nonsense' and 'you know what girls are like . . . Yes, she has a history of histrionic behaviour and she is working very hard at the moment, which might have something to do with it'. After such an interrogation would Miss Armstrong, like the abbot, have been suspended by the Governors from further duties, pending an enquiry?

What were the feelings of the novice at this very moment? Albertine wondered. Was he glad that he had publicly denounced a celebrated figure? Was he running alongside the tumbril cheering or was he frightened and ashamed of what he had done? Was he doubting the facts he had reported, or perhaps thinking that he had made the most terrible fuss about nothing, that perhaps it was normal, even desirable, that a teacher's feelings should sometimes spill over the boundary between affection and love, and from love to sexual arousal? He might even be thinking that it had been in a way an honour . . . Had this really been why she had never told, rather than because it would be too embarrassing? Should she have been proud to have been chosen?

In addition to being suspended, what would have happened to Miss Armstrong, in the unlikely event of Albertine being believed? She would perhaps have been arrested, and tried. Albertine would have had to give evidence and not only suffer the excruciating embarrassment but also see the agonised look of '*et tu, Brute*' in Miss Armstrong's eyes. She would perhaps have been sent to prison.

As it was, retribution had not come from the public but from her own demons. Albertine did not know yet – and it was perhaps what she wanted to discover – if the demons had been guilt and shame or jealousy and despair. Miss Armstrong had undoubtably been her own executioner and Albertine had escaped, wiser, in many ways, from the experience and certainly unharmed; or had she?

She realised that she was glad that she had not gone to the police as the novice had done, but she did not blame him. Had she had more courage or more knowledge she might have done the same.

She wished she had not taken the boat; she only very rarely drove it and now the wind had got up and the sea was very choppy. Within minutes she was drenched with spray; sharp needles of pain struck her face. It was getting dark. She was afraid that she would not be able to find the channel through the banks of sand and eelgrass to the dock. They never went out in the boat at night for this reason. The channel was only three feet wide and was difficult enough to find in daylight; at night they found it impossible and always took a water taxi if they did go anywhere. She was already blinded by the wind and water and the night was falling very fast. The pelicans flying dark and low were mere shapes and on the shore the lights were appearing one by one between the tall black palms silhouetted against the darkening sky. Other boats passed her, with more powerful engines, with more confident drivers. There was a fraternity among the boat people; in less hostile conditions they would wave to each other in passing, but tonight the drivers were crouched low in the stern, heads huddled against the driving spray.

Albertine was afraid. She was afraid that the engine would fail and that she would be driven onto the coral. She had no oars with which to fend herself off the treacherous branches or to propel herself home over the sand. She was afraid that, now numb with cold, she would be unable to control the boat; she was afraid, not of seeing Max, but of not seeing him. All her anger had disappeared and she found herself whimpering in the gale for his presence. She had been a fool and she did not care what he said to her if only he would be there.

The three tall palms of Tres Cocos, after which it was named, came into sight. She could see the lights from her house, from Albert and Elma's house, further up the shore from Bill and Ellen's house, and standing at the end of the dock was a figure waving a torch. She knew it was Max and relief washed through her body as forcefully as had the fear only moments before. Whatever happened now, she knew she would be safe.

She turned the boat towards the shore opposite the weak light from the flickering torch. She could hear that Max was shouting something but not the words, and he was waving his arms. As the boat ground into the sand she realised she had come in too much to the left. The channel was far right of the dock, but she was close enough now to wade. Lifting the outboard from the water, she slid over the side and started to pull the boat after her. She stumbled many times; floundering in the sea, which was still strong, she was

154

rammed and battered by the boat as it was swept forward on a new oncoming wave.

Max suddenly appeared beside her. She had been so intent on trying to stay upright she had not seen him come.

'Don't worry, darling. You get behind and push and I'll pull . . . we're nearly there.'

Together they worked and inch by inch and foot by foot they reached the dock. In silence Max made the boat fast and in silence she stepped onto the firm platform.

'You idiot,' he said. 'Why did you do it?' Although the words were strict his voice was gentle.

'It got dark so quickly,' she said, and burst into tears.

Back in the warmth of the familiar room Albertine shuddered. 'I'm sorry, I should never have gone.'

'No, it's my fault for walking out like that, it was stupid of me.'

'No, no, I shouldn't have stayed so long, you were quite right to be cross with me.'

'Anyway, it doesn't matter, you're back . . . Go and have a shower – you must be freezing.'

'So must you, you're just as wet as me.'

They showered together, taking turns to direct the jet of water on each other until the whole floor of the bathroom was awash.

'What were you doing going back anyway?' Max asked, once they were dry and sitting comfortably with warm drinks in their hands. Their unusual intimacy was shattered and, once again bound and separated by her secret, Albertine replied, 'I went back for the fish and your whisky. Stupid, wasn't it? Oh my God, after all that I left them in the boat.'

'Don't worry,' Max said, 'I'll get them.'

14

Albertine was unhappy about sneaking off again without telling Max where she was going. He had been unusually tender the night before. For the first time for many years she had lain in his arms when they eventually went to bed. He had not said much but she had felt that he was wanting to reach out to her in some way. She did not understand why he should have changed so suddenly. She had lain there unresponsively, certainly feeling protected from the storm, but knowing that whatever it was that Max wanted she could not give him. She was in the grip of an obsession and had no feelings or thoughts other than those that centred round Miss A.

'I'm just going for a walk,' she shouted to Max, who was in the bathroom. 'I won't be long,' she added without conviction.

She did not know and perhaps at the moment could not have even cared, that Max had been almost unbearably moved by the sight of her battling with the sea. When she was safe he wanted more than anything to tell her that he loved her but the words would not come. She had seemed so brave despite her tears, that for the first time that he could remember he felt the weak one. There had been something magnificent about her battle with the sea, about her determination, that he knew he could not match. He had helped her, but she would have done it on her own.

He did not hear her leave. When he had finished showering he was expecting that they would have breakfast together, that she would have heard the words he had not been able to utter and would want to be with him. When he discovered that she had gone without saying anything at all to him, instead of his usual anger he felt alone in a way he could not remember feeling since he had been left at his prep school at the age of eight. He sat on the balcony eating the sickly papaya, not even resenting the fact that she had forgotten to buy a pineapple or even wondering where she had gone.

The narrow path between the seashore and the impenetrable bush was strewn with rubbish. The road into Jerusalem after Palm Sunday must have looked like this, she thought. On top of the dead brown palms, like mighty ash leaves and soft under her bare feet, lay dried orange skins, broken sandals, coconut shells and, as a sign of the times, plastic bottles and empty cans. A further and more deadly sign of the times, small sealed plastic bags were drifting gently on the edge of the lapping tide. She had seen bags like these many times on the television screen, the commentator proclaiming 'the biggest drug haul ever'. The ones she saw now were logged with sand and water, their murderous contents washed away by the action of the sea. She wondered idly how many heroin-addicted eels there were dozing their life away in the dark caverns of the coral reef or if the frenetic darting of the angel fish was governed not so much by fishy *joie de vivre* but by the intoxicating excitement of their cocaine-mad brains.

As always after a storm, the sky was clear and the sea like glass. All along the shore the slaty-blue-legged and pale-beaked herons stood in the shallow waters. Like statues they stood peering into the drifting grass at their feet until, spying an unwary eel, their heads would dart in and out so fast it was impossible to follow the speed of their flashing beaks. Human beings are so slow, so lumbering, she thought, as her legs became heavier with every step she took towards Miss Armstrong's house.

She knew it was beyond the next bend and she paused in an attempt to gather her thoughts, which had become like a tangled skein of wool, the many knots concealing both the beginning and the end. If only she could find that one free strand, she felt she would be able to start the untangling process. She had a sudden vivid picture of herself and Miss Armstrong together untying the knots and of herself peacefully winding the thread into a neat ball from the skein held between Miss Armstrong's fragile hands. What the knots were, what she wanted to know, what she wanted to say to her – this was the elusive end she wished to discover; from this the rest would follow.

She walked round the corner and confronted the green house. For once it was not surrounded by children; standing slightly crooked, it was alone and silent. An odd bedraggled chicken was pecking its way through the debris thrown up by the night's storm. Very slowly, her hand on the rickety rail, she climbed the rotting stairs.

She tapped on the wooden frame of the mosquito-screened balcony door, which, being unlatched, swung slightly as she knocked. There was no answer. She waited in the doorway and knocked again on the solid wall of the house. The balcony itself was cram-full of furniture: mennonite chairs in varied states of disrepair and all bleached to a silvery grey from the salt and the sun; a large table, covered with overflowing bowls of bits and pieces – string, pencils, rotting fruit, burnt-out candle ends; on the ledge running round the sides of the balcony were flowerpots full of strange spiky leaves, none of which she could recognise, most of which were brown at the edges, dusty and uncared for. There were piles of yellowing newspapers stacked in the corners and, incongruously, three brightly coloured balls and an old tennis racquet, its head warped into a near semicircle. She knocked again, this time on the door leading into the house itself.

'Who's there? Come in!'

It was the voice of someone woken from sleep, but it was undoubtedly her voice, deep and rasping from 60 years of 40 cigarettes a day. Albertine pushed open the door.

'Miss Armstrong?'

The room was so dark it was almost impossible to see the shrunken figure in a low armchair.

'Who is it?' She had turned and was peering through the gloom, shading her eyes against the light flooding through the open doorway. Though Albertine had recognised Miss Armstrong's voice it was obvious that Miss Armstrong had not recognised hers. Why should she? Thirty years was a long time and Albertine had been prepared, Albertine knew it was her.

'Miss Armstrong, it's me, Albertine . . . Albertine Williams that was . . .'

There was a silence, a long, palpable silence. Whether it was due to shock or lack of recognition Albertine could not tell, but she wished she had not come. She had been mad to come. It was all too long ago and if Miss Armstrong had really forgotten her, how could she say to this frail old woman, you must remember me, you were my lover, I betrayed you.

'Albertine.' Her voice was almost fearful. 'You are Albertine . . .'

'Can I come in?' Albertine said, moving forwards.

'Where have you come from?' It was as if she was speaking to a ghost, and Albertine felt as insubstantial as if she had indeed been created from a fragment of Miss Armstrong's mind. She felt enveloped by a swirling mist, magnified like Hamlet's father by 'airs from heaven or blasts from hell'; she and Miss Armstrong seemed like actors in someone else's dream. Unreality enclosed her; the shock of seeing her so close and so familiar yet so different trapped her securely in the past, but a past at the same time haunted by a present equally unfamiliar.

'We, that is Max, my husband, and I are staying at Tres Cocos. I thought I saw you on the Banana Boat the other day . . . I wanted to see you again.'

She was trying to sound normal, as if this was an ordinary visit to someone she had not seen for a long time, but the words came out stumbling and hesitant.

'I asked Angel where you were living. When I told him I'd

known you he said I was to say he sent me to you . . . I went to the library as well. I discovered it was your creation . . . It is amazing. You've obviously done a terrific amount for San Pedro – everyone I've met says so – I felt very at home in the library.'

She was talking very fast now, still standing close to the door. Miss Armstrong was still sitting in her chair.

'You've hardly changed at all,' Albertine continued, which was not quite true; she was smaller, softer too. She was obviously at this moment paralysed by shock. Albertine smelt fear in the air too but did not know if it was Miss Armstrong's or her own.

'I'm sorry, I'm not being very hospitable,' Miss Armstrong said, suddenly roused. 'Would you like a cup of coffee or something? It's a bit early for anything stronger. It's such a surprise to see you.' She started to struggle from her chair.

'Don't move, I'll do it. Would you like some?'

'Thank you, you'll find everything by the sink.'

It was easier to talk to her with her back turned. As Albertine filled the kettle and lit the gas ring she could feel the tension in the room diminish.

'You've got a wonderful house. How long have you lived in it?' Her tone was now bright and conversational.

'Thirty-odd years, I suppose.'

'Do you still have milk?' Albertine asked.

'Yes, and two sugars, please.'

She carried the mugs to the table and sat down. The room was not only dark but small. Apart from the large table, which was covered in a thick velvety-green cloth fringed round the edge, and the one armchair, in which Miss Armstrong was sitting, the only other furniture was four upright chairs round the table and one or two small tables which were crammed with photographs and candlesticks. In the centre of the large table stood a paraffin lamp and on all the walls sconces of rather rusty metal, bearing burnt-out candles. The wall furthest from the door was totally shelved with books and in one corner stood a small Davenport, overflowing with papers, which Albertine thought she recognised from her house in Esher. She felt almost comfortable; the room was so very English when compared with the barren and rather foreign furnishing of their rented house. Miss Armstrong was sitting in front of her, backed against the wall, and Albertine knew that if she were a beast of prey she would only need one more pounce and her quarry would be hers. Miss Armstrong could not get away; she was cornered. Albertine could see from her expression that Miss Armstrong knew this too.

On one of the small tables Albertine noticed a photograph of Miss Armstrong and Maud standing in front of the house. They were much younger and were posed, smiling, their arms round each other's shoulders. They were both wearing knee-length shorts, Maud's fat little legs looking like bolsters beside the stick-like elegance of Miss Armstrong's.

'I see Maud was here. Was she just staying with you, or did she come and live here too?'

In saying this – in the same bright, conversational tone – Albertine knew she was the cat playing with the mouse; a little tap with her soft paw and Miss Armstrong would be sent spinning into her corner. She waited, still feeling relaxed and in control, for her reply.

'Maud came here about twenty years ago, when she retired. She is in a home in Belize City now, poor love. Her mind has gone but physically she is still very fit.'

It was not what Albertine wanted to hear. The tone was all wrong, Miss Armstrong had recovered her poise and Albertine was no longer sure that she was the predator. If Miss Armstrong was going to play the same offhanded game as herself, they were unlikely to arrive at any point of real contact.

'Oh, I'm sorry to hear that. From what I've seen of the city, it must have been difficult to find anywhere that could cater for someone in that state.'

'It was; but there's a very nice English ex-hospital nurse who's turned her house into a sort of nursing home. She's well looked after.'

Miss Armstrong was no longer on the run. She was

showing herself to be the carer, the one in charge, the one who looked after people, the one who honoured her responsibilities. Albertine almost felt that she was saying, 'You see, I look after people who are maimed, not like you, who walked away.'

'Are you on your own now or do you have someone coming in to help you?'

It did not look as if she did. The room was deep in dust and the wooden boards of the floor were inspissated with greasy deposits. If, as it seemed likely from the number of candles, she had no electricity, it was possible that she had no hot water, which would make any serious cleaning operation a Herculean task. The faint smell of old age was just discernible through the mask of her favourite eau de cologne, mixing rather unattractively with old cooking smells. Albertine had a sudden flash of memory to the kitchen in the house in Surrey which Miss Armstrong had shared with Maud. Maud had done all the domestic work there – cooking, the cleaning, the washing-up, the laundry – and Miss Armstrong had seemed quite happy to let her do it. Maud, too, had seemed to accept her role with satisfaction. She suspected that when Maud had been here the house looked quite different. There would have been nothing lying around, no dust, no dirt. The oppressive darkness of the house would have been lightened by open windows and the mosquito screens kept clean of dead insects; there would have been no dirty plates by the sink. She would not have allowed the broken chairs to remain on the balcony or the old newspapers. Albertine felt a sudden pity for Miss Armstrong; not for the guilt she might or might not be experiencing, nor for her exile, self-imposed or not, but for her old age, for her helplessness.

'I don't like having people messing around me,' Miss Armstrong was saying, her eyes moving vaguely around the room. 'I suppose it is rather untidy, isn't it, but I like it like this . . . I suppose one gets used to different standards here.'

Her fingers were tapping the arm of her chair, the only sign now that she was nervous. Albertine knew that she had

162

lost control of the conversation but as she still did not know where she wanted it to lead, she betrayed her own nervousness by the disjointed and staccato rhythm of her words.

'Do you ever go home?'

'No, never. This has been my home for a long time; there's nothing in England for me.'

'You haven't missed much. At home everyone is so busy being busy there doesn't seem much time for living.'

Albertine wished she had not mentioned home and went on quickly before Miss Armstrong could ask her where home was.

'One very nice thing we have noticed while we've been here is the almost total lack of either race or class consciousness. I've never been anywhere before where they seem to matter so little. England seems to be getting worse and worse.'

Miss Armstrong laughed. 'Apart from the dogs; have you noticed that the dogs belonging to white people only bark at the blacks and vice versa?'

They had noticed that. Only a day or two before she had been asked by a woman to walk past Ellen's dogs with her. These dogs had always ignored her and Max, but despite her presence with the totally unthreatening but black woman, they had gone almost berserk. It was possible to walk along the beach and to know which house was owned by blacks and which by whites from the behaviour of the dogs.

'Do you go out much?'

'Not any longer; I have a boat, but it is too difficult for me to start now and I have kind neighbours who shop for me. I go into San Pedro with them once or twice a week. Most of the friends I had are dead or, like me, very old.'

'When I was trying to find where you lived I had lunch with Tony and Melissa . . . they told me you still went to the library.'

'I don't go as much as I used to; the girl there is very competent so there is no need.'

'They were full of praise of you.'

163

'Were they? That's kind. They're a nice couple. Belize attracts the best sort of American. They bring some much needed energy but are not as pushy as some I've met elsewhere. Still, it was very different here before they came.'

Her expression became wistful as she thought of the gentleness and the slowness of the life when she had first come and how this in itself had soothed her where she had needed soothing and bolstered her when she had found that she could be useful.

Albertine wanted to ask her if she was lonely but decided that she was not ready for such intimacy. She was well aware that the conversation was too general and that if it continued she would not be able to alter it next time; she was determined that there would be a next time and that it would be then that she would raise the temperature. In military terms this meeting could be called a preliminary skirmish.

'I must go in a minute or Max will be worried about his lunch. Shall I do some of this washing-up?'

'That would be very kind. Now tell me about your husband.'

She pretended not to hear her. She did not want to talk to Miss Armstrong about her current life. She wanted to keep it uncontaminated. It was for this reason, she now realised, that she had never told Max about her and why she had not wanted him to know about her visit today or her enquiries yesterday. She was angry as she thought how easily Miss Armstrong could still manipulate her into behaving as if this was a casual visit, that their normal conversation was possible. That she had colluded with her in this only added to the irritation she was feeling with herself.

She had been far to impetuous. She should have waited for at least a week before seeing her. She should have allowed herself time to recover from the shock and to regain some emotional stability; then she could have planned precisely what she would say to her without giving Miss Armstrong the slightest opportunity to gain the advantage. She would have gone straight to the point, to the jugular, she thought, noticing a lump protruding from her stringy neck. The reason she had colluded so willingly was because she was still so uncertain of what the point was.

'There,' she said, drying the last mug, 'that's all right. I must go now.'

She did not know how to say goodbye. She could hardly shake her hand, she certainly could not kiss her; she stood awkwardly by the door and raised her hand in a tentative wave. She was outside before she had time to know if Miss Armstrong had said goodbye or not.

She walked back to the house as if in a dream. She noticed nothing of her surroundings and kept her head low, seeing only her feet and the soft wet mud squelching between her toes. She felt as if she was an egg about to hatch. The shell had cracked, there was unseen stirring within its brittle boundary. She did not know if what would emerge would be a damp, bedraggled chick or whether it would be a baby dragon, already able to breathe fire, already able to fly and lash its horned hail, already fully armoured in impenetrable scales. She hoped it would be the latter but the weakness in her legs seemed to indicate that she might be as helpless and as soft as a newborn chick, with down not scales and with wings as yet unformed.

After Albertine had gone Gerda remained in her chair. The small dark room which had been her home for so many years, which had been her haven in many troublesome times, seemed to have been swept through by a hurricane. She was surprised to see it unchanged; everything was still in place but she felt it altered. Each object, the books on the shelves, the photographs in their frames, the kettle on the stove, which before had been in some way a statement of her stability now represented an ominous threat. She felt very cold but it was a coldness which started inside and worked its way through to her outside where it met the warmth of her skin, sticking her thin clothes to her body with a clammy Gloy-like substance. She felt very alone and realised that in this life she had built for herself, which had seemed so fulfilled, so safe, there was no one to whom she could go now danger threatened, no one but Maud; there had never really been anyone but Maud, and Maud, who had been her anchor, was out of reach.

She had hardly thought of Albertine for years. From the moment she had arrived in Belize City, welcomed by her brother and his wife, thrown into a world so unlike her previous existence, a world of cocktail parties and official functions, of beach parties and jungle expeditions; where she was accepted as Geoffrey's sister and where no questions had been asked, the healing process had begun. Each day the pain had become less; she began to look forward rather than back until it almost seemed that the years at Hartwell had been nothing but a nightmare, a figment of her tortured imagination. She had placed all her memories of Albertine in a cupboard and thrown away the key.

Geoffrey and Patricia had two teenaged children and she had taught them, at first informally, but later when some of their friends had joined them, she held what became evening seminars, and children who might otherwise have achieved only moderate A levels had gone on to universities either in England or the States. She became respected not only for being Geoffrey's sister but as someone in her own right, who was able to make a valuable contribution to the strange world of the Colonial Service. Geoffrey never asked her about Hartwell. She never knew what Maud had told him but occasionally Patricia would refer rather coyly to 'women's problems' and she assumed that that was what Maud had told Geoffrey. If so, it was clever of Maud; Geoffrey would never refer to anything as intimately female as the menopause, and after a time she herself had begun to accept the diagnosis as the truth. When the time had come for Geoffrey to return to England, his tour of duty done, they had asked her to go back with them, but by that time she had become so contented and so liberated from her past she decided to stay. They helped her find the piece of land, they helped her a little with money and so she built her house. It was only a year or two later that Maud had

166

come and they had created the life which suddenly seemed about to be shattered.

Whether it was her internal peace that was threatened by Albertine's arrival or whether she was afraid that she would make some public statement, spread some salacious rumour which would destroy her outward reputation, she could not decide. For her, as for Albertine, their secret was a secret which she had never for one moment thought that she would ever have to look at again. She certainly did not want to look at it alone. She recognised Albertine as her avenging angel, Nemesis arrived finally to punish her, not only for what she had done with her but with others too. Until Maud had come there had been others; she could not help it. There had been no one like Albertine, but she remembered, as if they were characters in a play, that some had shone more brightly in the footlights, whom she had been more intimate with than perhaps she should have been. She could not help it, she had never been able to help it. She was paralysed by fear of the price she might have to pay for these small alliances and was overwhelmed by the knowledge of her weakness. Old age had stolen her steel and robbed her of her only ally.

'Almighty God, Father of our Lord Jesus Christ, maker of all things, judge of all men; we acknowledge and bewail our manifold sins and wickedness which we from time to time most grievously have committed against thy divine majesty' ... Had it been a sin? The familiar and rolling words of the Prayer Book revolved round Gerda's head. 'We do earnestly repent and are heartily sorry for these our misdoings, the remembrance of them is grievous unto us, the burden of them intolerable' ... That was not true; it was not the burden of sin she had found intolerable but the burden of grief. It had been the loss of Albertine that she had found intolerable – or had it been the burden of sin that had turned her mind? Why had Albertine come, and why now? Had it really been accidental, as she had said, or had she in truth been seeking her out, had she been stalking her for years and was she about to take revenge? But revenge for

167

what? She had seemed all right . . . She had been friendly, not apparently vengeful; she had seemed pleased to see her. Why should she be feeling so afraid? If Albertine wanted revenge she had had it all those years ago when she left her, when she had not answered her letters: but of course she had not been there to see that. Perhaps she was here now to watch and enjoy her suffering . . . but she was not suffering now, not at all.

'Forgive us all that is past' . . . To ask for forgiveness, either from God or from Albertine was to acknowledge the sin. There had been only one time, after a particularly awful Governors' meeting, that she had allowed lust to overcome her love. She had always tried to love her gently, not to frighten her. Was love not meant to be godly? If love was of God, where had been the sin? She had truly loved her, had felt blessed in her loving . . . or perhaps she had only persuaded herself she was doing her good by loving her so that she did not have to face the harsh reality of sin or wickedness. If she had indeed used Albertine as an escape from the horror of the institution and because she was missing Maud, that would have been indeed wicked. But it had not been like that; she had loved her and Maud had understood that. Maud had stood beside her, had not condemned her because she had known . . . Known what? Had Maud known that she would return to her because it was Maud she really loved and Albertine had been just an amusement? If anyone should condemn her surely it would be Maud.

And Albertine had been willing. She was not a child, she was 17 . . . some girls marry at 17. She had never said no; until the end she had always answered her letters. She had always come when she asked her. What about 'the remembrance of them is grievous unto us'? . . . Now that she was allowing herself to remember, there was nothing grievous in her memories. It had been a joy to love her . . . she had been so beautiful, so full of life. It was a joy to see her fulfil the potential that she had recognised and fostered. Albertine should have been grateful, had seemed grateful, until

168

the end. So why did she feel that Albertine had come to destroy her?

'Have mercy upon us, have mercy upon us most merciful Father' ... But it was not God she wanted mercy from, it was Albertine.

There had been something sinister in the blandness of the conversation, she had felt that she was being played on a line. It was only a matter of time till Albertine struck, and she would be landed, jerking on the shore as she had been once before.

15

Max spent the morning in a state of limbo. He walked as far as the river and back, he swam, he was unable to read; the thought did cross his mind that he might call on Bill and see if he would like to go diving but he quickly discarded this idea as he wanted to be there when Albertine returned from wherever it was she had gone. He had not gone so far as to wonder after all the years of marriage why this should be so; he just wanted her beside him. The image of her in the sea was still vivid in his mind; when he looked at the waves he almost expected her to rise from them, in a shell; he felt like a saint who has suddenly experienced a revelation of the divine. In a strange way he felt transformed himself, as if he had just shed his skin which lay dry and cracked and dusty on the ground as he emerged from it, soft and shimmering.

He had never performed a single domestic chore since he had been a fag at public school; he had not considered it his role and he had no idea how to make a room clean, but out of desire to please Albertine he began to sweep the floor. He did not start in the corners, and by the time the centre of the room was more or less sand free, round the edges it lay about half an inch thick. In trying to sweep the sand out of the door he only succeeded in spreading it all over the room again. His admiration for Albertine rose to even greater heights: she was not only brave, magnificent and beautiful she was also capable and modest. If he had felt anything when she was cleaning it was annoyance that she was disturbing him as she swept round his legs or asked him to move his chair. He had had no idea that the deftness with which she handled the broom was a skill he did not have. He had thought, as he thought about most things, that if he had to he would do it twice as fast and twice as effectively as she.

Defeated by the sand, he thought, Lunch! I'll make lunch for us both. He carefully sliced an iceberg lettuce into quarters and placed two tomatoes beside them. He thought it did not look quite right and boiled two eggs which he put, still in their shells, beside the tomatoes. He was well aware that his salad did not look like her salads but could not remember at all what she did to make the same ingredients look more appetising. He found a tin of tuna fish in the cupboard and emptied it onto the plate. The brine from the fish made the lettuce look even more uninviting; he poured salad dressing over everything, hoping to conceal the water but only succeeded in making the whole a sort of creamy lake on top of which floated strands of pale brown tuna and from which now jutted limp lettuce and rock-like tomatoes. I should have peeled the eggs, he thought but could not face doing so. His fastidiousness, despite his desire to please, prevented him from touching the slimy and slippery shells.

He laid the table and waited until at last he saw her walking head down along the shore. When she came level with the house she stood looking at it as if deciding whether or not to go in. Just as he thought she was going to come up to the house she turned and walked to the end of the dock and sat down, swinging her legs in the water, kicking at the orange sargasso swept inshore by the night's storm.

Albertine had hoped for a more dramatic encounter with Miss Armstrong and could not decide whether it had been so unsatisfactory because she had lost her nerve or because Miss Armstrong had outmanoeuvred her; she was dreading facing Max, who she knew would be angry with her again. She looked up at the house and saw him waving – or was he beckoning? She waved back and reluctantly got to her feet. She composed her face into smiling innocence, her story not quite prepared.

171

'Ah! There you are at last ... Did you have a nice morning?' There was not a trace of sarcasm in Max's tone, not even a suggestion of reproach.

'Yes thank you. I went up as far as Captain Morgan's and had a drink ... the girl in the bar is sweet. She comes from San Ignacio and she's one of twelve children. She doesn't like it here but apparently it's very hard to get work of any sort up there ...' Albertine had in fact had this conversation a few days before so she was able to describe it quite convincingly. What was not to convincing was the rush in which the words came out. But Max was not listening to her; she need not have bothered. She saw that he was looking at her expectantly, like a small boy waiting for the cry of approval after scoring a goal.

'Oh Max! Well done! You've made lunch ... how kind.'

Max was disappointed by her response. He had expected more. There had been something almost automatic in her thanks and he did not think she had noticed that he had swept the floor.

'I thought salad would be enough, or would you like something more after your long walk?'

'That's fine,' she said. 'It looks very good ... I might just take the shells off the eggs. They'll be easier to eat, don't you think?'

Quickly she washed them, peeled them, sliced them and mixed them into the dressing. 'There you are, *oeufs mayonnaise*!'

Max was astonished that doing something so simple could transform his odd-looking culinary attempt. He should have thought of it himself.

'What did you do this morning?' Albertine asked, still surprised at Max's lack of curiosity; it was almost as if he was restraining himself rather than that he had no interest in where she had been, and his preparation of lunch was completely out of character. He was often conciliatory after they had had a row in which he was to blame. This time he had not been solely to blame, and she had never known him take conciliation so far as to do anything domestic.

'This and that, nothing special. I saw Albert when I was taking a stroll. They've invited us for bridge this evening.'

Elma and Albert, who lived in the house nearest to theirs, had become good friends, despite having nothing in common apart from their age. They were Americans, like most of the foreigners in San Pedro. Albert had retired early, and after sailing round the Caribbean for ten years they had finally settled on Belize as the most congenial place to build a house and spend the rest of their lives. They were a delightful pair and if it had not been for them Max and Albertine's evenings would have been long and tedious. As it got dark at six o'clock, and with neither wireless nor television, their lack of conversation was more apparent than at home. Although Albertine did not much like playing bridge, having never fully mastered the rules, she was particularly pleased that tonight, when she wanted to plan her next visit to Miss Armstrong, she would not have to struggle through time-filling conversation.

'What do you feel like doing this afternoon?' He was looking at her intently, as if willing her to give a specific answer.

'Shall we go snorkelling? The sea's wonderfully calm. Or will it still be murky from last night?'

'I shouldn't think we'll see much. It was quite a storm. But we could try if you like.'

It was not what he had wanted her to say. He had been hoping that she would suggest a siesta and he would be able to hold her in his arms again, but he was fearful, as if courting a stranger, of moving too fast and frightening her away. They gathered their equipment and set off in the boat towards the reef.

There were buoys anchored at intervals along the edge of the coral; small white blobs of polystyrene which were only visible at close quarters. When they first arrived, Albertine, whose job it was to catch the buoy, had been very frightened that Max would go in too far or too fast, that she would miss it and the boat would be swept onto the branches of coral, some of which stuck out of the water like the burnt stumps

173

of trees left from a forest fire. Bill had warned them never to touch the coral, partly because it was dangerously sharp but mostly because it was so fragile that damage done to one piece could spread disease through the entire range. She was terrified of being responsible for destroying the greatest length of reef in the Western Hemisphere. Now she had become very skilled at leaning over the edge of the boat, snatching the bobbing white ball and deftly slipping the rope noose round its neck.

Safely tied, they put on the giant flippers that the salesman had recommended in favour of the more manageable ones which were about nine inches shorter. 'If you are going to be doing a lot of snorkelling, or even some diving, possibly, you will find these more satisfactory in the long run, though they are more difficult to manage at first.' Albertine had not learnt to manage them at all and bitterly regretted the excess of confidence which had led her to choose the whale-like fins she had difficulty even putting on. She had not seen a single pair of flippers like hers, not even in the professional diving shops. Once in the water, they dragged her legs down and were so heavy that she could not control their drift and was constantly having to stand in order to avoid crashing onto the coral. In trying to stand, which was difficult in itself because of the length of the fins, panic overcame her and she consequently ended up taking in gallons of water through her nose, down the snorkel and somehow behind her goggles.

Max never experienced any of these problems and was now floating happily in front of her. His legs, which looked white under the water were spindly like frogs' legs, his head was level with the surface of the water and his arms were outstretched, perfectly balancing the weight of his body.

Although the water was still a little dirty it was quite possible to see the fish, the sweet blue tangs with their wide fixed smile, the thick-lipped grouper, the shoals of snapper and the sinister barracuda suspended just beneath the surface of the water like shafts of steel. They had been told that barracuda were only dangerous, despite their razor-sharp teeth, when there was spear fishing going on around them. Albertine supposed that this was because they were excited by blood and hoped that the cut she had on her finger would not arouse them to a frenzy of aggression.

The fishy world that she always felt it was such a privilege to enter was as usual having a calming effect on her mind. As she watched a shoal of snapper swim past her, turning purposefully and swimming back as if involved in a complicated square dance with an invisible caller, she thought what it would have been like if her relationship with Miss Armstrong had been normal. How good it would have been if she had been first a mentor, then a mentor-friend and finally an equal. How good it would have been if she had not just come across her here, but had planned her holiday round a visit to her and if, after years of corresponding, they could have met again and each acknowledged the debt they owed to one another, a debt that would have been mostly of friendship. How satisfactory it would have been if she had been able to make Miss Armstrong godmother to Amanda so that the valuable mentor relationship could have been continued into the next generation. She fucked it up by fucking me, she thought, astonished that the word she never used should come to her mind so readily. Until now Albertine would have denied that by abusing the protégé relationship, she had also fucked her up. The intensity of her feelings since she had seen Miss Armstrong again was leading her to accept the possibility and at the same time allowing her to feel the anger that all those years before she had kept suppressed.

For there had been anger, she could see that now. Helpless, impotent anger that had had to be suppressed or it would have become intolerable, would have destroyed her. She was thinking that to be in the power of someone stronger than oneself must always be intolerable: hostages must feel it, countries overcome by invading armies experience it, it is the main pain of the adolescent child who has to break free from the domination of loving parents, it is at the root of the frustrated anger of the old faced by their own powerlessness. Of course she must have felt anger; she had only been able to deal with the whole affair, she now realised, by pretending that it was not happening, and with a cold, appalled horror she understood that pretending there was no domination where there was, was what she had done all her life; and not only domination, she ignored anything unpleasant but she stored it nevertheless. She allowed Max to dominate her and raged speechlessly when he did. It was this characteristic of allowing people to walk over her which had been at the root of what everyone, Max included, had seen as her admirable placidity; but it was the source of her depressing self-image, the whole Cheddar cheese, round, cracked and sweaty, on a plate, legless, ready to be devoured by the crawling mass of mice or rats who were gorging themselves to satiety on her readily available person. This is what she had learnt through all those nights in Miss Armstrong's bed, her hands and lips and tongue, like the mice on the cheese, feeding off her unresisting body. She had learnt not to say no, she had learnt that she was nothing unless totally available for other people's pleasure.

As her anger mounted she had a sudden memory of a time when Judy and Miranda had gone out one night to the cinema in Sheringham. There should have been plenty of time for them to get back before bedtime but the electricity failed. Instead of coming back, they stayed on in the hope that power would be restored in time for them to see the end of the film. They were not there to say goodnight to Miss Armstrong and there was the most terrible drama. She and Ruth were questioned over and over again. Of course they both denied any knowledge of where the others were. When they eventually returned, Miss Armstrong was in such a towering rage she was talking about expulsion and ringing their parents. They all took it with a pinch of salt, certain that once she had calmed down she could not possibly upset their future for such a small misdemeanour.

The next morning Albertine was summoned to her study before prayers; she was expecting an embrace to make up for not spending the night but instead she was met with a rage that she had not seen before, rage worse even than had been poured over the luckless Judy and Miranda. 'How could you have been so disloyal to me? I trusted you. Whose side are you on?' Albertine tried to explain that you did not rat on your friends, but Miss Armstrong said that love came before friendship, that to put casual acquaintances before her lover must mean that she did not love her very much. The last words she had said were, 'I've a good mind to expel them to show you what your disloyalty to me has done for your so-called friends.'

As she remembered that occasion, the only time Miss Armstrong had been angry with her, she felt a return of the fear she experienced then, that it was all because of her that they might be expelled; but how could she have done otherwise? Of course her loyalty was going to be with her friends. In order to save them, in order to keep the status quo, she had gone to her in break and said how sorry she was and how she realised that Miss Armstrong had been right and she had got her priorities wrong. She had hated doing it but she had seen no other way.

Although it was frightening to be confronted by so unfamiliar an emotion as anger, it was at the same time exciting. She began to swim strongly, not caring if she touched the coral, boldly moving through narrow gateways she would not have dared attempt before, coming into open spaces as if already free from a bondage she had only just recognised.

Getting back into the boat was an ordeal. The water by the buoy was not quite shallow enough to gain any leverage from the bottom and Albertine's arms were not strong enough to pull her up over the side. She had to remove the cumbersome fins in the water, and by half climbing up the outboard motor and with Max hauling her by the arms, she was landed like an enormous seal into the body of the boat. Her skin was bruised and scraped and her dignity damaged.

By the time they got back to the house it was nearly dusk. The no-see-ems were out in force, blown across the mangrove in the lagoon by a north wind. The wind was rattling

177

the palms, sounding as if it were already raining. The rain, when it came, would fall on the corrugated tin roof like thousands of ping-pong balls, forcing its way through the closed wooden slats which formed the windows behind the mosquito screens, making pools on the floor and channels of water down the walls. The screens were protection against mosquitoes but not the no-see-ems, fierce little biters which were only seen when, in the rain, they came through the screen and stuck to the white walls, making it appear as if the contents of a hundred ashtrays had been blown around the room, the grey flecks evenly and densely spread as on a screen print or engraving.

'Are you looking forward to tonight?'

Max's question was one that she knew did not require an answer; it was more a statement that he was feeling relaxed and at one with her. He was lying on the sofa and concentrating on rubbing a bitter-smelling insect repellent on every exposed part of his body. He was always very careful about these applications. Albertine found it irritating, but the fact was that he did not get bitten and she did.

'Actually I'm feeling rather sleepy, but I expect I'll wake up soon. I think I'll have a shower. That might help.'

'You've had quite a long day. Where did you go this morning? I can't remember.'

'I don't know why I ever bother telling you anything, you never listen . . . I said I went to Captain Morgan's.' She was quickly on the defensive, thinking that perhaps he was planning to trap her.

'Oh yes, so you did. Did you meet anyone interesting?'

'I told you that too; no one apart from the girl behind the bar. I'm going to shower now,' she said, to prevent him from pressing her further.

'Don't be too long,' he called to her. 'We should go quite soon. You know they like to eat early and do let's try to get there before this rain starts.'

Elma and Albert's house was furnished in a style that was both spartan and expensive-looking. The furniture was all new, dark heavy department-store mahogany, and the room was dominated by a large leather-topped table which might almost have been suitable as the boardroom table of a small company. There was not a single comfortable chair or cushion to be seen, no colour to relieve the unremitting sombreness of the brown, and although they had a television, Albertine could never work out where they sat to watch it. It was extremely tidy; she had never seen one item of clutter, no books apart from Webster's Dictionary on the glass-topped coffee table, nothing that pointed to either of them having any hobby, no letters or papers waiting to be dealt with. The cream-coloured walls were bare and there were no pictures or photographs to indicate that they had any other life apart from the one started that day in that just-moved-into, prepared house.

Albertine supposed that the extreme, and to her unnecessary, orderliness was the result of years of disciplined living on a boat, where their lives would have depended on there being nothing out of its place or lying around, but what might have been proper in a boat gave the room a cold, uninviting atmosphere, like an expensive Harley Street waiting room.

She also felt frustrated by her inability to imagine what they did when the door was closed. Guessing at lives led behind closed doors was one of Albertine's favourite fantasies. Being bad at casual conversation, she built her pictures from small hints, from photographs, from bills waiting payment, from the choice of ornaments, from that most revealing place of all, the bathroom cabinet, which told her whether her hosts were having an active sex life, what secret illnesses or complaints they suffered from, from piles to cramp, from mild anxiety to chronic depression. Evenings with Albert and Elma were always the same. Albert would hand out rum and Cokes and Elma would tell one of her endless and invariably garbled stories, a convoluted version of what she had picked up the previous day.

'You know those people from town who are building the

condos?' she began, 'Ya know, the ones by the Simpsons' . . . down by the beach? Ya know they're asking a hundred and seventy dollars US for those!. . . Waal . . .'

Her blue eyes widened and her voice dipped, they all waited expectantly, even Albert, who had almost certainly heard the tale already.

'Wall, ya know, I heard that their boat has been cut from its moorings . . . again . . . that's the third time in a month!'

Albertine had expected to have difficulty in detaching herself from thoughts of Miss Armstrong, but she found herself already genuinely engaged by the story Elma was telling. There was something about the way she told these stories, the pauses, the tense moment before the denoue-ment which was inevitably an anti-climax, her own obvious excitement in the telling and not least the concentration necessary to disentangle the main thread from the various subplots which she had a habit of introducing with no clear division either in her tone of voice or the punctuation.

Albert was entirely different from Elma. He seemed to have no interest in people. It was from him they learnt about the wild life. He identified the numerous different species of birds for them; the humming bird with his long beak who would vibrate above a flower for only a second before flying off, the brilliant jewel coloured oriole and the four varieties of woodpecker which along with many others would feed on the lot behind their house, 'thirty seven separate species, and that's not counting the migratories,' he often said with pride. He described the fishing habits of the herons, how they dealt with the eels they caught in the shallows, which wrapped themselves round the heron's beak as a python would wrap itself round a human form, by shaking their heads until the eel, no doubt dizzy and exhausted from its 'Waltzer' experi-ence would fall at their feet and be gobbled in one swift mouthful. They had a way of dealing with crabs too; they would catch them and rip off their legs dropping the cripple for later consumption. 'Kinda mean that', but Albert's foxlike face would light at the memory of having seen it. These herons were territorial birds and would not let another of

180

their own species graze in their waters, though they would tolerate others. Thus it was that there were so many different varieties of birds in the small stretch of beach-front.

He told them to keep an eye out for the osprey, which caught fish not with their beak but with huge talons which would sweep across the surface of the water like the giant clawed machines on building sights, sometimes taking fish as big as a foot long. He fed a family of raccoons which came into their garden every morning on boiled rice and tacos and was as concerned for their welfare as he was for their cats, who had been on the boat with them for six years without ever touching land and their dog who they had rescued from being destroyed on account of her unusually strong antipathy to black men. He could be seen for hours sitting on the end of his dock studying through binoculars the many different wading birds that stood like statues apparently unaware of his presence, large white herons, small white herons, large blue herons with yellow legs, small blue herons with pale blue legs, and the large grey, which sat hunched shouldered on the post which marked the entrance to their channel.

'Say Albertine, I nearly came and got you this morning, there was a beautiful vine snake in the plants in the front there.'

Albertine shivered, snakes were something, like rats, which she could not bear.

'They're really cute you know, not dangerous at all. You don't often see them, they mostly stay in the trees.'

'What trees?' she said in horror, imagining a snake leering down on her, unnoticed, when she was reading in a hammock they had stretched between two palms.

'Well, palms mostly,' he said, 'You'd be surprised what lives in those things.'

He was, or had been before he retired, an engineer by profession and was constantly engaged in practical things.

'How about some bridge then folks, are you ready partners?'

The two Alberts, as Elma sometimes called them, always

played together. They were the weaker partnership, but sometimes they managed to pull off unexpected victories and the overall score remained surprisingly level.

'Did I tell you about the carry on in the Pier Lounge the other day?' Elma was dealing.

'No, what happened?' Albertine asked, not feeling very interested in bridge and knowing that the story would delay play for quite a few more minutes.

Albert and Max looked at each other and both raised their eyebrows and shrugged their shoulders, the gesture very clearly saying, hold on, this is going to take some time.

'Waal,' her stories always started with 'Waal', the 'a' drawn out and followed by a decidedly 'pregnant pause'.

'Ya know that gal, the one who is married, . . . well she's not actually married, but you know what I mean . . . a native girl, lives with that guy up the coast, the one who's always in the Pier Lounge, sorta good looking, waal he's Sonia's son and she runs it . . . ya know Sonia? . . .'

Albertine certainly knew of her but like so many of Elma's characters she did not know if she had in fact actually spoken to her; to avoid a detailed description of her life she said she did, and Elma continued.

'Waal, ya know, this girl, his wife was in the bar . . . just kinda talking ya know . . . when this woman comes up to her and says, "that's my bracelet you're wearing" and this girl, Estelle I think she's called . . . she says, "no it's not, it's mine . . . I bought it in Corozal four years ago" and this woman says, "I lost it two days ago and I know its mine" . . . waal, you know what, she goes and gets the police, and Estelle is taken to the Police station and put in a cell . . . and isn't that just arful for Sonia, I mean she's nearly her daughter in law . . . well sorta, ya know.'

'The Police can't do that, they would have to have some proof before taking her away.' Max said, as if there was something he should do about it.

'Not here, Honey . . . not here.' And she laughed delightedly at yet a further example of her superior island knowledge.

All through Elma's story Max, though trying to appear interested in what she was saying, could not keep his eyes from Albertine. She was looking so wonderful tonight, her skin, which he had not noticed before, was the colour of golden syrup. She was sparkling, interested, she laughed in the right places and asked the right questions. He could see that Albert was fascinated by her as well he should be; she was like a thoroughbred and Elma was a cob. If only she would look at him, but her eyes were firmly fixed on Elma, he almost felt that she did not even know that he was there.

'Shall we get on with the game?' Albert said in a tone which meant he was resigned not to.

'Oh sorry, yes, I was dealing wasn't I?'

Once the chat about island life had ceased Albertine had more difficulty than usual concentrating on the cards. Her mind kept returning to the problem she had to face the next day. Whether to play a diamond or a spade seemed a small decision compared with what she was to say to Miss Armstrong. She was also extremely discomfited by the looks Max had been giving her all evening which she could not interpret. Even when Elma was talking she could feel his eyes like lasers boring into her back. She made a lot of very elementary mistakes even for her, and after she had gone down four in what should have been an easy contract, Max, although not her partner said,

'I think we'd better stop, Albertine is tired, do you mind Albert?'

'How about something to eat, then you get an early night gal.' And Elma started to prepare the Mexican tortillas.

They had their early night, leaving immediately after supper; but it was after two o'clock when Albertine at last fell asleep whilst Max lay for nearly all the night trying to understand how it could be possible that after thirty or more years of marriage he should suddenly be in love with his wife.

16

Foxy-faced Albert was sitting opposite her, the far side of a huge table. The other players were unidentifiable, their faces covered by white stocking masks, and separated by yards of dark green baize. Albert pulled out a card from his hand, very deliberately laying it face downwards and then with a leer which revealed all his teeth and transformed his expression from one of benign benevolence to one of almost inexpressible evil, he turned it over. It was the Hangman. The card played, he was himself again, smiling at her as if to say, 'that's a good card eh!' It was her turn to play. None of the other players seemed to have noticed that Albert was playing a different game. She looked at her cards which were weaving in and out, black to red, red to black, bowing and passing on, dancing a minuet of colour in her hand. They made no sense to her but she at last drew one out and placed it on the table, a prancing red Prince, bright and carefree. Now it was Albert's turn again; with the same deliberation he pulled out another card and laid it down. His nose became a snout, drawn back into deep creases, his teeth became fangs, dripping blood. He turned the card over. It was Death; sickle in hand the grinning skull seemed to be saying 'I want you.'

Suddenly Miss Armstrong appeared with two policemen. She was dressed in a tube of glimmering black silk and her face was the skull of Death. She pointed to Albertine and said to the policemen, 'That is her ... that is my life she is wearing ... arrest her ... take her away ... she must never be seen again.'

Albertine woke up sweating and shivering. It was morning, just. The sky and the sea were a pale silvery grey; the sun, just risen, a white disc like a gigantic Host held up by invisible hands above the altar of the horizon. There was no wind. The heavy palms hung limp and the only movement came from a single pelican gliding serenely a foot above the motionless sea. 'I'm going to kill her,' she thought.

Max was still asleep. She got out of bed and tiptoed to the stove. She did not let the water quite boil, knowing that the piercing whistle would wake him up. She did not want the distraction of Max while she made her plan. 'I don't mind if I do get cholera,' she said to herself. She took her mug of coffee onto the deck. It was too early to go to the green house. She would have to wait until it was at least nine o-clock and it was now only six-thirty. Three hours ... three hours to plan a murder, three hours before she would be free. She felt a surge of almost uncontrollable excitement, of energy flowing through her body like a rushing tide. This is what it will always be like, she thought, once she is dead.

Her father had had an expression which he used frequently to describe unpleasant situations. 'Like the inside of a chinaman's bed' he would say and as a child she had been able to see it in her mind's eye; a mess of tangled sheets, noodles and soy sauce, a smell of oil and spices and in the middle a fat greasy chinaman with chins and a stomach like the Buddha, bright yellow with slit eyes looking sinister but happy in the rank disorder of his nest. She knew for certain that Miss Armstrong had made a chinaman's bed of her life and only by destroying her, annihilating her completely would she be able to lie in peace, in laundered linen, the sheets pulled tight over the bed, without a wrinkle, hospital corners and plump pristine pillows. Only then would she sleep soundly, only then would her days and her life be under her own control.

Max shuffled onto the deck and stood beside her, his face crumpled by sleep, his eyes only half opened.

'You're up very early, what time is it?'

'I couldn't sleep. The kettle hasn't boiled for three minutes if you want some coffee; I didn't want to wake you.'

'You must boil it, you must ... how much have you drunk?'

He was very funny about disease, or about preventing disease. His maternal grandfather had been a doctor specialising in tropical medicine. Max was full of half remembered information about potential plagues that could strike them; cholera, typhoid, malaria, all Somerset Maugham types of illness. She had not noticed anyone they had met taking any precautions at all. Elma washed lettuce from the tap, took no anti-malarials and for all she knew they drank the water. If Max saw her clean her teeth in water that had not boiled for three minutes he nearly hit the roof as he was doing now. She thought by his irritation that he had a hangover. She did not know that when Max knew that she had drunk unboiled water, he had had an unrepressible picture of Albertine lying on the bed, with arms and legs like sticks and an expression of utmost agony as she died, imploring him for help that he could not give her. She knew none of this, she left him to his boiling and went to dress.

As for all important events she had the usual trouble choosing what to wear. She studied the pile of shorts and tee shirts which was all she had brought with her, wondering what colour would be the most suitable for murder. She would like to dress entirely in black, like the Miss Armstrong of her dream, but the pile of clothes in front of her had been chosen for frolicking in bright sunshine. There was a black tee shirt but all her shorts were pale blue or pink. She had one pair of long dark blue trousers which she had brought in case it should be cold when they went into the mountains, but they were designed for an English winter; heavy corded velvet. She did not think that she would be able to stand them in this heat. To arrive at the house puce and streaming with sweat was not how she imagined it. She wanted to be as cold and as clean as a barracuda with teeth of vengeance sharp and showing. She wanted Miss Armstrong to be frightened and to sense what was coming to her

186

and to know that she could not run away. She also did not want her legs bare; not only were they too fat, not at all like steel, but bare legs seemed somehow too frivolous for murder. She looked at Max's wardrobe. He had a pair of long pale grey trousers and a black tee shirt. She tried the trousers on; they were too tight round the waist and round the hips but the length was right and the tee shirt came far enough down to cover the gaping zip. She would have to find some string or something to act as a fastening. It would not do for her trousers to fall down at the moment she struck her.

She had been so absorbed in the thought of herself as an instrument of divine retribution she had not thought at all about how she was to accomplish it. Why had she thought 'struck'? There were many ways to kill someone; how should she do it? With a knife, with a blunt instrument, a gun ... with poison, should she hurl her from a great height or drown her; should she strangle her? She had only thought 'kill'. That had seemed enough. Poison she knew would be too slow and too chancey; there were no great heights here; she could not imagine saying to Miss Armstrong 'shall we go for a swim' and her agreeing, though the thought of holding her down in the water, seeing her struggling and gasping for breath and finally glassy eyed, becoming limp and then dead was rather satisfying. Strangling would be too intimate she thought, and too technical. She had an idea that for strangling you had to know more about anatomy than she did, that the windpipe had to be strictured at exactly the right point. She had no gun and she certaintly did not like the idea of the blood that would flow from a knife and anyway that involved anatomy too. In films people were stabbed all over the place without dying. She had been right to think about striking; it would have to be a blunt instrument. 'Long Time Resident of San Pedro Found Bludgeoned to Death' would be the headline in the *San Pedro Sun*. She could make it look as if she had been robbed ... throw stuff around the room, take some valuables and hurl them into the sea ... no, the sea was too shallow ... throw

187

them into the bush. She wondered how heavy the blunt instrument should be. She was certain she would find something along the beach, there was always driftwood of one kind or another.

It was nearly nine o-clock. The sky was blue now, the sun high and bright enough to draw out the colour of the sea which was dark in the shallows but where the sea grass ended was a deep rich blue until it reached the white foaming band of the waves breaking over the reef.

'I think I'll go for a walk. Do you mind if I borrow your trousers; I got terribly bitten yesterday.'

She tried to make her voice sound casual but it came out breathless and like a little girl's. Being bitten was the only reason she could think of for wearing Max's trousers. It was not a very likely excuse as the biters only bit at dawn or dusk or if there was no wind. As the sun had risen in the sky so had the wind resumed its gentle stroking of the long fingered palms. Her high pitched tone sounded to her so false she was convinced he would suspect something, but to her relief he only grunted, still, she assumed, in the stage of nursing his hangover.

Part of the equipment of the poorly furnished house was a walking stick with a large and interestingly knobbly head. It was not a specially crafted stick but a piece of wood, possibly a piece of mangrove which someone had obviously once thought would make a good staff, useful perhaps for fending off the attentions of racially prejudiced dogs. She considered it as she walked out of the house but decided it would be too light. She was not strong enough to inflict serious damage with such a delicate instrument. She set off down the path with determination in her stride and with her nose to the ground searching for her weapon.

Max was neither as hungover or as obtuse as she had hoped. He was in the grip of an obsession as great as hers and his antennae, so long dormant, were out, waving aimlessly before him and receiving no signals in return. She had not, as he had said to Albert and Elma the night before, been tired; despite an appearance of being interested in

Elma's stories, he realised now that she had really been distracted, the excitement radiating from her had nothing to do with the evening, she had been like someone who had a secret but she was not a secretive person and what possible secret could she have here that he would not know about. Unless ... the thought hit him with all the force of a blow from a sledgehammer; there could be only one possible secret she could have that would give her that look of suppressed excitement, only one secret that meant she was so continually and uncharacteristically going off on her own, and why, although her perpetual complaint was that he never listened to her, did he now have the feeling that her thoughts, whatever they were, had absolutely nothing to do with him. She must have found a lover. How or where, since they spent so much of their time together, he could not fathom but it was the only explanation for everything that had been so different about her over the last few days; her distraction, the many absences, her almost hysterical look, her lack of interest in what he was thinking or doing, even her failure to appreciate his advances towards her. Last night, when he had tried to hold her again she had shrugged away from him, turned her back and gone straight to sleep.

He was unused to any form of self analysis and although his mind was working furiously he could not make the connection between his newly discovered passion for her and her obvious absorption in someone else. He was quite unable to realise that it was her very lack of interest in him which had provoked his sudden obsession.

'I'll kill him!' He was dressing fast and unconsciously; rage was in some way alleviating the terrible pain he had experienced when the thought had first struck him, and being a man of action rather than of ideas he was invigorated by his decision, giving no thought to either the means by which he could accomplish the deed or the consequences.

The anger which had at first been directed only towards Albertine's seducer was now extending towards her. He was forgetting for a moment his recent feelings for her; he did not particularly like her, he was bored by her but she was not going to bore anyone else ... And she was wearing his trousers ... what was all that about, certainly not insects, there weren't any at this time of day. It was some horrible plan she had to humiliate him, going to her lover in his clothes, perhaps laughing with him about them. What a sick mind she must have to think up something so crude, so devious. As he left the house he grabbed the stick which was leaning against the wall; it would be just as well to have a weapon but who he would use it on he could not tell; his fury was dispersed, embracing everything he saw from the coconuts lying on the ground to the picture, like a Catherine wheel flaming in his mind, of Albertine rolling about in the enseamed sheets of some unknown man.

He could just make her out in the distance but he could not see clearly what she was doing. She seemed to stop every few yards to peer into the scrub at the side of the path. Once or twice he saw her stoop to pick something up and swing it round her head before throwing it away. She did not seem to be in any hurry. He was beginning to see how ridiculous he must look. Whenever she stopped he stepped aside from the path and hid behind a palm tree. If anyone saw him they would think it was he that was behaving strangely, not her. She had mentioned Captain Morgan's; perhaps her lover was a tourist staying in one of the cabanas on the beach; a perfect place for an illicit love affair he thought furiously; if that was so and if progress was going to continue at this rate it would take over an hour to get there.

She had now picked up a long stick and was hitting the ground with it over and over again. He felt a sudden surge of protectiveness; she must have seen a snake and was foolishly trying to kill it. He wanted to shout out, 'Leave it alone, they're all harmless here'; he knew her dread of snakes and felt the frenzy of fear she must be experiencing. He wanted to hold her trembling body and tell her how brave she was ... but now she was swinging it round her head again as she had the others. She seemed to be examining the end which had a protuberance as far as he could see, as large as a small coconut. She continued up the path, faster now, no longer looking at the ground and holding her stick or what seemed more like a sort of club, which she swung in the air as if taking swipes at unidentifiable objects.

She had got to the bend in the path where the green house stood on stilts almost at the water's edge. She stopped and stood looking up at it. Even from a distance he could feel a tension in her stance. She walked round the back of the house and looked up at the windows then back to the front again. She seemed to be in a state of indecision about whether to go in or not. Max felt the blood drain from his body leaving his head light and his stomach pulsating with the effort to stand upright as the full realisation of what this meant hit him. This was not a tourist's house, it was not a monthly or weekly let; this was a native's house. This was the house of someone who had lived here for years. There were chickens pecking round the steps, plants on the deck, a wheelbarrow and a sort of a garden. The boat moored at the dock was old and well used, not the kind of boat a tourist could rent by the day from Island Adventures. Albertine was having an affair with a black man.

What was she waiting for? Did they have some sign that meant 'All clear?' She was looking up and down the path as if to make sure she was not seen going into the house. Max was standing deep in the undergrowth and could not see the source of the female voice which was now coming from the deck. He heard the light slamming of the screen door and the sound of steps coming down the stairs. He could see that Albertine, obviously having heard the same voice was standing back in the shadow of the house. A large fat black woman passed his hiding place, singing and swinging an empty shopping bag. His wife ... the bastard ... he had told Albertine to wait until his wife had left to do some shopping in San Pedro. If she was walking there would be at least three or four hours before she returned; plenty of time for all kinds of sexual activity ... blacks were famous for it he knew ... what they did that was different he had never

191

bothered to find out but his imagination now triggered led him through lurid fantasies where the predominant image was Albertine's large white breasts being fondled, caressed and mauled by calloused black fingers, and a large black cock, as big as a horse's, thrusting its way between her flabby dimpled thighs; he could smell the disgusting rancid smell of sweat, sweet, fetid, stinking. She would have AIDS now, he thought. She is far too naïve to think of safe sex, which was what he had recently discovered was the modern euphemism for what he was accustomed to think of as a french letter.

He was quite right in his supposition. She was walking up the stairs now, through the screen door and without even knocking, into the house.

He had never encountered the emotion of sexual jealousy before. He was an attractive man even now and he had always been the one to end the brief affairs of his youth. The pain which now engulfed him was worse than any torture he could imagine. He felt garrotted, on the rack, torn inch by inch as the machine pulled him slowly apart. Every cliché he knew failed to express what he was enduring ... limb torn from limb, sinews ripped asunder, paralysed and rooted to the spot, seeing red ... he experienced it all and more as he was overcome by an attack of shuddering more powerful than any orgasm. He wanted to bay ... to lift his face to a full moon and howl.

Any idea he had of confronting the man, beating him, dragging Albertine by her hair down the path back to his lair, had all gone now that he knew her lover was a black man. Somehow everything was changed, he was in a territory he knew nothing of. He could not even understand what black men were saying. He was and always had been very fastidious in his relationships and the thought of confronting a Creole speaking nigger who had just ejaculated into his wife was impossible, but he had to know who it was. Stumbling blindly and to his shame tearfully back to the house he knew that first he had to have a drink and then he would think of a way to discover who lived there. He had three tumblerfuls of whisky, drunk one after another, undiluted.

The excruciatingly painful vision of Albertine in bed with another man was replaced by the even more painful memory of Albertine as she had been when he first met her, when he first loved her. His love had been instantaneous, not unlike the *coup de foudre* he had experienced when he saw her in the sea. She had arrived unexpectedly on his doorstep with his mother's god-daughter and had stayed for tea. She had been shy but immediately he had been certain that he had detected something in her reserve that he would be able to stir; she had not been at all like the debutantes of his early bachelor days, she had not been giggling or in the slightest bit flirtatious and no-one could have been more surprised than he was when after only three weeks and against the advice of both his mother and his friends who all said she was too young for him, he had proposed to her and been accepted. He did not realise that what he had found attractive about her he spent the next few years destroying. He had detected originality, but slowly and inexorably he had killed it, recreating in so far as he could, his mother; someone whose sole aim in life was to please him but not interfere with him, someone he could rely on but at the same time, slightly despise. He treated her as a child, at first kindly, later with a certain sense of exasperation without noticing that she had grown up and without giving her the chance to realise it fully herself. As he grew to despise her he had learnt to despise the feelings she had originally inspired and so had grown cynical about any form of emotion he could not easily explain.

The more he drank the less he could see what to do and the more he understood how much he had been to blame himself the more he drank. He sat slouched over the table, bottle by his side, and finally slept.

Albertine did not knock. She wanted to surprise her, she wanted Miss Armstrong to feel at her mercy; walking in unannounced she thought would give her authority, it would be a statement that she had a right to be there. She did not know what to do with her club. Seeing the woman who was obviously the neighbour Miss Armstrong had described as the one who helped her, had made her feel rather uncomfortable about her weapon. She decided to leave it on the deck for the time being.

Miss Armstrong was in the chair as before and was reading. Although the sun was bright the room was still dark and Albertine wondered how she could see. She looked up as Albertine walked in and smiled until she saw who it was when a look of horrified recognition passed across her face, swiftly countered by a polite but reluctant show of welcome.

'Oh it's you, Albertine; what can I do for you?'

It had been so easy in her imagination to confront her. In her imagination she was a dragon to be slain, a witch to be burnt, a destroyer who had to be destroyed. In reality and in the flesh she was an old woman with kind eyes and a bewitching smile who was frail and alone and who needed protection from violence. One did not attack the vulnerable at least Albertine did not. In that old woman too was the person who used to look at her with warmth and approval. She wanted to replace the look of cold politeness with the familiar expression which had made Albertine feel valuable and special. She had been driven to succeed by the desire to please not only herself but this woman who had driven her, driven her with love and faith and with exhortation, who had rejoiced in her success as if it were her own.

She was already being pulled into the sticky, dark depths of confusion which had always accompanied her relationship with Miss Armstrong. The bedroom scenes which had loomed so large in her recent retrospection suddenly seemed a matter of no importance; they had been there, they had happened, but now they were nothing. Now Albertine felt that she would gladly go through it all again if that was what it would take to win her approval. She felt particularly conscious of her body so ludicrously clothed in Max's trousers; she could feel the string that was holding

194

them up biting into her fleshy stomach. And still Miss Armstrong was simply looking at her, waiting.

'I thought it would be nice to see you again ... I hope you don't mind me bargeing in like this.'

Already she was using schoolgirl expressions; she felt that any minute she would say how super it was to see her again.

'I wondered if there was anything I could do for you but I saw your friend leaving so I expect she has done everything.'

Gerda visibly relaxed. She thought that Albertine had come with the intention of creating an emotional scene, that she was going to be forced to remember, to relive that terrible time that she had fought so hard to forget. Although the woman still standing awkwardly in front of her bore no resemblance to the girl she had loved with such devastating consequence she was always pleased to see anyone. Since she had become too old to drive her boat into town herself she was dependent on people visiting her, which they did, but not all that frequently. Without Maud she was lonely. If the conversation with Albertine could be kept in the present perhaps it would be all right, though to keep in an unknown present with so much unspeakable past was bound to be uncomfortable.

'Bernice has done everything, thank you; but sit down ... would you like anything, coffee, tea ... how about some lime juice? I think she made up a jug.'

'I'd love some, can I get something for you?'

'I'll have some too. You'll find some glasses in the cupboard to the right of the sink.'

There was silence while Albertine poured the juice into two long and heavy brown beer glasses with the word Belikin painted on the outside.

'You told me yesterday where you were staying, remind me again.'

'Not far from here, Tres Cocos, next door to Albert and Elma, do you know them?'

'I wouldn't say I know them exactly, but I certainly know of them. It is hard not to know the people who live here, it's such a relatively small community, but they came after I had to give up doing a lot of things,' she smiled regretfully, 'old age is a terrible handicap.' Her tone was without self pity; Albertine felt an immediate desire to look after her.

'They have been terrifically kind to us,' she nearly said absolutely super, 'introducing us to people, making us feel part of the place. Elma even takes me to play bridge at the ladies' bridge club on Thursdays.'

Albertine could not remember if Miss Armstrong played bridge herself or if she thought it a frivolous waste of time, suitable only for the middle class women she used to despise so vehemently.

'What do you and your husband, what is his name, find to do all day?'

'He's called Max, Max Stevens . . . I don't know, we read a lot, snorkel on the reef, go to San Pedro, play bridge with Elma and Albert . . . I try to do a bit of drawing.'

This was not strictly accurate. She had brought a sketch book with her and some special kind of pencils which turned into wash if they were wet, but she had not yet tried them out. She did not say that for the last three hours she had been planning ways of killing her. She realised how very dull their life was and felt a creeping sense of guilt and failure at the drabness of her existence. She would have liked to be able to say that she was writing a novel, or a thesis on some obscure literary text, something that would remind Miss Armstrong of the person she had once been, something that would say to her, 'You see, I have not let you down', something that would ignite a spark of interest and change the look of boredom on her face to one of enthusiasm and encouragement. She thought she sensed disappointment and tried to compensate for it by saying, 'I write a bit of poetry,' whch was not true but which she hoped might impress her. She had not written anything since Amanda was born. Such creative energy as she had was used up by her baby and by Max.

Gerda was not impressed. She was overwhelmed by sadness as she glimpsed a trace of the old Albertine. As if caught by the lens of a camera, through the weighty bulk of the middle aged woman emerged the girl, restless, excited, eager for life, for knowledge, for experience. Where had it gone, and had she had anything to do with its disappearance? She felt engulfed by regret as much for the loss of her own powers as for Albertine's. She wanted to ask if she had enjoyed Oxford, if she had used her degree, but she kept, as she had promised herself, in the present.

'What are you reading at the moment?'

Albertine wished she had not said that she read a lot. She did, but her reading consisted of light ephemeral novels none of which she remembered for more than a day or two. They provided for her an escape into a world where things happened; for the period that she was reading, the stories became her reality, the characters her friends and the richness of the invented lives compensated for the poverty of her own. She read with the obsessive compulsion of the bulimic who no sooner gorges herself to repletion and over satisfaction, on sticky cakes and junk food, than she vomits it up, ready for the next binge. She could not remember when she had last read the sort of weighty book she would be unashamed of and she could remember neither the title nor the author of the story of middle class domestic life she was presently engaged in.

'I am re-reading Trollope at the moment' she lied, thinking that she could just remember some of the tales enough to be able to carry on a conversation if she was required to.

'He is so splendidly relaxing for a place like this,' she added airily, and reminding herself of her mother who had for years put her off reading Trollope by saying he had got her through the war.

'Oh yes, which one are you reading at the moment?'

Albertine was beginning to feel as if she was in an exam, she felt as she had at the interview with the Principal of LMH who had asked her what she had read on the train journey to Oxford and which she then had to discuss. She had been prepared by Miss Larkin for this question and had deliberately chosen Virginia Woolf's *Diaries* which she felt happy to discuss at any length, having at that time a devouring passion for Virginia Woolf. She picked a title at random.

'*The Last Chronicle of Barset,*' she said.

'Oh yes, one of my favourites. I love the stubborn pride of the "Perpetual Curate".' She put the words Perpetual Curate in inverted commas and smiled reminiscently. The word Hogglestock flickered faintly into Albertine's mind, bringing with it a picture of total desertion and for some reason that she could not put her finger on, the colour red. She could see the interior of the house in which the perpetual curate, whose name she could not remember, lived. She could picture his faded exhausted wife with pinched pale features, seated on one of the few sticks of furniture. It was coming back to her, there was a daughter, Grace, but what did she do? And something about a postal order, but what? Was his name Frank Crawley or was that the nice Agent in *Rebecca* . . . She longed to make some intelligent comment but it was all too cloudy. She remembered a seemingly endless journey in a pony and cart but could not remember who was making it, or why.

One thing she could be certain of in a Barsetshire novel was that the Proudies would appear at one stage or another. She decided to risk it.

'Mrs Proudie is as wonderful as ever.'

'Oh yes, her death scene is gloriously described isn't it?'

Death? She could not remember Mrs Proudie dying. How fascinating, she would have to read it again when she got home. She could not ask Miss Armstrong how she died, but she could not imagine a Barchester book without Mrs Proudie. She realised she would have to change tack or she could get into serious difficulties.

'I don't suppose you get any British television here do you. They did a Barsetshire series some time ago and Anna Massey was brilliant as Mrs Proudie.'

Gerda very much wished that she would leave. The old Albertine would have become instantly engaged in discussing the different levels and different sorts of pride as represented in *The Last Chronicle*; the hubris which flawed the otherwise great character of the perpetual curate, the unchecked self certainty and self righteousness of Mrs Proudie and the self aggrandizement of the man sent to replace Crawley, all contrasting so beautifully with the touching humility of Grace and the chronic low self-esteem of the hen-pecked Bishop which rendered him such an impotent tool in the hands of his wife. They could have had some fun, but all she could say was who acted what part in a television series which she must have known she could not possibly have seen. The only Massey she knew was Raymond, who must be dead now and who anyway was male.

'If you don't mind I must ask you to go now; I have a friend coming from the city for lunch and I must prepare for her; do come in though, any time you are passing . . . and bring your husband, I would like to meet him.'

She was lying too. She had no wish to see Albertine again, it was too painful, the memories she evoked were too disturbing and she could not free herself from the idea that Albertine's visits had some more sinister motive attached to them than the desire of the middle aged to help the old. She had no wish to meet her husband either who must be the one that had taken away the joyful spirit she had loved so disastrously.

Albertine got up, clumsily knocking over her glass which was still half full of lime juice. She was blushing, embarrassed at being found so wanting over *The Last Chronicle*, knowing that she had blundered and suspecting, rightly, that Miss Armstrong knew she was not reading it, and feeling fairly certain, again rightly, that the friend from the city was a figment invented to get rid of her. The morning had not turned out as she had planned it. Miss Armstrong, as ever, had had her entirely in her grasp apart from that first moment when she had entered the house and Albertine had thought she saw an expression of fear in her eyes, a momentary flash which she had fast covered up with the awe-inspiring mask of distance.

199

Wanting to cry with frustration she picked up her club from the deck and threw it as far as she was able, which was not very far, into the bush. She had been so certain that this time she would deal with her, she had been so certain that her rage would last long enough to destroy her. With her weapon gone she was prey again to all the demons of disillusion, despair, hopelessness and hate; but now the hate was directed towards herself and she felt no wonder that Miss Armstrong despised her and no wonder that Max ignored her.

17

Max was still sitting at the table on the deck when Albertine returned, gloomily gazing out to sea but seeing nothing, his feelings numbed by his discovery of her unfaithfulness and by the whisky, a large tumberful of which he was drinking almost absentmindedly. His thoughts by now were too dislocated to unravel coherently; 'how could she do that to me' was welded to 'that bitch, I'll kill her' and 'wait till I get my hands on that man', but through this combination of rage and self pity still rose, accompanied by a surge of pain he found unbearable, the thought that at the very moment he had found her she was not there. Like a living man he had held out his arms towards a phantom whose embodiment was only an illusion and who remained perpetually just beyond his reach. When he saw her standing beside him he hardly knew if she was real or not, he looked at her without speaking, finally returning his unseeing eyes towards the sea.

Albertine had been expecting to have to defend herself again. She was feeling too discouraged to have made up any story to account for her early morning departure and stood beside him wanting to receive what ever was coming to her as quickly as possible so that she could go for a swim and rearm herself for the next encounter with Miss Armstrong. Only when he looked at her so strangely, almost as if she was not there did she notice that the bottle of whisky which had been full the day before was now nearly empty as was the glass beside it.

Max never drank in the morning, it was only since they

had been here that he had drunk at lunch time. She was filled with an overwhelming sense of disaster, every thought of Miss Armstrong vanishing into the pit of her sinking stomach. He must have had some bad news, a message from England, something had happened to Amanda . . . she was dead . . . or one of the children. Her legs began to tremble; in the space of a second she experienced the flight home, the funeral . . . perhaps they were all dead, three coffins side by side in the church, three holes in the ground and an eternal hole in her heart. She hardly dared ask him so sure she was of his answer, she wanted this moment, before her life was shattered irrevocably, to last forever; she did not want to know the truth. They were two people frozen by fear in infinity, divided by misunderstanding and falsehood.

'What's happened?' The banality of her question in view of the certain answer was ridiculous even to her in the unreal state she was in. Max did not stir. She thought he was asleep and frenziedly she shook him.

'What's happened for Gods sake . . . Is it Amanda?' He looked at her, bleary eyed.

'Is it Amanda what . . . what are you talking about?'

'Has anything happened to Amanda?' she screamed.

'Not that I know of, what the hell's got into you?'

Relief flooded through her, she was engulfed by anger with him to exactly the same extent as only minutes before she had been overcome by fear.

'What are you doing then? Why are you drunk? I thought . . .' and the thought of what she had been living through so vividly reduced her to hysterical tears.

'I don't know why you are crying,' Max said, 'and I should be the one to ask what you are doing, not you. You weren't going to tell me though were you. I had to find out for myself.'

The memory of his pursuit of her, when he had felt the fugitive when it should have been her, when he had felt the wrong doer when it fact it had been she, silenced him in full spate.

202

It was her turn to be confused. He must have followed her but why should he be so angry.

'What do you think you have found out?'

'You know what I have found out. When were you going to tell me. Would it have been never or when we got home, "Oh incidentally Max, I might as well tell you I had a wonderful love affair when we were in Belize while you were diving or sleeping or doing the housework",' he added as he remembered the afternoon he had swept the floor to please her. 'Or were you just going to tell your friends, "Max never knew but I found this wonderful black lover when we were away", or perhaps you thought you would stay here, creeping into his house every morning or afternoon while his wife was out, living off my money to satisfy your lust. You're disgusting.'

She was finding it hard not to laugh. The thought that she might have a lover was so alien to her idea of herself and so far removed from the real reason for her visits that it was difficult for her to relate to what she could see was his very real distress. That he could really be jealous she still found unbelievable, he was not the type she thought without having any idea of what 'the type' was. If he had not been so drunk she could possibly have laughed with him over his suspicions, but he was too serious in his conviction and too angry, she did not want to sound as if she was mocking him. In spite of still feeling shaky from the shock of discovering that her fears for Amanda were false she tried to allay his in as gentle a way as possible, leaving, if she could, his pride more or less intact though he had revealed too much for it to be totally undamaged.

'I'm very flattered that you should think anyone would find me attractive enough to have an affair with, but Max I promise you I am not.'

'You can deny it as much as you like but I won't believe you. I saw you and adding lies to adultery won't help you, you have told enough of those already.'

He was beginning to sound more like his usual self when

he was angry; calm, cold and disdainful. It was his disdain that usually frightened her in the same way as Miss Armstrong's had frightened her this morning. Although she knew she was innocent of what she was being accused she knew that she was not innocent of deception and that Max had every right to be angry with her. Her ability to turn everything around until she could be absolutely certain that she was to blame was the characteristic which annoyed all those who were close to her the most. She was unable to see that her desire for self immolation was only an extreme form of egoism and just as unattractive as if she tried to display to the world that she was better than everyone else.

'I have been lying to you, you are right and I shouldn't have done, but I have not been visiting a lover I have been visiting Miss Armstrong.'

'Who the hell is Miss Armstrong?'

'She's the headmistress I told you about, the woman we saw on the boat. I wanted to make sure it was her and when I found it was I have been to see her, twice.'

'Why didn't you tell me then, why lie to me and why on earth do you have to wear my trousers to visit your headmistress, is she a muslim or something that you have to have your legs covered? I have never heard such a ridiculous story in my life. Why haven't you invited her here to meet me, why didn't you suggest I came with you? Am I so unimportant in your life? I don't believe a word of it, you'll have to do a lot better than that my girl!'

'Honestly Max it's true. I didn't tell you because I didn't think you'd be interested and because I wanted to see her on my own. You would have been very bored listening to us reminiscing, you know you would.'

She was trying to sound forceful and convincing but the knowledge that she was still lying and that she had not answered his main question was undermining her tone of conviction.

'Well, if what you say is true, take me to see her now. If you are not prepared to do that I will know that you are lying and will be forced to make my own conclusions.'

'I can't do that, she is expecting someone to lunch which is why I left her when I did; in fact I wouldn't be at all surprised if that boat that just passed wasn't her friend. She was coming from the city and the flight must have arrived about half an hour ago.'

'There you see, I knew it.'

He had won but the victory was sour. He did not know how to proceed, to go on arguing about whether or not she was lying was self defeating if she continued to hold to her story. He would have to ask Albert who lived in the house and when he had incontrovertible proof that it was not the mythical Miss Armstrong he would confront her again.

'I don't know what you are going to do but I am going to have a shower and then I will go to sleep; I suggest if you know what is good for you that you are not here when I wake up. Go and see Miss Armstrong! Hah!'

She went down the path towards the river. Passing Albert and Elma's house she saw Elma waving and beckoning to her, raising a cupped hand to her mouth indicating a drink; she walked on pretending not to have noticed, she was in no mood for Elma's pleasantries. She walked until she came to a large clump of Mangrove jutting into the sea, making small inlets like caves. Here she sat hidden from the passers by, tourists laughing on battered bicycles, old men laboriously collecting coconuts and young men in brightly coloured trousers and rasta ringlets swaying to the sound coming from large tape recorders swinging from their arms.

What had Max meant when he said don't be here when I wake up? Did he mean ever? Did he want her to disappear never to return and if he did, did she mind? It would be very silly if her marriage broke up completely because he did not believe her, anyway that could be easily remedied, all she had to do was to produce Miss Armstrong and Max would feel guilty for maligning her. He was bound to find out whether she told him or not; whatever he was feeling now would not last so there was not much point in thinking about it. On the other hand when he had said 'don't be here' why had she felt that little quiver of hope, caught a glimpse, like a shadow seen from the corner of her eye, of a freedom she had forgotten existed?

She stripped and sank into the sea. Out of the shade of the mangrove the water was translucently clear and she could see ribbons of rainbow, like the strings of a giant maypole, rippling over the sandy bottom which was dotted with miniature treelike growths, oak trees seen from a great height with little stalks for trunks and round blobs for foliage. She turned and floated on her back wondering what to do next and how long it would take for Max to discover that she had been telling the truth even if not the whole of it.

Max did not sleep after his shower. He lay on the bed wondering what he should say to Albertine if he discovered from Albert that she had been telling the truth as he was now beginning to believe she had. He was realising that it was only his new feeling for her that had made him overreact so violently, careering after her like a teenager, accusing her with no proof. It would have been completely out of character for her to indulge in a casual liaison. She had never seemed interested in sex for sex's sake and had frequently commented adversely when she found that some of her friends had. He could not believe that in such a short space of time she had found a lasting passion. He was feeling ashamed of himself, a feeling he was unused to and which was making him extremely uncomfortable. He dressed and went to see Albert.

Albert was watching CNN News which flickered through a blinding snowstorm. All the American programmes were pirated and the reception was invariably misty if not like now, near invisible.

'Hiyah Max! Come on in. Elma, fix Max a rum and coke.'

'Just coke please,' Max said. 'I'm not feeling too strong this afternoon.'

206

'Not your stomach?' Elma said, 'I hope it wasn't the food last night.'

'No, no, supper was delicious, I am afraid I over indulged in the Glenlivet after we left.'

They sat in silence for a while. Albert was still watching the television out of the corner of his eye and Max felt that it would be churlish to engage him in conversation until the news was finished. He felt that although Elma could certainly tell him what he wanted to know it would seem more natural for him to ask Albert. Albert would not want to know why he was asking which Elma certainly would, to stir Elma's inquisitiveness towards him was the last thing he wanted. He wished she would leave the room. When at last the news was finished, trying to sound as casual as possible though to his own ears failing, he said,

'I've often wondered who lives in those houses beyond Bill and Ellen's. Albertine and I were walking up there yesterday and realised we haven't met any of them, are they let to tourists or are they locals?'

Elma was immediately engaged; without giving Albert a chance to speak she embarked on a detailed description of every house, the inhabitants' lives and characters vividly brought to life, their idiosyncracies, their affairs, their relations, including the sins of their fathers and the wayward-ness of their offspring. When she had finished she had still not reached the green house.

'And beyond that?' Max said. 'Isn't there something beyond them, what about that double storied one, the green one?'

'Oh yes! You'd be interested in her, that's Gerda Arm-strong, she's English, you'd like her very much, she's a character, one of the oldest residents. Well I mean she is old, but she's lived here longer than any other foreigner I think, hasn't she Albert?'

'Ya, she came here when the British left, if not before, no well before now I come to think of it.'

And so as not to appear to have lost interest Max

continued his questions for another three houses and so as not to be too abrupt in his departure he asked Albert what his views on Bill Clinton were now.

'There's no doubt he's under the thumb of that wife of his. She wanted the job for herself so she pushed him into it; the man's not up to it though and soon everyone will realise it.'

'Well, I must be going now, thank you for the drink, we'll be seeing you.'

It was seven o'clock and nearly dark by the time he got back. All he could think of doing was to go to bed before Albertine returned. Even if he was not asleep he would pretend to be so which she would not be surprised by since he had been so drunk. In the morning he would think of some way, if not exactly to apologise, at least to admit that he had been wrong. He would make up for his mistake in some way, he would buy her some flowers or take her out to dinner. He would not mention what had happened but she would know that she had been at least in part to blame and that he had forgiven her.

18

'You what?' Albertine had returned from the ladies' bridge club which she went to every thursday with Elma. Max, to her relief, had been asleep when she had at last returned the night before and she had deliberately gone into San Pedro very early so as to avoid having to speak to him.

'I said I'd had a very pleasant afternoon with Gerda. She's a fascinating woman, you were very lucky to have someone of her quality and calibre as your headmistress. I can't understand why you've never talked about her; she is not only extremely intelligent she is also very charming. She talked a lot about you when you were young which was very interesting.' Albertine's initial red hot fury was rapidly turning to ice.

'Oh, yes, and what did she have to say about my youth?'

'She said how intelligent you were and what high hopes she had had of you, things like that. We didn't only talk about you if that's what worries you, we had a long conversation about colonialism in principle and Belize in particular, she's very knowledgeable. She talked about Diderot as well; she told me a lot about the encyclopedists I didn't know. I haven't had such an interesting afternoon for a long time.'

He did not seem to notice her mounting anger and was sitting back in his chair with the self satisfied look that said he admitted his mistake and had made reparation. He had woken in the morning inspired with the idea of visiting Miss Armstrong; he had been certain that Albertine would be pleased that he was taking a real and constructive interest in her life and was delighted with himself for hitting on a less predictable way of apologising than flowers, he thought it was just the kind of thoughtfulness she was always complaining that he did not show. He had not begun to consider that she might have had a reason for not telling him where she was going.

'Did I say you could go and see her?'

Max looked at her with astonishment.

'What on earth do you mean. Do you think you own her or something? You went off to play bridge and I went to have tea with an old woman who incidently happens to have been your headmistress, and we had a nice chat. What the hell's wrong with that and what could possibly be more natural? I should think she was surprised that you hadn't introduced me before.'

'I didn't want you to meet her.' She was nearly crying.

'Well you've made that perfectly obvious, but I don't see why I shouldn't. I think she's quite lonely up there all by herself and I got the impression she enjoyed having me. I really don't see why you should keep her all to yourself; she's certainly more interesting than most of the people here.'

'And I don't see why you should think that you can have everything of mine.' She realised how idiotic she was sounding but continued, 'She's not what you think, you know; I can see she's charmed you as she does everyone and that's how she gets away with it.'

'Gets away with what? You aren't making any sense at all.'

She knew she wasn't. The reasonableness of Max's response was making her even more angry but her emotions were in such turmoil she did not know what she was saying or feeling. The picture of Max and Miss Armstrong sitting together, talking about her, wooing each other, exercising their charisma on each other was completely intolerable to her. She did not know if she was frightened that Max would take Miss Armstrong away from her or if Miss Armstrong would take Max for herself as she had taken her. All she could see was that there two powerful people in her life

210

were in collusion with each other against her, and ensnaring each other and herself in yet more deception.

'You don't understand anything . . . and you're not even sensitive enough to know that if it was simple I would have told you.'

She did not know which of them she was most angry with.

'I'm going to see the bloody woman and put an end to it once and for all.' She ran out of the house and for the third time, up the beach to the green house, this time seeing nothing on the way and with no thought in her mind other than revenge.

'I expect you're really happy now aren't you!'

Gerda was sitting in the darkening room thinking how pleasant it had been to have an intelligent conversation with an educated man for a change. After some initial anxiety that Albertine might have told him about their relationship, when he had made it quite clear from his conversation that she had not, she had relaxed happily into the sort of academic dialogue she missed so much and which she had been disappointed not to have had with Albertine on her previous visits. She was glad that Albertine had found such an interesting man to marry as it showed that she had not become quite as inert, dare she say stupid, as she had appeared to be. But now she was standing in front of her, purple in the face, sweating and heaving in a singularly unpleasant and undignified manner. Yet again she was forced into wondering what on earth she had ever seen in this woman who was appearing at the moment more like a fish wife than an educated woman and she wondered how Max, who had seemed so particularly civilised, could live with her.

'Are you . . . are you happy now? . . . You took my life and now you're trying to take my husband.'

'Albertine, calm down for goodness sake, you have no idea what you are saying . . . I haven't "taken" your husband . . . he, very charmingly, came to see me and I gave him tea. I was delighted to meet him.'

211

'Yes,' she said, 'he thought you were charming too . . . that's how you do it isn't it, with charm . . . but sometimes you do it in other ways too, don't you . . . do you remember those nights, those endless nights when I had to suffer your disgusting hands all over me, your disgusting tongue in my mouth and in my cunt . . . did you ever think what it was like for me to have to stroke your skeletal body with its sagging breasts and purple scar . . . you didn't worry about that did you? . . . no, you knew that you would be able to charm me into acceptance, and you did . . . whenever you thought I might be getting away from you, you charmed me back with gifts and with flattery and sometimes, may you be forgiven, with odious self pity, so I felt I had to comfort you, to understand you . . . I suppose what you really meant was to forgive you . . . I was seventeen for God's sake and I didn't know anything.'

Every word that Albertine spoke was printing itself on Gerda's mind as if her tongue was a branding iron, she could almost smell the burning flesh and Albertine was transformed in front of her eyes from vulgar fish wife to an avenging Fury.

'I'm sorry,' she said, and for the first time she began to realise what it was she had to be sorry for and that to be sorry was not enough, either for Albertine or for herself.

'No you're not, you can't be sorry because you don't know what you did . . . do you want to know . . . or are you happier to just say you are sorry and then forget about it? How dare you say you're sorry. If you're sorry now why couldn't you have been sorry thirty-five years ago, why couldn't you be sorry enough not to start it?'

'I do want to know. I thought it was the same for you as it was for me.' But as she spoke she knew in her heart that she had never thought that, she had wanted to, she had per-suaded herself that it was so, but all the time she had really known.

Her voice was very quiet and Albertine responded. She stopped shouting and said with cold deliberation as the words she had tried to find all week appeared whole and ungarbled in her head.

'You made me who I was . . . you created the person you wanted me to be and then you took me. You left a shell without a kernel . . . when you "took me" in the biblical sense, when you fucked me . . . I was left not knowing who I was. You always used to say to us we had to "Know thyself" . . . do you remember that . . . you made it sound like an exciting quest . . . but when I escaped from you, which I did, I was left without a shape . . . If I wasn't the person who was loved by you, who was I? I have been looking for that self ever since and Max has not been able to help. He loves, or used to love, the shell, but he couldn't love the kernel because you've still got it . . . and do you know? . . . when I heard that you had been ill, had a nervous breakdown or whatever you want to call it . . . do you know . . . I felt guilty,' her voice was rising again, 'I felt that I should have gone on and on and on letting myself be your puppet, not ever letting you know what I really felt so that you could feel O.K. about it.'

'It wasn't your fault, it was mine.'

'Oh yes, I know with my head it was yours, but that does not change what I felt in my heart or soul or guts, wherever it is that one feels things. Do you know that when I came here yesterday was it, or the day before, I still felt sorry for you . . . To see you old and alone I still felt that I should not have left you, should have answered all those endless turgid letters you wrote when I left school, and yesterday, when you were so cold and patronising . . . I had intended to kill you . . . do you know that . . . I was going to batter you to death . . . but in about two minutes you made me want you to love me . . . *love* . . . what did you think you meant by love . . . making me climb that fucking broom cupboard every night . . . saying those ghastly prayers which I can see now was your way of trying to justify what you *must* have known was wicked . . . was that your idea of love, did you ever, just for one moment ever think about me?'

213

'I did love you Albertine, you must believe that . . . Yes, in retrospect I was wrong . . . I know that, I suppose I always knew that . . . but I let myself believe that I was not all that wrong . . . you were too young and I did not realise it, did not want to realise it . . . in some ways you were so mature . . . but you must believe it wasn't just your body I loved, it was you.'

'I know it was me,' Albertine was screaming again, 'that's what I'm saying . . . don't you understand . . . it was *me* you loved and *me* you took . . . I want *me* back and you're the only one who can give me *me* . . . you're the one who has always had *me.*'

She was sobbing and Gerda was silent. She could think of nothing she could either say or do to help her. She was also, in a curious way, swathed in relief; perhaps this is what she had always been waiting for, knowing that one day the fateful sword would fall upon her and without knowing from where it would strike she had become closed too, fearful and lost a little. She had come to this country to escape and to start again, she had tried to work with the children of San Pedro in an effort to redeem herself, but she had always known that the Fates did not work like that, 'Vengeance is mine, saith the Lord, I will repay.' There was never a time limit on the Almighty's vengeance and now at last it had come. She had never expected it to come in the person of Albertine herself but now she was here she saw it could have come no other way.

'What do you want me to do?'

Albertine was exhausted; the rush of adrenalin that had finally propelled her into this confrontation had died as suddenly as it had come.

'Do? I don't know what you can do . . . it's just that I have always felt so hopeless, and when I saw you the other day . . . on the boat . . . I thought it was all because of you . . . but I don't know what you can do about it . . . It's too late really, isn't it? I'm sorry, I shouldn't have said all those things to you, it was all so long ago . . . seeing you brought it all back. I suppose it's up to me really . . . it always has been . . . I

214

thought if I got away from you I would be all right ... but I wasn't, so perhaps it wasn't you after all.'

'What did you mean when you said I still "had" you?'

'I don't know; it was just that you were the only person who ever seemed to believe in me, and I believed in me because you did, so I sort of thought that I was nothing really because you probably only believed because of the sex thing ... or you were pretending to believe because you wanted to get me into bed with you ... something like that I suppose ...' and her voice which was subdued again, trailed feebly. It all suddenly seemed terribly unimportant. She felt flat and wanted to walk away.

'But that was not true Albertine, Miss Larkin believed in you, JPC always believed in you, I wasn't the first.'

She knew that this was true.

'No, I suppose you weren't the first, but you were the most important, I suppose because of the bed thing, and you made it seem to me as if the others were just following you.'

The room was completely dark now; their voices disconnected from sight had taken on a disembodied quality. Honesty had crept into the darkness giving off a brighter light than any number of candles. But there was more than honesty, suddenly, for the first time there was equality, without hysteria, without youth, Albertine was able to speak to her as an adult, without anger and without fear, neither trying to please her nor to berate her, only trying to understand.

'You see I loved you too in way, at least I think I did. I certainly admired you and I loved what you saw in me and sometimes I even loved what you did to me. You were the first to bring not only my mind but my body, alive. But I did not know what you were doing because I did not know about sex ... it seemed exciting in a way, but also disgusting, and I felt bad about being so enthralled by something that was so revolting ... and secret. I was frightened and exhilarated, but also terribly confused ... do you understand? That you prayed before making love was confusing too. It made me wonder if I was wrong to think that what you were doing was not right, would you who always advocated honesty above all things, be so hypocritical that you would pray before you sinned?'

Gerda understood. She saw Albertine suddenly as if she was the wounded Christ, carved in stone on his mother's lap, and she knew that she was the one to have pierced her side and crowned her head with thorns. For the first time she was able to see her pain and in the darkness she wanted to reach out and touch her.

'I was terribly wrong to make love to you, terribly wrong ... and everything you have said is true and you are right about the prayers too. I suppose I hoped that if I brought God into it, it would make what was wrong somehow right; I loved you and if God is love He must have been there somewhere, at least that must have been my reasoning but of course in fact it made it worse, turning sin into blasphemy. God will not tolerate being mocked. I suppose I have never properly repented ... felt remorse perhaps, but mostly for myself, not for you ... when you came the other day, the first time, after you left I was still trying to justify it all, comfort myself by saying to myself that you were not a child, wondering if you had been damaged and convincing myself that you hadn't been, convincing myself that I had given you more than I had taken ... no, more than that, that you loved me too . . . I would not see my sin . . . or your wounds.'

'But you did,' Albertine was crying, 'You did, you gave me so much, that is why I thought I must have loved you in a way . . . without you I would have just drifted.'

She cried more because she knew she had drifted anyway and that she had been blaming Miss Armstrong, an ideal scapegoat for her own inadequacy.

'Without you I would never have been excited by learning ... never have experienced the thrill of thinking ... that's what has been so complicated ... I have not known whether to hate you or be grateful ... whether to kill you or ask you to be my friend ... whether to forgive you or ask for forgiveness.' The tears were flowing now. 'I'm sorry, have you got a handkerchief?'

'Look,' Gerda said, exhausted too, 'let's talk about it again later. Why don't we have some light. Let's have a glass of sherry. I think we've both said enough for now.'

They lit the candles together, and the hurricane lamp. The room became a mysterious cave, full of warmth and flickering shapes.

As Albertine sipped her sherry she said,

'Do you remember when you used to give me sherry at school. I hated it, but I felt so grown up.'

Max knew that he was out of his depth. He had never been able to properly understand women: one of the most attractive qualities about Albertine was that unlike so many women he had met, she did not seem to be ever demanding 'understanding' she just was, and until he had begun to find her boring it was this aspect of her character he had found particularly soothing. She was like a cow grazing in a meadow and seemed more interested in pleasing him than being 'understood' herself. Her emotions had been no more complicated, as far as he could see, than a child's. She was sometimes, though rarely, angry; she liked his attention and sometimes sulked a little if she did not get it, though on the whole she accepted his rare kindness with an undue display of gratitude which left him thinking that perhaps he should pay her more attention. The most reassuring thing about her was that she was always the same. Her hysterical fury over his spending the afternoon with Gerda was completely inexplicable.

There was something in Albertine's history which revolved round Miss Armstrong, that much was clear, but until she was prepared to tell him what it was, and it did not look at all likely that she was going to, he decided his best strategy was to pretend everything was normal and ignore her peculiar conduct as best he could. He took the book on animal behaviour, lent to him by Albert, and settled back to read about the mating habits of bullfrogs. His mind was only half on it, the other part was restlessly revolving round how to make himself visible to her, how to woo she who had become so unexpectedly desirable. He was wishing in a way that he had a large bull neck that he could puff out, that he could make loud croaking sounds that she would find so attractive she would come to him without the necessity for words which he realised he was not good with if he was trying to express his feelings or even his lack of them. Whatever he said he seemed to upset her, he either said too little or too much and whatever he did seemed to be wrong too. It had not been like this before, he wondered if it was the menopause, he would take her to a doctor when they went home.

When at last she returned it was dark. He was relieved to see that she appeared quite calm, totally unlike the virago of an hour before.

'I think I need a drink ... have we got any plasters? I forgot to take a torch in my temper and I cut my foot on something coming back.' He could see that blood was pouring freely from her toe.

'Stay there and I'll get you some.'

Having washed and bound the cut which seemed quite deep, he poured her a glass of wine and waited. When she did not say anything and feeling that it would sound unnatural not to mention her absence at all, he asked rather nervously, dreading another screaming attack,

'How did it go, was she in?'

'Max,' she was looking serious, 'I think I must tell you all about Miss Armstrong; I think I can now ... I couldn't before and I'm sorry to have been so angry with you ... you must have thought I was quite mad.'

'Well something like that I suppose,' and his laugh did not quite conceal his tension or the fear of what was coming.

'Well' ... she paused a long time, not knowing how to say it and having no idea how Max was going to receive it.

'From when I was seventeen, just, until I was eighteen and a half, Miss Armstrong ... Gerda ... was, well I suppose you could say she was my lover.'

'She was your *what*?!'

'My lover, you know ... my lover ... I went to bed with

218

her ... we fucked, did what lovers do ... had an affair ...
do you want me to spell it out?'

Her voice rose to a pitch. Max had no idea what he was
going to say. It was the last thing in the world that he could
have imagined, not only of her but of Miss Armstrong as
well.

'I don't believe it.'

'You see ... that's why I never told anyone; if you don't
believe me now, who would have believed me then?' There
was a wistfulness in her tone that Max responded to without
thinking.

'My poor love, I did not mean I don't believe you are
telling the truth ... I meant how incredible and how awful
... she didn't seem like that at all ... I mean I didn't think,
when I was talking to her yesterday, this is an old Lezzy.'
Max had a very traditional view of lesbians. He found them
rather pathetic people, with their collars and ties and short
hair cuts he saw them as imitating men because they had
failed to get a man. He had never bothered to think what
they did if and when they were in bed together and certainly
not what they must feel. He saw them as freaks and gave
them the benefit of his compassion as he might a severe
cripple or lunatic. The thought that Gerda, whom he had
found delightful, was one of those and had actually taken
Albertine into her bed was so disgusting his stomach went
into spasm, he found it almost impossible to remain dispas-
sionate which he knew he would have to be if she was to go
on. He did not want her to go on, he wanted her to unsay it.
He wanted the events and the feelings of the last two days to
turn out to be a dream, but he had to let her continue.
When she had said they were lovers had she meant that she
had been in love with her as well, and if she had been, what
would his feelings be towards her then. Would he ever be
able to feel the same about her or would she join the ranks
of the people he found disconcertingly different and whom
he avoided if he could? How was it that he had been married
to her for over thirty years and had not known this? He
looked at her familiar face, her middle aged body of which

219

she was so self conscious, her eyes, pleading, for what, was it recognition or comfort; she seemed the same but that she looked the same was worse in a way. Had he ever known her at all and if this had happened what else might there be in her life that he also did not know about? He hardly listened to her as she was talking.

'When I saw her on the Banana Boat the other day I think I went sort of mad . . . I can't begin to describe what it has been like . . . I haven't thought about her for years and there she was looking almost exactly the same, though older of course . . . even I think wearing the same clothes . . . or ones almost identical . . . I knew I had to see her . . . talk to her . . . something . . . but I had no idea really what I wanted to say to her. One minute I wanted to kill her, that was yesterday . . . but when I got there I wanted her to love me again . . . you've met her, you know what she's like . . . and now she's so old she seems so vulnerable . . . I found it very difficult to be angry with her.' She paused. 'But tonight, when you said you'd spent your cosy afternoon with her, something snapped . . . my fear of her I suppose, or my regard . . . anyway, I charged in and told her how I felt and how I'd felt then and what I thought she'd done to me . . . it was awful really, some of the things I said . . . but then we talked a bit and it all went away, at least some of it . . . the anger anyway . . . I am not sure that I can really forgive her, but I could see that she in a way had been hurt at the time as well . . . she hurt herself by denying to herself what she was doing to me.'

'Why on earth should you forgive her . . . she abused you.' He felt a great relief at that, it did not sound as if Albertine had wanted it. 'And what's more she abused her position outrageously. She should have been sent to prison.'

'I know all that, but she did do other things as well, and it is the other things I can begin to remember now without the accompanying revulsion or fear, things that are in some ways more important.'

'What do you mean?'

'Well, when I left school I refused to see her again, and

220

because of that she had a breakdown, that is why she came here ... but refusing to see her, although she pleaded and pleaded, made me feel very guilty, made me feel that I was responsible for destroying her. I have felt guilty all my life but could not really face up to it. I wanted to see her but was afraid to, I was afraid to confront what I had done because I could not undo it. Over the years I have been far more conscious of what I did to her than what she did to me.'

'Umph!' Max grunted, 'more like she destroyed your life as far as I can see.'

'No, tonight I was able to tell her what I thought about the bad bits, the sex bits ... and somehow that gave me access to the memories I had kept submerged because they were tied up with the sex ... do you understand ... the good bits. I'm not being very clear, but tonight it was as if a dam had burst and the water which has been pent up for years can now flow freely and give life to a desert, to me, the dried up me ... it really feels like that ... but the plants that can now grow in me were planted by her ... do you see, without her there would be nothing to grow even if it was watered ... or that's how it feels and that's why the last few days have been so complicated.'

He did not really understand what she was saying. He was still feeling too shocked by the idea of Albertine being in bed with a woman. It was a different sensation from the one he had had when he thought she was in bed with a man, but it was almost more disturbing. That she was being so calm about it in a way was making it more difficult for him. He could not express disgust if she was talking in this flowery and exaggerated way about dried up deserts.

'When I followed you yesterday you might have thought it was out of curiosity or a possessive jealousy. It wasn't, it was because I love you and when I believed that you had found someone else I realised how much I need you. When you told me you hadn't been meeting a man at all I did not want to believe it because I felt such a fool and also I realised that I couldn't really blame you if you had had a lover; I have not behaved towards you as I should have done or respected

221

you as you should be respected. I have been selfish and ignorant but I want you. I want to show you how much I love you and I want your love in return. Forget about Miss Armstrong, whatever happened then has nothing to do with us now.'

But it does, she thought. It has everything to do with us now. In a sense Max had become Miss Armstrong in her mind, everything that she had been he had been and still was. Although his words were more than she had heard from him for years, behind them she detected a plea for sympathy which reminded her forcibly of Miss Armstrong. She felt as manipulated by what sounded like self pity as she had been by Gerda. I love you so you must love me, I need you so you must fulfil my need, I order you and I must be obeyed. She had allowed herself to be manipulated by Miss Armstrong because she had not known how to avoid it or even that the stranglehold she was gripped in was manipulation. She did not have to repeat the pattern, recognition at last gave her the key to resist.

'I don't think it is quite as easy as all that Max. You can't suddenly say you love me just because you thought I might have found someone else; that is what it sounds like to me and if anything it is insulting.'

'No, it's not like that. I realised I loved you before yesterday, it was because I knew that that I followed you; not because I thought you had a lover, at least not at first, but because I wanted to know where you were going all the time. I wanted to be with you.'

'You have just said you followed me because you thought I was going to someone else.'

'Well, I didn't really think it, it was just one of the possibilities. You must believe me, it's true.' She looked adamant, he had never failed to win her round if he had really tried and he was trying now as he had never tried before but still her expression seemed carved in stone.

'Well, true or not I don't think we can talk about it now. Let's have some supper and go to bed.' She did not want to go on talking to him; she did not like the mixture of self pity

222

and arrogance he was displaying, she knew that he was thinking that she would succumb to his attentions as she had always done, perhaps she was a little afraid that if she allowed him to continue he would be right.

There was nothing in the cupboard except one tin of refried beans and a tin of tomatoes and nothing in the fridge other than two eggs.

'I don't want anything to eat anyway, let's have another drink and go to bed. It's been a pretty exhausting week hasn't it, one way or another.'

Max was sure that when they were in bed he would be able to make love to her, that she had resisted him before was because she, very naturally under the circumstances, did not want to be seen to succumb to his advances too easily. Now that she knew that he knew everything she would not have to pretend any more, they could start again, she would understand why he had been horrified and understand why he had been angry with her for her deception, she would certainly accept that she was in many ways to blame and she would want to show him that she forgave him.

When she came to bed and immediately turned her back towards him and switched off the light the sense of power-lessness, had he been a child, would have reduced him to tears. As it was he raged inwardly and his thoughts were all directed towards how he could force her to be a proper wife to him, how he could make her realise that she owed everything she had to him and that it was her duty to put his desires before her own and his needs before the selfish and self indulgent behaviour she had been displaying all week.

19

When Albertine woke she knew at once she felt different. The heavy weight of a new day which always accompanied her waking was not there and the dazzling clarity of her dream was still with her. She had seen a Red Indian standing poised on the edge of a high cliff. She knew that he was being pursued by forces which would inevitably destroy him, and that to jump would be instant suicide. She watched him, in her dream, stand for only a moment, gathering his strength and his purpose before leaping, the feathers of his headdress flung behind, no help to him in his plummeting fall. He flashed before her eyes like a kingfisher in mid-dive, a brightly coloured dart of courage. She did not see his pursuers, but halfway through the death-defying plunge she became him. She felt the sensation of falling through the air, weighted by the feathers pulling on the tight band round her head, the tomahawk, the heavy leather clothes, and knew that her only hope of escaping a horrible death would be if she could land in water, a deep still sea which would receive her and offer her slowly back to the surface. Below her, the ground which had been too far away for her to see but which she was sure was a rocky canyon on which she would be broken, became the sea she desired, her one hope of salvation. It took her down into its fathomless depths, cradling her in darkness and then slowly and gently returned her to the air.

She knew she needed a boat and straight away a raft appeared, bobbing on the waves, which were no more than ripples. She clung to the edge and it dipped towards her, plunging her back beneath the surface, filling her lungs with salt water as she struggled to take enormous gasping breaths. The fear of her pursuers had lifted and she was now overcome by a greater fear. The weight of her sodden clothes, the unwieldy headdress hanging heavily on her shoulders and the weapons strung round her waist were pulling her under. Her arms were weak from the effort of staying afloat and panic was flooding her body as she realised she had not the strength for this last effort. She was going to drown. 'Take them off!' came a booming sound from the ocean. 'Take them off,' echoed the tiny voices from the circling terns. 'Take them off,' whispered the breeze. And she cast them off. The heavy feathered headdress, the weapons, the sea-soaked garments all fell away from her and feeling light and strong she sprang onto the raft in one easy movement.

She felt wonderful and powerful and in control. She knelt on one knee at the front of the raft, lean and brown, with strength that was definitely male, muscles sharply defined. She was full of energy, and looking round the empty sea, she knew she could go anywhere. She travelled swiftly; the raft swept through the still water, ploughing a furrow of white foam. She felt the sun on her naked body and as she approached different stretches of land she could feel they were not right. She experienced the powerful exhilaration of knowing without any doubt that it was her choice alone where she landed and that she would keep travelling until she found the place that she would know at once was hers. She felt no fear and no impediment, driven by a gentle wind towards the cloudless horizon.

Awake, she hugged the dream to herself, not wanting to lose the sense of strength it had given her. She felt it was an omen of such import she could not bear its dissolution. She knew that somehow, eventually, she would be that much in control of her life. She could take off the sodden clothes of her imagined fears which weighed her down, she could leap from those that bound her, trusting in her own strength to find another way; she could rely on her own instinct to judge

225

correctly when she had found her goal, and she would find the power to achieve it. The same strength that had lifted her to safety on the raft would land her safely on her chosen piece of land.

She felt drunk with excitement, the same excitement as the Israelites must have felt as they crossed the Red Sea into the Promised Land. She had been enslaved by the fear of not knowing who she was, of being nothing; and now she was free. It did not matter how long she spent finding her destination; when she found it she would claim it; she would land and till the soil until it yielded up what she would choose to grow. Meeting Gerda has been like the sea in the dream, she thought. I will not be broken on the rocks; if I go deep enough I will be returned whole.

Max was waking up now. He groaned. Sleep had driven away his anger of the night before and he reached for her. He had not done that for years, she realised. They had woken separately, got up separately and lived their lives separately, though on the surface together. But in the conversation last night, Max had been trying to reach her at a level that only a few weeks before he would have been ashamed to admit he even knew about. Walls built over the years with bricks of secrecy were tumbling just as surely as the Berlin Wall, with possibly just as many uncertain but hopeful beacons of light breaking through to guide them in the re-creative process. But when walls collapse, chaos and confusion can reign in their place, and without solid foundations nothing can be rebuilt. It was the lack of foundation that Albertine was most aware of. Perhaps her Indian was saying something to her about her marriage. The leather clothes which bound her like a second skin could be discarded. *Take them off* were the words she had heard in her dream. *Take them off.*

'I'm getting up. You go back to sleep. It's early but I'm going to see her again and I need to think what I'm going to say to her.'

She did not want to be trapped by any more declarations of love which were so transparently only made because he could feel her distancing herself from him; she felt much the same as she had felt when Miss Armstrong had given her presents. He had simply found a new way of exerting control; she was expected to be grateful and therefore unable to avoid it.

'I don't want you to go, but if you think you have to, that's OK. Come back soon, though,' and he rolled back into sleep. As she took a cup of coffee to drink on the dock, at the back of Albertine's mind was the image of the eucalyptus tree whose regeneration is only accomplished by destruction. The kernel can only be released by a forest fire. She felt that for her whole life she had been waiting, and only the fire of the last few days could have broken the shell surrounding the kernel of her being. If she had been asked what she was waiting for she would have been unable to answer. The waiting was quite unconscious; she had not in any way played a waiting game, it could be said that she was waiting to discover what the game was. The nearest game she could have thought of would have been grandmother's footsteps. She had waited for too long on the starting line; if she had crept forward at all to capture the waiting grandmother it had been too late, she had waited as if expecting the grandmother to capture her, and the other players, braver in stealth, had inched passed her while she had waited, waited for the right moment, which had never come, as right moments never do. Moments have to be made, or sometimes snatched unawares.

Before what she thought of as 'Miss Armstrong' she had made moments, made things happen, sometimes too many things, sometimes moments she had regretted in what is referred to as the cool light of day. She had charged through her childhood like a subaltern in the doomed Light Brigade, slashing with her sabre to right and to left, perhaps knowing in her heart that she would eventually meet the cannon head-on but pressing on regardless of shell and shot, mindful only of the charge. Had it been Miss Armstrong or was it simply adolescence that had made her so timid, so uncertain, so craven; so expectant of something happening to her rather than making something happen herself? Leaving Oxford so precipitately had been her only creative act; after that she had waited, regretting perhaps, not knowing what to do and not caring all that much if she did nothing.

What had happened to her was Max. He wanted to marry her so she married him; he wanted to live in his mother's old house so she did, he wanted only one child so she had only one child. She had waited for him to change her and when he had not done so she had waited for him to change himself. All the time she was receiving her life so apparently placidly she was really simply waiting for it to begin.

When she told Miss Armstrong that she had taken her life and kept her self, the words had sprung into her head and out of her mouth quite involuntarily; once out, they had sounded completely mad and she had tried to unsay them. Now, as she sat on the dock waiting for the dawn, surrounded by an orange carpet of sargasso, she realised that everything she had said was true. Not only had she been waiting ever since for her life to be returned to her, she had been waiting alone. She had had so little sense of herself that she had been unable to communicate either her thoughts or her desires to anyone, even herself. With nothing to give she was unable to receive; the barrier she had sensed round others had been really round herself. At 55 she was no longer waiting for life, she was waiting for death without ever having lived. She felt a surge of energy as strong as that which had driven her to Miss Armstrong's door with murder in her mind. I'm not going to go on doing it, she thought.

The unsatisfactory conversation with Max the previous evening had made her see that whatever words were spoken, nothing could change the way they were with each other. They were too firmly set, like portraits in a plastic mould, unbreakable. With felt tip the image could be altered but the change could not be permanent; the slightest touch would smear the new face and a single wipe would make it clean, leaving once again the picture that had been laid there so many years before. The night she had come back from Gerda convinced that the light she had seen through the torn curtain of their relationship would let in light on her whole life was, she could see now, just a fantasy. Max's unexpected admission of jealousy and of his love for her was nothing more than a knee-jerk response to the emotional fever of the last few days and she could tell he was already beginning to be a bit ashamed of it. In any case, it was too late; she had to be completely free. She had been bound, first by Miss Armstrong and then by Max; but she had also bound herself. To have a clean sheet on which to write her life, she had to be physically alone, to re-create herself she had to have no luggage to weigh her down, she had to stop waiting and start living. She would be like a bird, not like the frigates who glided in air currents without moving their wings and lived on fish caught by others, but something like an eagle, purposeful, strong and king of the sky, or like the Indian of her dream, naked and alone seeking a chosen shore.

The sun was risen now, revealing a day which she knew would be heavy and overcast. The sky was lumpen and there was no wind; even the breakers over the reef appeared as just a dark thin line painted across a silver canvas, and the leaves of the palm trees hung still, like tattered shrouds. It was the stillness before the storm; the clouds would gather, the heat of the day would bring with it a sense of foreboding as the people looking at the sky would shutter their houses, sailors would stow loose objects and reef their sails. Albertine felt a greater dread for what was to come, for the storm she was about to unleash she could not hide from. She would have to walk out into it and be battered until perhaps she could no longer stand. It would topple the roof, shake the foundations and she would have to watch the destruction of her life, knowing that she, not the gods, was responsible. Would Max recognise the warning signs? Could she warn him? *Should* she warn him and give him the opportunity to shut her up, to bar the door, chain her down until the danger had passed, until her resolve was weakened by waiting?

She did not trust herself. She would walk away from Max as she had walked away before, she would not look back and see the devastation, she would not grieve for 30 years lost as she had grieved for her innocence, she would not be like Sisyphus pushing his rock up the hill for eternity, never reaching the summit. It would be hard, but birth is seldom easy and she felt that she was labouring with a child she wanted to be born whole and healthy, a child she had learnt to love *in utero*, a child she would recognise when it emerged, whatever it took in pain and sweat because the child she laboured with was herself. But first she had to see Gerda one more time.

'Gerda, it's me. Can I come in?'

Albertine knocked on the door this time. She was amazed that her Christian name, which she had never been able to use before, came quite easily, naturally, without her thinking.

The door opened and Gerda was standing in front of her, smiling. 'I hoped you'd come this morning. Come in.'

Albertine smelt coffee; the table was laid for two and in a bowl was a mixture of fruits – pineapple, papaya, mangoes and oranges. The word *Agape* flitted into Albertine's mind, a feast of friendship and reconciliation.

'I didn't make any toast in case you didn't come, but I'll do it now, if you want some?'

'Thank you, yes please.' She suddenly realised how hungry she was. Supper last night was not the only meal she had missed in the last four days.

'How did you sleep?' Gerda was asking her.

She wondered whether to tell her about her dream, but decided not. She thought its power might become lost in the telling. Also, although she was feeling very different from the other times she had seen her, she was well aware that undue intimacy with this woman could easily lead to the manipulation of which she was the master. She wanted to bury the past, possibly even to be friends with her, but she did not want there to be a future with her and she certainly wanted Miss Armstrong to know that she had no more power over her. She did not trust herself enough yet to be certain that her influence was well and truly broken.

'Very well, and you?'

Gerda had not slept well – she had hardly slept at all. She had lain awake all night wondering how it was that Albertine's attack, her sometimes quite horrifying flow of accusation and incrimination should have left her feeling so free. She did not accept Albertine's statement of love, which she thought she had made only to comfort her and which had in fact made the consciousness of her sin even greater. She had been guilty of everything Albertine had accused her of, and more. For the first time she was washed by something close to repentance; it flooded over her like waves of warm water, seeking out the deepest crevices of resistance and leaving her exhausted and exhilarated at the same time. She almost felt young again, as if the arthritis in her bones was being dissolved by the tingling warmth of some life-giving energy. 'Lord have mercy upon me,' she had prayed, and imagined forgiveness loosening the bond she had been so unwilling or unable to see.

They ate in silence, each with much to say but both of them uncertain where to begin.

'I found this extraordinary stuff on the beach when I was walking up this morning. I left it on the deck – I'll just go and get it.' Albertine got up. 'What is it, do you know?' she said, returning with a block of something that looked like yellowish wax.

'Oh yes.' She smiled. 'That's ambergris, a nice bit too.'

'What is ambergris, exactly?'

Gerda rose and went to the bookcase. 'Here it is,' she said, taking down an encyclopedia and reading aloud, '"Ambergris is a concretion (whether normal or pathological is still debated) formed in the intestinal tract of the sperm whale. It is believed by some to have its origin in intestinal irritation caused by the indigestible horny portions of the squid and cuttle fish on which the whale feeds. Fresh ambergris is soft in consistency, black in colour and has a

231

disagreeable odour. Exposed to sun, air and sea water, however, the material hardens, its colour fades to light grey, and it develops a subtle and pleasing fragrance."'

They looked at the lump of slightly yellowing grey matter between them on the table, a metaphor for what was happening and had happened in that room, the indigestible events which had lain submerged in both their minds, at last regurgitated, and even as they sat, beginning to exude a subtle fragrance, the fragrance of forgiveness – or was it more like the smell rising from the river Lethe? – could they both, through the power of the strange odour, forget the past?

'I've still got all the books you gave me . . .'

'Have you? I thought you might have destroyed them.'

'Definitely not. Do you remember giving me Traherne's *Centuries of Meditation*? . . . "You'll never perceive the world aright till the sea floweth in your veins, till you are clothed in the heavens . . ."'

'"... and crowned with the stars",' Gerda joined in. 'Magnificent, isn't it?'

'I always loved that particular bit. It helped me understand, more than anything else, what you tried to teach me about socialism; you know, when he says something about being "sole heir of the whole world, and more than so, because men are in it who are every one sole heirs as well as you . . ." That says so much more about the equality of man than any number of political tracts, more powerful than even "all men are equal in the sight of God". There is something about this place that makes me think of that piece – the enormous sky, the brightness of the stars and the endless rumbling of the sea . . . God here is somehow a very big God. Do you know what I mean?'

Gerda did know, but did not want to interrupt her.

'Organised religion tries to contain the vastness of God, in making Him edible the churches try to make the indigestible digestible; do you remember that wonderful scene in *The Royal Hunt of the Sun* when Atahualpa says in a tone of absolute disbelief something like, "So you turn your God into a biscuit and then eat him." It seems that we try to contain the universe in a pouch, God in one's pocket to be used as coinage when necessary. Religion, in a vain attempt to make God intimate has reduced Him from an ocean to a stream . . . What do you think?'

It was rather nice to be talking like this to her again, Albertine thought. It was easy, too. Although she was conscious that she was in a sense still being a bit adolescent, it made a change from the day-to-day conversations she had with Max. She could not remember ever talking about God to him although he was a regular church attender, being vicar's warden and on the PCC. She had no idea at all what, if any, were his beliefs. He considered church an extension of his commitment to the village; the way of life he had been brought up to meant that the people in the Big House were expected to set an example. She went with him because he expected her to but her religious faith, which she had never really lost, she kept to herself.

'Do you still go to church?' Gerda asked her, remembering her regular attendance at 'eight o'clock'.

'I go, but I'm increasingly annoyed by the pettiness of Church of England politics, by their crazy pursuit of political correctness.'

She was just about to say, and I hate the pederasty which seems endemic in the clergy, when she just managed to stop herself.

'How about you?'

'Oh well, they are all Catholics here,' Gerda answered, and wondered if that was really the reason she had stopped going to church. 'Have a mango or some pineapple.'

'Are those mangoes?' Albertine said, looking at the small yellow oval-shaped fruit. 'I think we must have been trying to eat them before they were ripe. The ones we've been getting are green.'

'You have to wait until they are pink or yellow, otherwise it is very difficult to get the flesh out. Try one. Tell me about Oxford. Did you go in the end?'

'It wasn't what I was expecting, I only stayed a year. I had

233

a very idealised and completely unrealistic idea of what it was going to be like. Still, I wish I'd stuck it out . . . You and Miss Larkin spoilt it for me, in a way. Your teaching was far more challenging than anything I found there and I got bored. I'd been expecting something like the medieval schools in Paris, sitting at the feet of someone like Abelard . . . Do you remember the passion I had for Abelard and Heloïse?' she said, the juice from the mango dribbling down her chin. 'I went to visit their graves in Père Lachaise when I first went to Paris, after I left . . .'

They both remembered the *Letters*, and when Gerda had given them to her.

'I've still got the *Letters*,' she said, wondering why she had not thrown them away along with the letters from Gerda herself, which she was now wishing she had kept. The longer she sat with her the more unreal the previous relationship became. Could Gerda really have written that endless stream of wailing letters?

When Albertine mentioned the Abelard letters Gerda felt she was being forgiven for that night too and she felt a gratitude of such magnitude she was speechless; she put out a hand, which Albertine took but wished immediately that she had not. She was being seduced; the welcome, the breakfast, the conversation, so bland at one level yet so tinged with memories, were leading her away from everything she had determined to say.

'What I really want to know is how you could have done it, why you did it.'

'Because I loved you.' Her answer was pat, too pat.

'You might have loved me, but what about the sex? If you had really loved me, surely you would have wanted to protect me not abuse me.' She was beginning to feel anger stirring again.

'It developed so slowly and I didn't see it as abuse. A teacher often becomes emotionally involved, especially if the person you're teaching gives back. You were rewarding to teach because you were endlessly questioning, you didn't just wait to be fed the information, you were responsive, you made me feel that I was doing my job well; so my interest in you grew until interest turned to love and love eventually grew to needing to make love to you. By that time all the inhibitions that should have stopped me were secondary to the obsession.'

'I understand the interest part and how that can become emotional – I felt it as well. I loved your lessons, I felt challenged and wanted to do well, to please you; I felt your interest and wanted to live up to it, I wanted to give back. When you praised me I felt wonderful. You were an inspiration but it was an intellectual inspiration; to confuse that inspiration with sex was as bad as confusing parental love with sex. I don't see how you can say that just because you loved me you had to take me to bed.'

'But Albertine, look at it in another way. If we had been in ancient Greece, in the Platonic age, what happened between us would have been the norm; it was expected then that the mentor–protégé relationship would develop into sex, they recognised that to teach well there had to be an intensity in the relationship which would inevitably, if it was strong enough, become sexual.'

'But we were not in ancient Greece we were in Norfolk, in nineteen fifty and it was not the norm it was a criminal offence. It is outrageous of you to try to compare the two. You had a power over me which had nothing to do with love or sex. It came from your hierarchical position. How could I possibly have said no to you?'

'You could have done.'

'Of course I couldn't. You were my lover, but first and foremost you were the Head. "She who must be obeyed". You had authority and I didn't. The only way I could have got out of it was to have told someone. What do you think would have happened to you if I had gone to the Governors or the police? Do you ever see the English papers here? Did you read about the abbot and the novice who went to the police? I was thinking about him the other day. He was ruined because the boy told. What would you have done?'

'Well, I suppose I would have denied it – I would have

235

had to. If I had admitted it I would have betrayed the school, Maud, my profession . . .'

'But you did betray all of those, and more, every day by what you were doing; you betrayed me and my family too. I don't know which was the worst of your many betrayals. My family entrusted me to your care and you abused that trust. Maud loved you truly and you betrayed that love; more than that, you insulted her love by taking me to her home. If it had come out, the reputation of the school would have suffered terribly, everything that JPC had given her life to would have been destroyed. And you betrayed me too, you used my innocence and my naivety, my powerlessness, to your advantage and to feed your obsession. You were – are – a great teacher and you abused that gift by using it to pursue your lesbianism. Being caught would not have betrayed them; you were betraying them every day by what you were doing.'

'I know I did, but you are right to use that word, it was an obsession. I couldn't have stopped; you were all I thought about, day and night, month after month. Have you never loved like that?'

'Never,' she said.

But she could imagine it. She had seen people so obsessed that no number of obstacles had been able to stand in the way of the steamroller once launched. She had often felt envy for the excitement of the emotion but not for the results that so often followed. She had not believed they were in love, certainly not in the love that she had always dreamed of, which was a love that developed slowly, that grew day by day, not perhaps in height but in depth, fed by understanding and familiarity until it became natural to consider the other person before oneself, not in a self-sacrificing way, because there can be no self-sacrifice in real loving. The obsession Miss Armstrong was talking about led to the overriding desire for possession, to jealousy, to greed. The obsessed, lacking the compassion of real love, wanted everything from the object of the obsession, wanted to take, as Miss Armstrong had taken, without any thought of her needs, with no thought of giving other than timely bribes to secure her compliance.

'Do you remember when I stayed with you, how angry Maud was? I didn't understand why then, you know, I had no idea that you and she were lovers, I just thought she was a very bad-tempered friend and I couldn't work out why she was always so cross ... banging away with pans and never speaking.'

'Poor darling, it was a terrible time for her. I was so entranced by having you there, all to myself, all day, that I didn't give her a thought ... She was wonderful when I was ill, as you so delicately put it ... I wouldn't have survived without her.' She sounded almost smug.

'You turned her out of her bed, didn't you, for me? How could you have done that to someone who loved you, someone you loved and trusted and had done for years, who you knew would look after you when it all went wrong? I find it impossible to understand how you could have done that.'

'Maud understood, she really did. She was a wonderful person. It was hard for her at the time but she never blamed me.'

Albertine felt that Miss Armstrong accepted this sacrifice as her due, that although her words were full of sympathy for Maud, she had not, even now, really understood what it was she had done to her. Miss Armstrong had been even more ruthless with her than she had been with Albertine. She sensed that Miss Armstrong felt that she deserved everything that Maud had done for her because she was 'in love', though Albertine knew that it was Maud who had loved in the way she understood the word. Had she ever loved Max in that way or Max her? She thought not. She had stayed with him and done what he wanted out of fear as much as anything deeper; and Max had not considered her at all, as far as she could see – he had simply accepted that she was there.

'Did I really do you that much harm?' Gerda asked suddenly.

'I don't suppose it is possible for me to say whether you did me harm or not,' Albertine said slowly. 'I don't know what I would be like now if it hadn't happened, and no one can say for certain if what I am now is because of you. I'm sure that to use intellectual inspiration for sex was wrong and confusing, and if I was harmed it was due to that confusion. When I left school, sex was by that time inextricably tied to an older person and to feelings of admiration. I'm sure I married Max because he was older than me, because he was mature and I looked up to him. Because of you I was looking for a mentor figure and when I married him I thought I had found one; but Max was not looking for an intellectual relationship, in fact I was amazed when he came back from seeing you to hear him talk so enthusiastically about Diderot; his mentor role, if he had one in our marriage, was to try to turn me into a substitute for his mother. Sexual relationships should be between equals and I could never be your equal and I have never felt that Max was an equal. He kept me in a little-girl role and I allowed him to do it, mostly I think because you taught me. Maybe the sex in itself was not harmful, and as you say, in some cultures it might have been the opposite, the sex in our case was surrounded by deceit and secrecy, and from secrecy comes shame and guilt, which are enormous contributors to low self-worth, which I have suffered from all my life since then. Everything I have done has had the tint of shame.'

'If anyone should have felt shame it was me, I suppose I blocked it because I had to, for my own survival.'

Albertine was no longer listening to her, she was irritated that Gerda was still trying to justify herself, as if being in love was a legitimate excuse for everything regardless of the pain she had inflicted. The way she had spoken about Maud showed so clearly that it was not only her survival she had been interested in but her own desires; she had always been like that and she was still. But Albertine was not angry; she was seeing everything which had been dark suddenly illuminated and was determined to say everything that came to her. Miss Armstrong would never be sorry, she could not or

238

would not see what she had done, she would always wriggle, and even her so-called repentance was just another way of getting herself off the hook. 'I think another thing I learnt in your bed which has been bad for me is compliancy. I was never compliant until then, if anything I was rebellious, but I've been compliant ever since and it's prevented me from moving on. I've been so busy complying with everyone else I've been unable to see or admit to having any desires of my own. There's always this feeling that if I don't do whatever it is that's required of me by other people, something terrible will result. What happened between us fixed me perma- nently in the role of a child; I suppose that's really what I meant when I was screaming at you yesterday that you still had me. Today I'm beginning to feel adult for the first time.'

She was angry with herself for letting the experience, by remembering it, digging through it, become so important. In doing so she was renewing Miss Armstrong's power over her, by trying to see what had happened, through her ridiculous desire to forgive her, she had been saying, 'Go on, do it to me again, see how much you can muddle me, have a go at destroying me and feel good about it because to love is to be good.' At last she could see that she had neither to forgive her nor to be forgiven, she had to accept not only the happening but Miss Armstrong herself, as she was now and as she had been, and only by accepting Miss Armstrong could she at last accept herself as she had been then, as she was now and would be in the future. It had happened, that was all, Making it so important only pro- longed it. She had been touched by Gerda's loneliness but there was nothing she could do about it. She could do nothing for Gerda's life and Gerda could do nothing for hers. They had shared something once but they shared it no longer and reminiscence was turning out to be a sterile exercise. It was not the words they spoke that had healed the past for her but that they had been spoken, and there was no reason to pick at the fresh layer of skin that had grown over the weeping sore. She could not tell what Gerda was feeling and she did not care. She was responsible for her own feelings and her own salvation, not Gerda's. There was only one more thing she had to say to her.

'Was I the only one or were there others?'

Gerda paused, and in that pause Albertine felt as if she was looking at a huge wave in the distance; as it came closer, slowly and silently the waters gathered, and she knew that very soon it would dwarf its predecessor and come crashing at her feet.

'No, you were the only one,' she said.

But she had paused for too long. With her words the wave crashed and all Albertine's emotions of the last week, when she had swung from hatred to near love, from desire for revenge to what had been in the end a stronger desire to forgive, were dragged like pebbles into the rumbling backwash, drawn into a tumbling noisy confusion until the wave dribbled into non-existence and the stones settled in a new place as if they had never been moved.

The truth was at last so plain and yet Miss Armstrong was continuing to speak, declaring with total sincerity how her love for Albertine had been a unique and perfect experience. For the first time since she had known her, Miss Armstrong's words meant nothing; for the first time Albertine saw her as she was. She no longer saw the charm, she no longer felt the fascination or the pity, no longer was she drawn irresistibly into her web. She saw a ruthless old woman lying her way out of a difficult moment and she remembered with loathing a ruthless younger woman lying and charming and bewitching her way into achieving what she wanted, without a thought or care for anyone but herself. Albertine realised she had never had a chance. Rocks can survive the onslaught of the waters but Albertine had been the smallest of pebbles, a shingle or a grain of sand. When Miss Armstrong had extolled, as she often had, the moral virtue of self-sacrifice, she had been brutally sacrificing her powerless victims; when she had spoken of love she had used her lovers like toys, pulling off the wings of childhood and leaving creeping cripples in her wake. Albertine saw not only herself but those like herself; it was as if between her and the woman sitting in the chair opposite her lay a path made of corpses. How many like herself had battled all their lives to find the self that Miss Armstrong had stolen ... or destroyed? How many had struggled all their lives to find a relationship that was not built on compliance, not built on the fear that something dreadful would happen if they said no?

'I think you're lying,' Albertine said, interrupting the remorseless flow of her thoughts.

Miss Armstrong looked at her. Her mouth opened into the wide smile which had always seemed so honest, so generous, but her eyes were calculating. Had her eyes always betrayed her in this way and had Albertine never noticed before?

'Well, apart from Maud, of course, which was different, you were the only person I have ever loved.'

Even now Albertine wanted to believe her: she almost did. Surely she had been loved a little bit, surely it had not all been a lie? But still she saw her eyes. She saw too with unerring certainty, as if picked out by spotlights on a stage, the girls who had preceded her, who had stood outside her door with expressions of secrecy on their face, who had been as she had been, summoned to the Head at all times of the day ... Rosemary Lockhart, Jane Keir and Sheila Worthington. Why when it had been her turn had she not remembered them? Why had she believed that she had been special?

'Loved? How about used, how many people have you used?'

'I don't use people, Albertine. You know that.'

In the old days she would have put on her headmistress voice as she said this, Albertine thought, but she was too old and had lost her authority. Albertine was no longer afraid of her. She was hearing her words but she was still looking at her eyes. She could almost hear her thinking, I have never failed with this one, I'll win her round.

'If I had been just using you, would I have been so

241

devastated when you didn't answer my letters? Would I have been made so ill?' She was almost pleading.

'I should think that even if I had written to you, you would have dumped me as soon as you'd found some other gullible girl to take my place.'

'Of course I wouldn't, darling. It's not in my nature to be as ruthless as you were. I'm not blaming you – perhaps you were right – but you said you found it difficult to forgive yourself. I forgave you. I've always forgiven you. Although it nearly killed me, I let you go and I was happy for you.'

Albertine stood up, 'Stop it! Stop it! Stop lying, stop! I hate you, I hate your hypocrisy, I hate your lies, I hate your devious destructiveness, your dishonesty,' she screamed.

She picked up the piece of ambergris and threw it with all her strength, not caring or even seeing where it went. Miss Armstrong cringed in her chair, as if afraid of her, as if Albertine was going to hit her. As she ducked her head, the ambergris glanced off her temple. Albertine went to her and grabbed her by the arms and shook her, and shook her again. Miss Armstrong's head lolled; she was limp and made no reply to Albertine's screams.

'Tell the truth, for God's sake! For once in your life just tell the truth!'

Miss Armstrong's silence was suddenly more deafening than Albertine's screaming. She stopped shaking her, and Miss Armstrong slumped forward in her chair 'Gerda?' she said, 'Gerda, answer me. I'm sorry. Are you all right?'

She lifted the crumpled body, resting her head on a cushion. She noticed a nut shaped swelling on her temple. 'Please answer me . . . please. I didn't mean it. I'm sorry.'

All the time she was saying she was sorry she knew that Miss Armstrong was dead. Whatever it was that had made Gerda who she was was no longer there. All that remained was a limp grey bundle, a rag doll flopped, just flesh and clothes and a startled expression. She wanted to close the unseeing eyes but she could not bring herself to touch her again. Already Miss Armstrong's fingers seemed yellow, more twig-like than ever, the nicotine stain on her forefinger a dark knot on pale wood.

'Oh God, oh God, what have I done?' Albertine said out loud and her voice seemed to echo in the tomb-like room.

She wanted to leave but could not move. I am a murderer, she thought with horror, forgetting that only a few days before she had been in this same room with murder her intent. She could not believe that only a few moments before she had been holding that dead hand with nothing but forgiveness in her soul.

She picked up the lethal lump, the solidified excretion, the indigestible horny bits of squid, the sweet-smelling murder weapon which she thought should turn back to foul softness in her hand. A murderer's first act was to get rid of the weapon, she thought, and remove all fingerprints. Without looking at the body, like an automaton she proceeded to wipe away all traces of her presence. She washed her own breakfast plate and cup and saucer, leaving Gerda's untouched. She felt an overwhelming sense of grief as she thought of the care and the love with which Gerda had prepared her last meal, remembering how she had thought it was to be a feast of forgiveness and reconciliation and that Gerda must have thought so too. She remembered the excitement in Gerda's voice as she had said that she hoped Albertine would come, with no idea that it was her death she was hoping for so innocently and welcoming so wholeheartedly.

She was shaking uncontrollably as she dusted the table, the door handle, the chair she had sat on; she removed her cigarette ends from the ashtray so that only Gerda's remained. She watched herself like a character in a bad film clumsily removing the evidence; as she was doing it she knew that even the policeman from San Pedro would know that someone had stayed there long enough to cover the traces of their murderous deed. She felt she should stay by the body, if not grieving at least honouring the dead; she the murderess should keep vigil, but at the same time she knew that no one had seen her come, no one knew that she had anything to do with her. Only Max.

What would Max do? He was a JP, not only a law-abiding citizen but a dispenser of justice. Would he make her go to the police? Did she want to go to them herself, to own up, to be punished rightfully for what she had done? It had been an accident, she had not meant to kill her, she had not even meant to hit her, but how could she explain the cut, the bruise on her head, how could she explain such violence towards an old and frail woman? Max would not hand her over; she was sure that he would know she had not meant it. He would protect her, he might even say that Miss Armstrong had deserved it, that justice had been served, however roughly.

Or perhaps she need not tell him, and save him from having to lie on her behalf. She could go back now and say that she wanted to go home immediately; she had made her peace but she did not want to see Miss Armstrong again. She could persuade him that she was now only thinking of them and their lives together. But she knew really that they would not get a flight straight away and that by tomorrow the whole island would know what had happened. She could imagine Elma's excitement as she told them the news and she could feel herself already trembling at the thought of trying to express surprise and shock and innocence. But Max would know; he would know but he would not tell.

Who apart from Max knew there was any connection between them? She cursed herself for telling Angel and his sister that she had known her. She could not remember if she had told Tony and Melissa why she wanted to know about the old woman on the Banana Boat. But even if she had, would they think for a moment that she had killed her? No, of course not. When her body was found everyone would think that it had been a mugging, someone had broken in and stolen something. She knew she should make it look as if that was what had happened but she could not bear to touch anything more. She was stricken with fear, paralysed into immobility, like the dead body beside her whose basilisk stare seemed to see right through her, judging her, condemning her. How could she have been so self-righteous, telling Gerda that she had been wicked to do the things she had done? Only a few minutes ago she had set herself up as judge and jury, feeling perfectly entitled to be both, and now she was the hangman too.

The storm which had been brewing all morning was nearly broken. The sky was black now, the wind was ripping through the palms and the sea was in ferment. If only they had not come here; if only she had not seen her on the boat. If only life could be as it had been and never could be again.

She had always known that there was a world beyond the narrow confines of her existing environment, a world she had looked at through plate glass, knowing that its joys could never be hers. Somehow she had never been able to express the emotions she felt so strongly and had thus been barred from participation. This morning she had almost cracked the glass, realising that the life she felt caged by was of her own making, that her Indian was showing her that the world beyond could be hers, she had only to open the door and walk through. The bars had been in her imagination; she had only to have courage and they would vanish. She had experienced the power and the space of freedom as if it were already hers, had tasted the wide salt sea on her lips and felt the changing wind brush her naked body.

She had never wanted revenge. Perhaps she had wanted Gerda to atone in some way, but not with her death. She had wanted to be able to hold her hand without hatred, she had wanted to be free from memories, to look back with understanding and without pain. But now it would never be. What had been imaginary chains were now real ones, what had, in her head, been bars made of guilt and shame and uncertainty and fear would now be bars created of mortal sin. In her temper she had cracked the glass which could never be mended. There had been safety behind that pane; now she would never be safe again. If she confessed she would be punished, she would be behind real bars, made of iron; padlocked doors and implacable guards would enforce

245

the punishment she had called upon herself. The inescapable truth was that by trying to embrace freedom she had brought about death and would never be free again; an eye for an eye, a life for a life, that was justice. Now forever she was bound not by leather garments, to be put on or discarded at will, but by Milton's 'adamantine chains', not free to find her shore but manacled to Max. They would both be trapped by a new secret of Miss Armstrong, more awful by far than the first, pursued by the forces of fear and guilt from which she could never escape, with Max as both jailer and her only protector. Even in death Miss Armstrong had won.